I0645806

The Laura Black Scottsdale Mystery Series

Books by
B A Trimmer

~~~~

The Laura Black
Scottsdale Mystery Series

Scottsdale Heat

Scottsdale Squeeze

Scottsdale Sizzle

Scottsdale Scorcher

Scottsdale Sting

Scottsdale Shuffle

Scottsdale Shadow

Scottsdale Secret

Scottsdale Silence

Scottsdale Scandal

Scottsdale Sleuth

Scottsdale Spy

~~~~

The Aloha Lagoon
Mystery Series

Hula Homicide

Homicide Honeymoon

Scottsdale Spy

Scottsdale Spy

B A TRIMMER

SCOTTSDALE SPY
Copyright © 2025 by B A Trimmer
All Rights Reserved

HULA HOMICIDE
Copyright © 2022 by B A Trimmer
All Rights Reserved

Without limiting the rights under copyright reserved above, no part of this publication may be reproduced, stored in, or introduced into a retrieval system or transmitted in any form or by any means (electronic, mechanical, photocopying, recording, or otherwise) without prior written permission, except in the case of brief quotations embodied in critical articles or reviews.

This is a work of fiction. Names, characters, places, brands, media, incidents, and dialogues are products of the author's imagination or are used fictitiously. Locales and public names are sometimes used for atmospheric purposes. Any resemblance to actual events, companies, locales, or persons, living or dead, is entirely coincidental.

Editors: 'Andi' Anderson and Kimberly Mathews

Design & derivative cover art by Janet Holmes using images under license from Shutterstock.com.
Portions of Hula Homicide reprinted courtesy Gemma Holliday Publishing, Inc.

ISBN: 978-1-951052-40-9
Saguaro Sky Media Co.
060125pb

Email the author at LauraBlackScottsdale@gmail.com
Follow at www.facebook.com/ScottsdaleSeries

To Katie Hilbert,
who always pushes me to reach for the stars.

Thanks to:
Catherine Bertoldi, Bonnie Costilow,
Jeanette Ellmer, Barbara Hackel,
Millie Knight, Judith Rogow,
Gail Shillito, Sherry Troup,
Tony Tumminello, and Sherri Vaughn

Scottsdale Spy

Introduction

If you've never read a Laura Black Scottsdale mystery, you may want to start with *Scottsdale Heat*, the first book in the series. If you'd instead like to begin with this book, here are a few of the key people in the story:

Laura Black – A Scottsdale native with a degree in philosophy from Arizona State University. She's five foot seven, skinny, and has shoulder-length medium brunette hair parted down the middle. After working for a few years as a bartender at Greasewood Flat, she now works as an investigator in a Scottsdale law firm. She wants to make the world a better place, but she also has bills to pay.

Sophia Rodriguez – Laura's best friend, who also works in the law office as the paralegal. Sophie is a former California surfer chick and a free spirit. She's currently exploring the concept of only having one boyfriend, Milo.

Gina Rondinelli – Laura's other best friend. She's a former Scottsdale police detective and the law firm's senior investigator. She has a strict moral code and likes to play by the rules. She's currently dating a former Navy SEAL named Jet.

Leonard Shapiro – Head of the law firm and Laura's boss. He's miserly and always pads his bills. He has few morals, loose ethics, and no people skills, but with the help of Laura, Sophie, and Gina, he usually wins his cases.

Max Bettencourt – Laura's boyfriend and the head of the legitimate resort side of the former DiCenzo crime organization. Before coming to Scottsdale, Max was a covert operative for the U.S. government, mainly in Eastern Europe. He had needed to keep their relationship a secret for Laura's safety, but that is slowly changing.

Deborah Thompson – A pleasant middle-aged woman and the new receptionist and administrative assistant at the law firm.

Anthony "Tough Tony" DiCenzo – Retired head of the local crime family. He likes Laura and almost thinks of her as a daughter. Through various adventures over the past year, he owes Laura several favors.

Gabriella – A former government assassin from Russia. She currently works as a bodyguard for Johnny Scarpazzi, the new head of the local crime family.

Chapter One

As I sat on a bench next to a statue of a giant green parrot, I reflected on how my life had led me to this moment. The parrot looked down at me with a slightly sarcastic expression, as if it were mocking me for some of my questionable choices over the past few years.

On my other side stood a statue of a colorful, bare-chested pirate who had a monkey perched on his shoulder. The pirate was smoking a black pipe and seemed unconcerned that the monkey had stolen his spyglass and was using it to snoop on visitors across the crowded amusement park.

I'd chosen this particular bench because it would give me a clear view when Lyla Fuller, her friend Sarah Drew, and their five kids entered the park. I'd also chosen it because it was in the shade of three enormous Mexican fan palms.

Even though it was nearly four in the afternoon, the mid-May temperatures were still hovering in the upper nineties. Being outside in Arizona is all about finding shade, and I wasn't going to move until I had to.

I was at Castles N' Coasters, a roller coaster theme park located at the old Metrocenter in northern Phoenix. It's been marketed as Arizona's largest amusement park and has been a prime destination for group birthday parties and family gatherings for as long as I can remember.

I was waiting for Lyla and her friend to buy their entry tickets and come in. The plan was to follow them around and wait for Lyla to behave badly.

Three weeks before, Lenny Shapiro, my boss, had been contacted by Brenda Montoya, the head of the Commercial Claims Adjustment department for Bis-Sure Inc. This was a local company that specialized in business insurance. Brenda was an occasional client we'd been working with for several months, and we still had a sizable chunk of her original retainer that we needed to use up.

Brenda suspected that Lyla Fuller was trying to pull an insurance scam on The Critter Corner, a local pet supply store. Since Brenda only wanted to pay the claim if it was legitimate, she asked Lenny to find out whether Lyla really had been hurt or if she was merely faking an injury so she could collect a huge payout.

From the accounts in the paperwork, Lyla had slipped and fallen when she'd stepped in a puddle of dog pee in a store aisle while shopping for chew toys for Dudley, her labradoodle. According to Lyla's attorney, the injuries had resulted in her permanent inability to work.

They'd asked the court for over four million dollars in damages to cover future lost wages and medical expenses, along with a further payout for pain and suffering. They were also in the process of filing a negligence claim against the pet store for an additional five million dollars.

I'd spent the past two and a half weeks following Lyla as she went shopping, hung out with her friend Sarah, and took her kids back and forth from school. Unfortunately, she hadn't done anything overly suspicious, and I'd started to doubt if I was going to be able to shed any new light on the insurance claim.

Even though I'd been hot on Lyla's heels every time she

went out, I'd only come close to getting caught once. Lyla, her kids, and Dudley the doodle took an unexpected turn as they exited the Chaparral Dog Park the week before, nearly running into me while I was taking a video with my phone.

Lyla had given me a sideways glance, and I'd pretended I was merely taking pictures of the dogs in the play area. Fortunately, after looking at me for several seconds, she decided it was only a coincidence and let it go.

Today, I'd followed the two women to the amusement park, doing my best not to be seen. After pulling into a parking space near the entrance, they started dragging out bags and unloading their combined five kids from Lyla's ten-year-old Chrysler Pacifica minivan.

Since Lyla was supposedly injured, she wore a neck brace, her left arm was in a sling, and she walked with a pronounced limp. Fortunately, this slowed down her movements considerably and gave me enough time to buy an "Elite" all-access pass and hustle inside ahead of her.

Lyla's group was easy to spot as they spilled into the theme park. The target of my surveillance had chosen a ridiculously bright neon pink shirt. It was almost as if she knew someone would be watching and was doing her best to assist them.

I was a little disappointed when they headed to one of the miniature golf courses. The kids appeared to be between eight and twelve years of age, and I'd been hoping that they would have made a beeline for one of the roller coasters or the log ride instead.

My goal was to get a video of Lyla riding on one of the park's high-speed thrill rides. One or two videos of these types of activities would likely be enough evidence to invalidate her insurance claims. As it was, a mild round of mini-golf with the kids wasn't going to help me at all.

Crap.

Knowing they'd be occupied with golf for at least forty-five minutes, I called Sophie. Sophia Rodriguez was not only my main best friend but also the paralegal at the law firm.

"Hey, Laura," she said when she answered. "What's going on? Did you get the video of Lyla Fuller yet?"

"I'm working on it," I said. "But if you aren't doing anything tonight, I need your help. Lyla and the kids ended up at Castles N' Coasters, and it's starting to get crowded. I'm afraid I'll need to stay so close that she'll end up spotting me if I try to take videos of her."

I then heard Sophie talking to someone in the background. Unfortunately, with the surrounding sounds of music, laughing children, and the roar of a roller coaster flying over my head, it was hard to make out what she was saying.

"I just talked with Debbie," Sophie said a moment later after switching to speakerphone. "Neither of us is doing anything tonight, and working a stakeout at Castles N' Coasters sounds like fun. I love the churros at Tacos n' Stuff, and maybe when we're done, we can hit the arcade and play some video games. I'm sure Lenny won't mind paying for everything if we can get some good evidence first."

"That would be great," I said. "Try to leave as soon as you can. Even with the light summer traffic, it'll still take you a while to get up here."

"Keep your shirt on," Debbie laughed in the background. "We'll be there in half an hour."

Thirty minutes later, Sophie and Debbie walked into the park and joined me where I was still sitting on the bench.

Although Debbie had only worked at the law firm for a few months, the middle-aged office manager seemed to fit right in, and I'd already used her several times to help me with surveillance assignments.

"Lyla's the tall, athletic woman with the long sandy blonde hair and a neck brace," I said as I nodded to the group who'd just started the seventeenth hole of course number four.

"After mini-golf, they could either scatter or head out as a group. I need a video of Lyla on one of the fast rides or even the bumper cars."

"That seems simple enough," Debbie said. "Between the three of us, we can keep her surrounded.

"Wear your headphones and stay on the line," I reminded the ladies. "We'll all need to be subtle and keep a low profile. Lyla's been acting a little squirrely tonight. She's been glancing around every few minutes like she knows something's up."

"Don't worry about it," Sophie said. "We'll give her the ol' triple team. She won't know what hit her."

Debbie and Sophie positioned themselves to intercept Lyla and her group after golfing. I decided to keep my place on the bench, right outside the exit to the mini-golf area. Even though the crowd levels had risen considerably, I now felt like we had a good chance of keeping up with her.

After finishing, Lyla, Sarah, and their children headed across the park toward the Patriot roller coaster. Although it was definitely a fast ride, I was a little disappointed.

The Patriot was considered more of a family attraction that even smaller children could enjoy. A video of Lyla riding this may not be judged as conclusive proof that her injury was made up, but it would definitely be a good start.

The three of us took positions around the ride and waited

for Lyla to climb onto the coaster. Between her neon pink shirt and white neck brace, she was easy to spot, even from a distance.

I took a video of Lyla standing in line and caught her looking around at her fellow riders. I knew she suspected that someone was watching her, but the three of us were far enough away that she couldn't make any connections.

I began to hope we could quickly get the evidence we needed and call it a night. Earlier in the day, I'd promised my boyfriend, Max, that I'd call if I would be available for a late dinner with him.

Unfortunately, when Lyla got to the front of the line, she watched as Sarah and the kids loaded up in the coaster train, but then she veered off to wait for the group at the exit.

"Well, that's a little disappointing," Debbie muttered into her headphones. "For a minute, I thought we had her."

"Yeah," Sophie grumbled in my ear. "Maybe I should walk up and give her a fast slap or two, then one of you can take a video of her chasing me through the park."

"Umm, you might want to rethink that strategy," Debbie said, doubt creeping into her voice. "Sure, slapping her around a little might be fun. But Lyla looks pretty athletic, and I bet she can run really fast. If she caught you, it could get a little messy."

After the roller coaster, Lyla led Sarah and the five kids to the food court for a snack. It was located in a pretty area of the park, surrounded by dozens of shady palms and a big splashy fountain.

The three of us positioned ourselves at the exits from the area and waited to see what they would do next. I heard Sophie groan with desire when Sarah got in line at Coaster Cakes, a snack stand that sold freshly made funnel cakes.

"Let's hurry up and get the freaking videos," Sophie growled into the phone. "Otherwise, I'm going to need to call a time-out and go over there myself. I didn't eat lunch today, and a hot funnel cake to munch on while we're walking around the park sounds like a damn good idea."

After Sarah returned and handed out the snacks, Lyla and one of the older kids went to the bathroom. A few minutes later, the kid came back and rejoined the group.

Sarah gathered up the trash, and everybody got up to walk to the next ride. That's when I realized I hadn't seen Lyla come out of the bathroom.

"Do either of you see Lyla?" I asked.

"She went into the bathroom a few minutes ago," Debbie said in my earpiece. "She should be out soon."

"Yup," Sophie agreed. "She hasn't come out yet. Although you're right, it's been a minute. Maybe she ate something that didn't agree with her?"

"Alright," I grumbled. "New plan. You two follow Sarah and the kids. I'll wait for Lyla to come out. Hopefully, she'll rejoin the group in a few minutes."

"Okay. Good luck," Debbie replied.

When Lyla didn't come out of the bathroom after another six or seven minutes, I began to get nervous. I decided to partially break my cover by heading in to make sure she was still there. Unfortunately, the only people in the room were a mother and her two young children.

I hurried out, returned to the food court, and did a slow 360-degree scan, but it was no use. Lyla had disappeared.

Crap.

"I've lost her," I moaned into my headphones. "She somehow made it out of the bathroom. Keep your eyes open.

She could be anywhere."

"She's not with the rest of the group," Debbie reported. "They're all heading towards the Magic Carpet ride. Sophie and I have them flanked on both sides."

"Jeez, how could you lose her?" Sophie asked, sounding frustrated.

"I know," I admitted. "But she has to be here somewhere. I'm going to start a sweep. You keep an eye on the rest of the group. Let me know if she shows up."

I spent the next twenty minutes going from ride to ride until I'd made a circuit of the entire park. I assumed Lyla would be easy enough to spot, but I didn't see her anywhere.

I then went out to the parking lot to see if she'd perhaps taken her minivan out for a spin. However, it was exactly where they'd left it earlier in the day.

"I can't find her," I said into my headphones as I reentered the park. "Debbie, stay with the group in case Lyla comes back. Sophie, let's split up and look everywhere."

Sophie and I scoured the park, looking for Lyla. It was beyond frustrating that we couldn't find her.

After half an hour, I was about to call it a night when I spotted Lyla. She was in line for the Desert Storm roller coaster. This was a double-looped monster and the fastest ride in the park.

The reason I'd missed her was instantly obvious. While in the bathroom, Lyla had changed out of her pink shirt and was now wearing a light brown top that made her seamlessly blend in with the crowd.

In addition, she'd removed the neck brace and the sling. She even tucked her long blonde hair under a floppy sun hat and put on a large pair of pink plastic sunglasses. This forced me to look at her several times to confirm that she was indeed the person I'd been combing the park to find.

"I've got her," I shouted into my headphones. "She's about to ride the Desert Storm. I'll take a video of her on the coaster. You two take positions at the exits and take a video if you can. She's changed outfits and is now wearing a brown shirt and a white sun hat."

"She's a sneaky little thing," Debbie chuckled. "You gotta like her style."

"I guess she figured out that she was being watched," Sophie said. "We'll need to be careful. She'll for sure be on the lookout for people taking her picture now."

I hurried to a position where I could use the zoom on my camera to catch Lyla as clearly as possible. I felt a tingle of excitement when I was able to get a video of her climbing into the coaster train and then removing her hat and sunglasses, stuffing both into her bag.

After the three of us got videos of Lyla riding the coaster, we spent the next twenty minutes following her around the park, our cameras going the entire time. She first hit the Splash Down log ride, then eventually ended up at the Ram Rods bumper cars.

While she was in line, Sarah and the kids joined her. While on the ride, they spent the entire time smashing their cars into each other, laughing all the while.

"You know," Sophie said into her headphones as we took pictures of Lyla and Sarah crashing headfirst into each other. "There has to be a better way to take videos of people other than holding up a phone. I mean, what we're doing is pretty obvious, even from across the park."

"Maybe Lenny could spring for some sort of high-tech spy gear," Debbie piped in. "You know, like James Bond or Tom Cruise always seem to have."

"Yeah," Sophie agreed. "I could go for those glasses with a built-in video system or a shirt button with a secret camera lens. Anything would be better than walking around with my phone over my head, taking videos."

Once the bumper-car ride was over, I placed myself thirty yards off to the side, next to the Sea Dragon, where I could catch the group walking past me. Although it may seem silly to an outsider, I always prefer my video evidence to have a clear beginning, middle, and end, much like a documentary film.

After this final shot of Lyla, Sarah, and the kids leaving the violent ride, I figured that between the three of us, we likely had enough video evidence to create a compelling story—one that would make even Lenny happy.

After they exited the bumper cars, the group walked by my position, seemingly without a care in the world. Unfortunately, Lyla must have caught something amiss out of the corner of her eye.

Her head snapped around, and her eyes locked onto me. My phone was raised, and it was obvious that I was taking a video of her.

I could see the gears turning in her head, and then the connection snapped into place.

"You!" she yelled out, her finger pointed in my direction. "You were taking pictures of me the other day at the dog park. What the hell?"

Even as she berated me for violating her privacy, the real reason for me taking pictures must have fallen into place. With a look of panic in her eyes, her hands reached up to her throat, where there was no neck brace. She then turned and looked back at the bumper car ride, where she'd been crashing into her kids and best friend only minutes before.

With me still taking a video, Lyla stood as still as a statue for almost twenty seconds. I could see from the look on her face that she was envisioning her entire insurance scam unraveling and that she had just lost several million dollars in the process.

Lyla's face, which had initially taken on a sickly white tone, gradually flushed to dark red. She started taking deep gulping breaths, and her eyes bugged out, making her look somewhat like a cartoon fish.

Her eyes then narrowed as she started to shake with fury, staring directly at me the entire time. I could tell that she suddenly didn't care about anything except taking her anger out on the person who had just ruined her chances of obtaining a fortune.

"Uh oh," I heard Debbie mutter. "I don't think she's taking this very well."

"Yeah, watch out," Sophie added helpfully. "The shit's about to hit the fan."

"You goddamn dirty bitch!" Lyla screamed, her fists balled up at her sides.

She took off in my direction. Slowly at first, but after only a few steps, she'd kicked it up to a full run.

I quickly came to the conclusion that I didn't want to get into a fight with someone I was supposed to be secretly watching from a distance. Instead, I dashed off at full speed towards the park exit.

Chapter Two

"Come back here, you dirty slut," Lyla yelled as I ran past both the parrot and the pirate statues. "I'm going to take that phone and jam it up your stinky ass!"

Fortunately, from a lot of previous experience, I'd worn a comfortable pair of cross-trainers and easily dodged around the groups of people gathered at the park exit.

Lyla wasn't so lucky, having worn a pair of slip-on sandals that caused her to crash into parents and kids alike as she smashed her way towards me. I could hear from the angry shouts of the people she collided with that she was getting closer.

As I ran through the park, I had the presence of mind to hold the phone over my shoulder. It made running a little awkward, but I knew a video of a seriously pissed-off Lyla running through the park without her neck brace, her arm sling, or her limp would be more than enough to discredit the insurance claim.

I made it through the exit and into the parking lot about twenty yards ahead of Lyla. I thought, at this point, she would have given up. She must have known that she'd already blown up her insurance claim, and there wouldn't be any point in continuing.

I ran three rows into the lot and darted behind a pickup

truck, so I could catch my breath. Lyla flew through the exit and took off in the opposite direction. For a brief moment, I thought I might have lost her.

Instead, Lyla sprinted to her minivan, wrenched the door open, and began rummaging through her center console. I was concerned that she'd pull out a pistol but felt only slightly less alarmed when she slammed the door, screamed, and started running at me again.

In her upraised hand was a high-heeled shoe. I recognized the pump as one of her knock-off Louboutin stilettos that she had worn at dinner a few days earlier while on a date. Unfortunately, it had a four-inch spiked heel, and it looked rather dangerous.

Why do they always come after me with a shoe?

"I'm going to stick this in your eye, you cheap floozy!" Lyla yelled as she again came after me. "Maybe then you'll think twice before taking videos of people who only want to be left alone."

Far from calming down, Lyla's fury had only intensified. One of her eyes was staring a hole through me while the other one was pointed in a slightly different direction. Her face was almost purple with rage, and spittle was flying from her lips.

I still had a good lead on the crazy woman, but I knew I needed to move quickly. From the twisted look on Lyla's face, she wasn't going to stop until she either jammed the stiletto heel in my eye or dropped dead from exhaustion.

Before I took off running again, I checked to make sure the phone was still recording a video. For once, everything seemed to be working properly.

As I ran for my life, I veered toward a nearby Wal-Mart, again making sure to have the camera pointed over my shoulder at Lyla as she came after me.

"Stop running and take your medicine, you stupid fat cow!" Lyla yelled. "This heel is going in your freaking left eye, and I'm going to jam my thumbnail into your right eye. Then I'm going to stomp your ugly face."

Fear shot through me as I heard the slapping sounds of her sandals as she ran. She must have been operating on pure adrenaline because she quickly closed the gap between us.

How can she run so fast in slip-on sandals?

Not wanting to get caught by the psycho woman gave me an additional burst of speed. I'd almost made it to the store's entrance when Sophie's yellow Volkswagen convertible appeared next to me.

"Get in, quick," she yelled at me as the car slid to a stop. "I don't think that Lyla chick is too stable after we messed up her chances of getting all that money."

I hopped in, and Sophie floored it. It wasn't a moment too soon, as Lyla had already caught up with us.

She took a hard swing at me but instead hit Sophie's car with her shoe. I winced as I heard the *thump* of the stiletto making solid contact with the back passenger fender.

"My baby!" Sophie yelled as we flew down the aisle. "I swear, if that bitch so much as put a mark on my car, Lenny's going to pay to have it buffed and detailed."

Sophie drove about fifty yards through the parking lot, swung the car around so we faced Lyla, and then stopped the convertible. I think we both wanted to see what would happen next.

When Lyla realized that she couldn't get to me and it started to sink in that her cover was blown, her resolve finally crumbled. Her face fell, and her shoulders slumped. She then walked to her van slowly and climbed inside.

She must have called Sarah because the entire group came

out to the vehicle about ten minutes later. They sat there for about five more minutes and then took off.

Since the video evidence had been successfully gathered and Lenny's credit card had already purchased an all-access park pass for both of them, Sophie and Debbie decided to stay. They then headed to the massive Castles Arcade center.

I knew Sophie's favorite games were first-person video shooters. She particularly loved any game where she could shoot zombies in the head.

Debbie said she'd been a lover of video arcades since they became popular in the seventies and that she'd been pretty good "back in the day." She went in hoping to find a Black Knight pinball machine or a Centipede video game.

I'd had enough fun for one night, so I decided to take off. The evening was still relatively early, and I had hopes of having dinner with Max.

My name is Laura Black. I'm a Scottsdale native, and I've lived here pretty much my entire life. After graduating from Saguaro High School, I picked up a degree in philosophy from Arizona State University, down the road in Tempe.

I was married for a bit after college, but that only lasted a few years. Fortunately, we didn't have any kids, which made the divorce a lot easier.

I'm not opposed to having children, and maybe I'll have one or two, someday. But that's a problem I'm saving for later. Much later.

After bouncing around as a bartender for a few years, I ended up as an investigator at a high-end boutique law firm in Scottsdale's historic Old Town district. My boss, Lenny

Shapiro, can be self-centered and greedy, but my coworkers are great.

If I'm being honest, the job mostly sucks. It ranges from being dull and boring to being yelled at, chased, beaten up, or left somewhere for dead. But as time goes on, I seem to be getting better at it.

Through some good luck over the past couple of years, I don't have to pay rent on my apartment, and I have a nice car that belongs to me rather than the bank. Even with the pitiful paychecks I get from Lenny, I have enough to get by, and my credit cards are paid down.

Well, they're *mostly* paid down.

I drove over to the Scottsdale Tropical Paradise, the huge golf resort that was also the headquarters of Max's company, Scottsdale Land and Resorts Inc. On the way, I'd called Max to see if he was free, and he asked me to meet him at the Dreamland Cove Bistro for dinner.

When I walked in, my boyfriend was at his usual table. It was in a secluded corner near a waterfall, surrounded by ferns and tropical plants.

The only table close to ours was occupied by Carson, Max's assistant and bodyguard. From what I could gather, Carson and Max had both served in the same special ops unit, and the tall, muscular blond had helped me out several times before.

Max saw me and stood to give me a long hug. It still felt a little weird being able to hug him in public, but I was slowly getting used to it.

He was wearing my favorite cologne, which started to give

me tingles and naughty thoughts. Unfortunately, I knew we only had time for a quick dinner. Then, he'd need to take off for his nightly wrap-up meeting at nine.

"How'd your surveillance go?" he asked as a server brought over two glasses of scotch.

"It went great. Sophie and Debbie were with me, and all three of us got some incriminating videos of our target doing things that would be impossible if she really had been injured."

"I'm glad to hear you're finished with the assignment. Do you think you'll get any time off before the next one?"

"Why? Are you getting lonely sleeping in that big, soft bed all by yourself?" I teased.

"As a matter of fact, I am," he kidded back. "These surveillance assignments you get wreak havoc on my love life. Hopefully, you'll get a weekend off sometime soon. I'd enjoy taking you somewhere nice."

"I'd love that. We haven't been on a trip since we went skiing in Vail, and that weekend was cut a little short. Unfortunately, Sophie says I'm getting another assignment first thing in the morning."

"Well, hopefully, this one lets you work in a couple of sleepovers at your boyfriend's. He has needs, you know?"

"Oh, I know all about his needs," I laughed as I again started to tingle at the thought of spending the night with Max and helping him out with his problems.

Our conversation was about to turn into me describing all of the inappropriate things we'd do the next time we were together, but the server appeared with our dinners, and I restrained myself.

"What's going on with Johnny and his group?" I asked when she had left. "Do you still think that Las Vegas will be making a move into Arizona?"

"It's possible. So far, Johnny hasn't noticed anything amiss, and I know his entire organization has been on the lookout."

"What are they looking for?"

"The opening move in taking over somebody's territory is no different than any other business. They would first need to establish a physical presence."

"Like moving guys over from Nevada and having them open a casino or something like that?"

"Nothing that obvious," Max said with a shake of his head. "More likely, a few new street gangs will start to pop up throughout The Valley. Maybe they'll sell drugs, steal cars, or even rob houses. Nothing that would stand out as anything unusual. The individual members of the gangs might not even know who they're ultimately working for."

"But when it comes time for Las Vegas to make their move?"

"Then they'd have a small army of guys already in place to do whatever is required."

"Okay, I can see why that would be hard to detect. You won't have any idea it's happening, until it does."

"Exactly," Max said with a sigh. "It's going to be very challenging for Johnny to grow his business while also trying to keep track of outsiders trying to move in."

"Do you think they would have anything to do with your side of the business? There might not be a lot you could do if they started to put up a new golf resort."

"So far, I haven't heard of anything like that. But you're right. It would be an expensive gamble on their part, but it would be a simple way to have a hundred of their guys move into Scottsdale."

As Max was explaining this, he had his hand lightly resting on my leg underneath the table. He wasn't doing anything overly naughty, but just his touch was enough to get me going.

"Um, let's not wait too long before we get together," I said. "You being my boyfriend comes with a lot of responsibilities. You don't want to shirk your duties, do you?"

Max grinned and playfully squeezed my thigh, sending tingles all over my body. "Oh, I know what you want," he chuckled. "Wrap up your next assignment for Lenny quickly, and we'll plan a few days together."

Yum.

All things considered, I was feeling pretty good as I took the elevator up to the third floor of my apartment building. Between the three of us, we'd taken upwards of an hour of high-definition videos of Lyla doing things she shouldn't.

Lenny would be happy, as would Brenda Montoya, our client. Sophie had said I was due to get another assignment in the morning, but I wasn't going to worry about that. At least, not tonight.

I'd even managed to have a quiet dinner with Max, which was a great bonus to the day. As always, I could tell he had a lot on his plate, but overall, he seemed like he was doing okay.

I'd almost made it to my apartment when I heard the distinctive sounds of *The Voice* coming from behind the door to Grandma Henderson's.

I knocked hard enough for Grandma to hear me, then waited. After a moment, the TV's sound dropped, and I heard a pair of feet walking to the door.

After the deadbolts were flipped and the safety chains removed, Grandma opened the door.

"Well, hello, Laura," she beamed. "I'd recognize your knock anywhere. It's been days since we talked. Come in. What have you been up to?"

"I've been on the same stakeout for the past couple of weeks," I said as I walked into her living room. "But I finished it tonight."

Marlowe, the cat I share with Grandma, was asleep on his afghan in his designated chair. When he heard me walk in, he yawned and rested his head back on the blanket. His greeting wasn't overly enthusiastic, but I'd take it.

"That's good, dear," Grandma said as she stood back to look me over. "I trust nobody shot at you this time?"

"Not this time. I had to run from a crazy woman who wanted to jam a stiletto heel in my eye, but that was about the worst of it."

"And you get paid to do that?" she asked with a puzzled laugh.

"Well, not much," I admitted. "But it's enough to keep the lights on."

"Hello, cookie," Bob called out from the kitchen. He had a *Kiss the Cook* apron on and looked like he'd just finished doing the dishes.

"Hi, Grandpa Bob," I said with a wave. "How have you been?"

"I'm doing swell," he said with a chuckle. "But it's high time I hit the rack. You gals don't stay up all night," he said to Grandma.

She hugged him, and he disappeared into the back. "I'm about to have a Jamaican Jerk," Grandma said as she walked

22

into her kitchen. "Would you like one as well?"

"Sure," I said, not wanting Grandma to have to drink alone. Besides, her unique concoction of Diet Pepsi and Appleton rum had become one of my favorite cocktails. "Is your arthritis acting up again?"

"No worse than usual, but I hate to take too many of those damn pain pills. A Jerk or two at night takes the edge off and lets me sleep."

As Grandma and I chatted on the couch, I noticed that one of Grandpa Bob's living room chairs was missing. It gave the room a feeling of being more open.

"What happened to the chair?" I asked. "It gives you more space, but I thought keeping it was part of the deal you made with Bob a couple of months ago."

"Well, it turned out that one of his kids was shopping for something similar last weekend, and Bob decided to give it to them. I look at it as a win-win."

As we were chatting, Marlowe sneezed. It's something he sometimes does, and I figure he has some sort of cat allergies. But this sneeze sounded a little gurgly.

"Has Marlowe been doing that a lot?" I asked.

"He's been sneezing off and on all day," Grandma said with a shake of her head. "I hope he's not getting a cold."

"Do cats even get colds?" I asked.

"Of course they do," Grandma said. "I used to have a cat that seemed to get a cold three or four times a year."

Grandma and I had been talking for about twenty minutes when Marlowe sneezed again. This time, I noticed there was a glob of snot on his face.

"I think you're right about him catching a cold," I said. "Can I borrow a tissue?"

"Of course, dear," Grandma said, handing me the box.

I grabbed a tissue and wiped Marlowe's face. Normally, he hates it when I do this, but this time, he tolerated it fairly well.

"I'd better take him home," I said as I picked up the limp cat. "I don't want him to get boogers all over your chair."

"I think I'll head off to bed myself," Grandma said. By this time, she'd already had two Jerks, and I knew it wouldn't be long until she fell asleep. "Goodnight, dear."

Chapter Three

I made it into the office the following day at about eight-fifteen. Gina Rondinelli, the law firm's senior investigator, was in her cubicle in the back offices, typing on her laptop.

Due to her background as a detective with the Scottsdale Police Department, she gets most of what Lenny considers to be the "important" cases, but I'm good with that. As an investigator, she's a cross between Miss Marple and Wonder Woman.

Unfortunately, that leaves me with most of the wacky, oddball, and sketchy assignments that come through the door. I try not to take it personally that I'm constantly called on to take explicit photos of people doing sleazy things, but it sometimes wears me down a little.

Gina spun around in her chair when I plopped down at my desk. She had a broad smile and a twinkle in her eye.

"I heard that you, Sophie, and Debbie were able to get some good evidence on the Lyla Fuller assignment last night," she said as she leaned closer. "It feels great to nail down a case like that, doesn't it?"

"Thanks," I said with a nod. "And you're right. Lyla tried her best to throw everyone off with a disguise. But between the three of us, we should have more than enough video of her on the rides for the judge to dismiss the insurance case."

"Sophie said you're getting another assignment today. That sucks. Hasn't it been like three weeks since you've had a day off?"

"Tell me about it," I moaned. "I haven't even had time to do the laundry, and I'm starting to run out of things to pull from the back of my closet."

"Is that why you wore that bright green sweater last Friday?" Sophie asked, not even looking up from her tablet. "I was going to tell you. It looked a little funky."

"Summers are usually when things start to ease up around here," Gina said, ignoring Sophie. "But this year, it's been non-stop assignments ever since we took on the J. Barrett Knight case, and that was almost six months ago."

"I know," I said, also ignoring Sophie. "The past couple of months, I've been lucky if I can get a full day off in between assignments."

Sophie was at her desk, flipping through her tablet, mostly trying to ignore Gina and me. I knew she was going over the Southern California surf reports. I've seen her do this almost every day since I started working here, even though she hasn't been surfing in several years.

In addition to being our paralegal, Sophie handles most of the accounting duties. Unfortunately, she looked a little rough today.

Her hair was a hot mess, and her eyes were halfway closed as she sipped on a big coffee from QuikTrip. I couldn't tell for sure, but she might have still been wearing the same makeup as the night before.

She looked up at me and yawned. "Hey, Laura. Don't forget, we have the new client in about half an hour."

"That's why I'm here," I said. "Why do you look so beat up this morning? Didn't you get any sleep?"

"Not hardly," she scoffed as she yawned again. "After Debbie and I left the park, I went home and started watching Netflix. I then called Milo and told him to come over and service me. He was due to be there by ten-thirty, but something came up at work, and he didn't show up until almost midnight."

"That seems pretty late to have a guy over," Gina said, looking up from her laptop. "You'd think he would've waited until he could make it at a more reasonable time."

"Well, he said he'd come over another night, but I told him to show up, no matter how late it was."

"Why'd you have him do that?" I asked. "Were you looking at some old Aston Kutcher videos again?"

"No, this time I'd started watching a Ryan Gosling movie. I swear, that man gets me going every time I see him."

"How late did you keep Milo up?" I asked.

"I'm not sure," Sophie laughed. "But it was starting to get bright outside before I let him go to sleep. He's probably still in bed."

"You mean over at your place?" Gina asked.

"Yeah, he has the morning off, so I told him he could stay there until he felt like getting up."

"You normally don't let him spend the night at your apartment, especially not by himself," Gina pondered. "I don't even let Jet do that, at least not very often. It sounds like things are kicking up a notch between you two."

"Well, don't read too much into it," Sophie said as she took a noisy sip of her coffee. "But now that I'm exclusive with Milo, I'm giving him some extra privileges. I wanted to let him know that he went beyond what was expected last night. I had some exceptionally spicy needs that I made him take care of, and he didn't complain about it too much."

"Thanks for coming out to the park last night," I said. "I'm not sure if I would have gotten the videos of Lyla if you two hadn't been there as well."

"It's no problem," she said with a yawn. "Besides, having Lenny pay for us to play pinball and shoot aliens seemed like a good trade. Debbie's pretty good at those games. We even went out and rode a couple of the rides afterward."

"I'm glad you enjoyed yourself," I said.

"It's kinda weird that Lyla thought she could get away with riding those roller coasters last night," Sophie said. "She must've known that someone could be watching."

"I don't think she knew," I said with a shake of my head. "She showed up wearing that bright pink shirt so she'd be easy to track and did nothing that would have put a strain on her neck. She kept glancing around at the people next to her but never saw that we were taking videos. After an hour or so, she must have thought the coast was clear."

"I guess that would explain why she was so shocked when she found you taking a video of her," Sophie said with a chuckle.

"Yeah, probably," I laughed. "But the woman was bright enough to change out of the pink shirt and hide her hair. We nearly didn't spot her, even though we knew for a fact that she was somewhere in the park."

"Still, I seriously don't get that Lyla chick," Sophie said. "Sure, I could see that if you were shopping for Dudley the Doodle at the pet store, slipped on a puddle of pee, and fell on your ass, you might ask for five or ten thousand dollars to cover the medical bills. But asking for several million dollars was stupid. It only pulled the insurance company into it. If Lyla and her lawyer hadn't gotten so greedy, she would have made a nice chunk of change."

Gina took off to work on one of her assignments while Sophie continued to scan her tablet, her eyes only half open. I turned on my laptop and tried to focus. After a few minutes of scanning my emails, I closed the lid and looked at my best friend.

"Sophie, let me ask you something. Do you think what we do here is meaningful? Do you think we end up helping people more than we hurt them?"

"What are you talking about?" she asked as she looked up. "You aren't trying to discover the meaning of life again, are you?"

"I mean, have you ever thought about what we do? Every time we take on an assignment, some people win, and some people lose. I was thinking about that as I was watching Lyla and her kids playing mini-golf last night."

"Well, yeah," she agreed. "There are winners and losers. So what? We get paid to make sure our clients are the winners."

"Okay, sure, but look at it this way. Other than being a liar and a violent psychopath, Lyla didn't seem so bad. I've been watching her for almost three weeks as she took her kids out for lunch and went shopping for them. She seemed like a good mom, and I never saw her splurge on herself, even though she expected to get a huge insurance payout."

"Are you saying we shouldn't have taken the videos of her when she was clearly trying to cheat the insurance company?" Sophie asked, her head cocked to the side.

"Nooo," I sighed in frustration. "I'm not saying that. But it does get me thinking sometimes."

A little before the client was due, Sophie and I went up front to the reception lobby to talk with Debbie. As always, she greeted us with a friendly smile.

When Lenny hired our new receptionist a couple of months ago, he moved Sophie to a cube in the back offices. This had led to a month of Sophie grumbling about having to work in the back. She thought working in a cubicle was akin to some sort of sadistic prison sentence.

Debbie had been an office manager for various businesses around Scottsdale for the last thirty years, and she was good at it. She'd learned what kind of boss Lenny was during her first few weeks on the job, but fortunately, she hadn't decided to quit. At least, not yet.

Other than running a credit check on the client, Sophie hadn't heard any details about the new assignment. I asked Debbie, but she didn't know either.

I hoped the new case would involve more than taking naked pictures of cheating spouses, but I've learned not to get my hopes up. Every time I think I'm going to be able to do something interesting that will have a positive effect on society, I end up stuck in a hot closet listening to naked people having sex.

It's not that I'm opposed to sex, God no. But having to listen to other people going at it is only fun for a few minutes. After that, all I want is for them to finish.

Right at nine, a man in his mid-thirties came into the office through the front door. He was holding a manila envelope and a small black book, reminding me of a traveling missionary. From the way his eyes darted around the office, we could tell he was the new client.

He had a nice Arizona tan, green eyes, and a pretty smile. He stood a little over six feet tall and had a solid-looking body. His light brown hair was a little longer than most guys wear, but it looked good on him.

"Hi," I said as I walked over and shook his hand. "I'm Laura Black, one of the investigators here."

"Lance Tillman," he said with a strong voice. "Good to meet you, Laura Black."

"This is Sophia Rodriguez, our paralegal," I said as I pointed to my best friend.

Sophie smiled and gave him a little wave. From the way she was giving him the once-over and biting her lower lip, she seemed to approve.

"And this is our office manager, Deborah Thompson," I continued.

"Call me Debbie," she said, flashing a warm smile. "Mr. Shapiro is finishing up a phone call, but he should be ready for your appointment in a few minutes."

"Thank you, Debbie," he said. "Some issues have recently come up, and I'd like to talk things over with an attorney before I do anything."

Two minutes later, Lance, Sophie, and I were seated in front of Lenny's desk. After shaking hands with the man and sizing him up, Lenny didn't feel the need to offer the new client a drink.

"How can we help you, Mr. Tillman?" Lenny asked.

My boss had a yellow legal pad on his desk and was holding his black and gold Montblanc pen. He struck the classic pose of an eager attorney gathering information for an important new case.

"It's probably best if I first give you the background on my family," Lance said. "The main thing is that my mother, Valerie Bacchus, walked out on my dad and me when I was in the third grade. I haven't seen her since."

"Do you have any idea why she would do that?" Lenny asked. "Even if she was unhappy with the marriage and wished to end the relationship with your father, it's unusual for a mother to leave her young child."

Lenny was talking in the low, deep, steady tones of his *concerned lawyer* voice. We often hear him practicing this in his office with the door closed.

"For a long time, I assumed my dad did something terrible to her," Lance said. "Something bad enough that she felt like she had to leave both of us. Over the years, I've tried to accept it as one of those things that simply happen."

"What was your father's reaction to her leaving?" Lenny asked.

"Her taking off like that completely devastated my dad. He reported her missing right away and spent months trying to track her down. Over the years, he spent a lot of time and money looking for her so they could try to patch things up."

"Did your mother leave him a note to explain her actions?" Lenny asked.

"She might have, but if so, my dad never talked about it."

"You said your mother's last name was Bacchus?" Was that her maiden name? Did she decide not to change it?"

"Mom's name turned out to be a tricky issue. My parents lived together for over ten years, and they had me right away, but they never married. I have memories of them arguing about having a wedding."

"Was your father hesitant about formalizing the relationship?"

"It was the other way around," Lance said with a shake of his head. "It was my dad who wanted to get married, and my mother wanted to put it off. The most she would compromise was that she agreed to become engaged."

"Do you have any idea why she was opposed to marriage?" Lenny asked.

"I've gotten a few bits and pieces from my dad and grandmother over the years," Lance said. "My mom was somewhat of a free spirit and was unconventional in a lot of ways. Unfortunately, my dad, William Tillman, was murdered almost a year ago during a home invasion. I never did get the full story from him."

"A home invasion? In Scottsdale?" Lenny asked, looking up from his notepad. "That's quite unusual, although I think I remember the story on the news last summer. Did the police catch the perpetrators?"

Lance scowled and again shook his head slowly. "They're officially still working on the case, but they've never come up with a suspect. The current theory is that it was a random burglary gone wrong."

"Is that what you wanted our help with?" Lenny asked.

"Not directly. It's about this."

Lance took the black book he'd been holding and slid it across the desk to Lenny. It had a soft cover, and, until now, I'd assumed it was a bible.

"You asked if my mother had left a note. About a week ago, I was digging through my storage room to find an extra suitcase and came up with one that had once belonged to my mom. When I started to put my clothes in it, I found this, hidden under the lining. It's my mother's journal."

"I assume you've read through it?" Lenny asked as he picked it up and began flipping through the pages.

"I've probably read the entire thing five or six times by now," Lance said with a small smile. "It's the story of the last eighteen months she lived with us."

"What did she write about?" Lenny asked.

"Most of it talked about the day-to-day activities she had with my dad and me. Going to the park, painting the house, how I was doing in school. Those sorts of things."

"That makes sense," Lenny said with a nod. "What else was in there?"

"There was a lot that I didn't understand, of course. She talked about a group of people she called 'the wankers'. They were apparently looking for her, and they seemed to frighten her. She mentioned the 'wanks' every few pages and was constantly on the lookout for suspicious people watching her or even following her."

"Do you know who these people were or what they wanted with your mother? Were 'wankers' the name of an actual group, or was she using it as a more general type of insult for a particular set of people?"

"It's not explained in the journal, and it was the first I'd ever heard of them."

Lenny paused while he made some notes on his legal pad. Sophie flicked her eyes toward Lenny and then over at me.

I knew what she was thinking because she tells me about it after every new client meeting. She doesn't know why Lenny bothers taking notes since she's the one who keeps track of the names and important points of all the latest cases.

"Was there anything else of note in the diary?" Lenny asked.

"She also talked about somebody named Morgan," Lance said. "I don't know if he was a member of the wankers or if that's a first name or a last. She mainly referred to him as 'the asshole'."

"Do you have any idea why there was a conflict between them?" Lenny asked.

"No, but even though she thought he was a jerk, she still

seemed troubled by what had previously happened between them. But the reason I came in is on the last dozen pages," Lance said, now clearly uncomfortable.

"Take your time, Mr. Tillman," Lenny said. "Would you like a drink while we discuss this?"

Chapter Four

"No. I'm alright," Lance said with a slight shake of his head. "My mother wrote that Morgan had found her, although she didn't say how. He called her at home while Dad was at work and told her to meet him at a bar near our house."

"What happened during the meeting?"

"According to the journal, Morgan told her that she needed to come with him or else he'd kill both my dad and me. He then gave her three days to decide what to do."

"How long ago was that?"

"I was in the third grade when my mom left, so roughly twenty-five years ago."

"What else did your mom say about Morgan?" Lenny asked.

"The last few pages were mainly my mom trying to decide what to do. She didn't want to leave my dad and me, but she was convinced we'd both be killed if she didn't go with him."

"Did she mention going to the police?"

"Yes, but she ruled it out. She wrote that this wasn't anything the police could deal with."

"Unfortunately, the statute of limitations on kidnapping in Arizona is only seven years," Lenny said. "There are a few special circumstances that could have extended that, but I don't think we're looking at any of those."

"I was afraid of that," Lance said. "I had some vague notion that we could hold a threat of bringing charges over Morgan's head if we found him. But from what you're saying, it doesn't look like it."

"Why didn't your mother take the diary with her?" Lenny asked. "It's full of incriminating statements. I wouldn't think that she'd want to leave something like that for you or your father to find."

"I remember the day she left," Lance said, now sounding distant. "I was playing in my room after school, waiting for her to come home from work. It was St. Patrick's Day, and I was still wearing my leprechaun hat. She worked in a coffee shop, the Scottsdale Daily Drip, and would usually come home about the time I got back from school. She would always find me right away and give me a hug. It was a sort of game we'd play."

"What happened when your mother came home that day?"

"She came into the house but didn't even try to look for me, and I guess I knew then that something was wrong. I heard her banging around in her bedroom, and when I went in to talk to her, she was throwing things into a suitcase. She was crying and had the most horrible look on her face, like she was scared to death."

"Did she give any sort of explanation of where she was going or what she was doing?" Lenny asked.

"She told me she had a sick friend and had to go out of town for a few days. I remember that this bothered me at the time. Even as a kid, her explanation didn't seem to ring true."

"Did she give any other reason behind why she was going?"

"She only said that Dad and Grandma would take care of me until she got back. Then, she almost ran out the door. In her rush, she didn't have time to take more than a few things, mostly clothes and some personal items. She likely didn't realize she was using the wrong suitcase."

"Did you ever hear from her after she left?" Lenny asked.

"Not directly. The first couple of years, I'd get a box in the mail around my birthday. There was never a card or a return address, but I've always assumed they were from her."

"It's an odd coincidence that your mother received death threats directed toward you and your father, and your dad was later killed," Lenny said. "What can you tell me about what happened to him?"

"There's not much to tell," Lance said, his tone now bitter. "After my mother left, Dad threw himself into his business and became quite successful. Emotionally, he seemed to have good months and bad months. I remember that the month before he was murdered, his mood swings were especially bad. He was in a great mood for a week, then spent a week in a deep depression."

"Do the police have any idea why the burglars targeted your father's house specifically?"

"For the last several years, my dad had started collecting works of art, mainly paintings, along with a few sculptures. The detective thinks that perhaps word about the valuable items had gotten out to the public somehow."

"What else have the police found out about what happened?"

"According to the doorbell camera, two men in ski masks broke in a little after ten that night. Dad apparently grabbed a pistol and confronted them. During the altercation, they shot and killed him. He'd already pushed the panic button, and the police showed up right away, which scared off the men. Unfortunately, they got away cleanly and have never been found."

"That's a terrible loss," Lenny said, shaking his head. "Was anyone else in the house at the time?"

"No. After I moved out, my dad lived alone."

"Were there any other clues in the diary to indicate where your mother went or anything about the people who were trying to harm her?"

"A few things stood out," Lance said as he picked up the journal and flipped through the last few pages. "The day after this Morgan guy called, my mom wrote this."

"I talked to Jess last night. I said that I might need to hole up somewhere for a while. She said to come up to the ranch and stay as long as I needed to."

"Who's Jess?" Lenny asked.

"I hadn't heard the name before," Lance said. "I asked my grandmother about it, and she thought it might have been Jessica St. James. She remembered that my mom had a friend with that name who once stayed with us for a few days. Grandma says she only remembers the woman because her name was similar to one of her favorite actresses at the time, Susan St. James."

"Ah, I loved McMillan and Wife," Sophie said half to herself, a pleased expression on her face.

Lenny gave her a sour look and shook his head in disapproval. Sophie frowned and went back to taking notes.

"Does your grandmother have any idea where Jess is now?" Lenny asked.

"I asked her, but she never got more than the name," Lance said as he shook his head slowly. "But I guess my mom kept in contact with her, at least occasionally."

"What else did you find in the journal?" Lenny asked.

"Well, a few pages before the end, right after Morgan found her, I came across this," he said as he again picked up the book.

"Damn, it looks like it'll happen again. No one to blame except myself, of course. Karma is a wheel, and my life keeps repeating, but this won't make things any easier."

"Do you have any idea what she was talking about?" Lenny asked.

"No clue at all," Lance said. "But it seemed to be one of the main things weighing on her mind right before she took off."

"Would you happen to have a picture of your mother?" Lenny asked. "I realize the most recent ones you have would be at least twenty-five years old, but it would give us a starting point."

"I brought in several," Lance said as he undid the string from the back of his manila envelope and pulled out a half-dozen five-by-sevens and a few four-by-sixes. Lenny examined each photo and then passed them to me.

The pictures were of a pretty woman in her early twenties to early thirties. She was medium height, pale, and very thin, almost to the point of looking gaunt. Her eyes were light blue, and in most of the pictures, she had faint purple lines under them.

I took the pictures and lined them up on Lenny's desk in order of her age. In the early images, her curly, sandy-blonde hair had been cut very short, but she gradually wore it longer as she grew older.

In about half of the pictures, she was with a young boy and sometimes with a man. I could see that the boy was our client, and I assumed the man was Lance's dad.

"You have a very compelling story, Mr. Tillman," Lenny said, still using his *sincere lawyer* voice. "And you've brought up several areas of concern. The diary outlines the fact that your mother was coerced to leave her family under the threat of force. Do I take it that you're mainly interested in having us locate her? What about Morgan and the murder of your father?"

"I feel that my life has been a long series of unanswered questions," Lance said. "I'd like to get closure on everything I can. But I'd mainly like to find out the real story of what happened to my mother. I think that knowing the answer to that would bring me some level of peace."

Lenny sat back in his chair, steepled his fingers together, and thought for several moments about what Lance had requested.

"This could be a rather lengthy investigation," he said. "Digging back through twenty-five years will likely involve a lot of research and legwork. For something like this, you could possibly get away with a private investigator. Why come here? We'll be glad to look into this, but there will be some substantial costs involved."

Lance took a deep breath as if he'd been pondering the same thing. "I've thought about going the private investigator route. My dad actually did have some agencies look into this in the past. However, depending on what you find, some legal issues may come up. If that happens, I'd rather not start from scratch with someone new."

"Fair enough," Lenny said. "Sophie will set you up with the paperwork and collect the initial retainer. I'll have Laura start on this right away. She'll have some questions before you leave. If people have looked into this in the past, it would be helpful for us to have copies of the reports. It might keep us from running down the same dead ends."

"I'll give you everything I have," Lance said.

"I'll review the journal before we do anything. But assuming there are no surprises, I'll advise you to let us send a copy of your mother's diary to the police. If the investigation into the death of your father is still active, it may prove useful to the detectives."

Lance nodded. "Of course, that makes sense. The threats she wrote about in the journal happened a long time ago, but they may be related to what happened last summer."

"Alright," Lenny said. "This should be enough for us to get started."

He then reached over and got on the intercom. "Debbie, would you show Mr. Tillman into the conference room? Sophie will have some papers for him to sign. Then, would you make some high-resolution copies of the photos he has? I'd also like you to make a digital scan of a journal he'll give you."

After Lenny stood to shake the client's hand, Debbie came in to lead Lance away.

"Alright," Lenny said, looking between Sophie and me. "Let me figure out what to do with this one."

He then sat at his desk, opened his top drawer, and pulled out a pack of Dunhill Blacks, a glass ashtray, and a gold Zippo. As Lenny shook out a cigarette and sparked up the lighter, I opened the window to let in a hot breeze.

Sophie stuck her finger in her mouth while making an exaggerated gagging motion. She then went to the switch on the wall and turned on the overhead ceiling fan.

Lenny puffed on his cigarette while he absent-mindedly stared out the big picture window at the shoppers and tourists walking down Fifth Avenue. It was annoying to wait while he went through his ritual of going over the new case in his mind, but we've learned that things go much quicker if we don't interrupt.

"Unfortunately, we're talking about a twenty-five-year-old case, and nothing about this will be straightforward," he finally mused, smashing the remains of his cigarette into the ashtray. "Your only piece of evidence is a recently found diary that is nothing but hearsay, and the only witness is a man looking back with the memories of a small child."

I nodded and shrugged my shoulders. Assignments like this tended to be long and frustrating, but at least I wasn't getting any obvious red flags about angry, naked people being involved.

"I can see this one racking up some serious hours," Lenny continued. "Gina's already fully committed, so this will limit us from taking on anything overly complicated for a few weeks. But the client seems devoted to us doing this, and he has some deep pockets. Sophie, give him a forty-thousand-dollar initial retainer with a twenty percent discount."

Sophie nodded, then took off. I'd seen her yawn a couple of times during the meeting and was surprised she was still awake.

I'd halfway expected to see her head fall to her chest and then bounce up as she was startled awake. It's happened before. *Several* times before.

I was about to leave as well when I had a question. It's something that's always bugged me.

"Why do you always give clients a discount?" I asked. "You almost never charge the full hourly rate. It doesn't make a lot of sense."

Lenny gave me an odd look as he plucked another cigarette out of the pack and stuck it in his mouth.

"It's basic marketing," he said, as if it should be obvious. The unlit Dunhill bounced up and down in his lips as he spoke.

When I still looked confused, he shook his head in disappointment. He lit the cigarette with the Zippo and gestured for me to sit in the chair in front of his desk.

"Look, my hourly rate is one of the highest in the city," he said slowly, as if I were a five-year-old. "People can easily look up my fee structure on the internet. There are websites that track that sort of thing."

"I've seen them," I said. "You're right at the top of the list."

"Exactly," he said, pointing his cigarette at me as he talked. "Potential clients see how much I charge, and they know I must be one of the best attorneys out there. It's one of the main reasons they come here to ask me about their problems. The initial consultation is free, and they think they're pulling a fast one when they come in to get my opinion about something."

"Okay," I said. "I guess that makes sense."

"But then I give them a substantial discount off the full rate to have me work on their problem. Even though they're still paying a ton, they don't feel like they're getting ripped off. In fact, they often feel like they're getting a pretty good deal. It keeps them from shopping around to find somebody cheaper."

Go figure.

Chapter Five

I went into reception and entered the conference room, where Lance had signed the last form and given Sophie a credit card. He had the slightly dazed look that most new clients have when they realize they've handed over enough money to buy a nice car.

"Before you go, I'd like to get some more background on the assignment," I said.

"Of course," he replied with a sigh. "I'll tell you anything I know."

We spent the next half-hour going over the facts of the case. I tried to bring out some more details of the events surrounding his mother's departure and his dad's murder. Although I could sense that Lance wasn't holding anything back, it was also clear he didn't have a lot of new information.

"I'll need the reports from the other investigators," I said. "From what I gather, they didn't learn where your mother had ended up, but they might have gone down some paths that may be useful."

"They're over at my house," he said. "I have an appointment at my office in about half an hour, and I'll need to take care of that first. I can either come back here afterward, or we can meet at my place. I'm back to living in the home I grew up in."

"Let's meet at your house," I said. "It would be good to see where everything happened. What time would be best for you?"

"I'll be back over there by three or three-thirty at the latest. The address is in the paperwork I just signed. I'll meet you there."

After Lance took off, I asked Debbie about lunch. It was only ten-thirty, but I was starting to get hungry.

"Lunch sounds great," she said. "Whatever you're in the mood for. Give me a call when you're ready to go."

I went into the back offices and found Sophie asleep at her desk, snoring loudly. She must've heard me come into the room because she woke with a start and quickly looked around. She then relaxed when she saw it was only me.

"Is the client gone?" she asked as she yawned and stretched. A strand of her dark hair was plastered against her face, and she peeled it away. "It's a shame about what happened to his parents, but he's kinda cute. Much better than the usual clients Lenny picks up. Let me know if you need any help with this one."

"Don't you literally have Milo sleeping in your bed right now? Why would you want to start hanging out with the client?"

"Hey, I didn't say I wanted to date the man. Although it would be nice to go out with someone and not be forced to meet their parents. Whenever a guy starts bugging me about meeting his parents, I know it's time to end the relationship."

"Really? Has Milo ever asked you to meet his parents?"

"His family lives back east, New York or somewhere, and they think Scottsdale's too hot to visit. He went out there about six months ago but didn't invite me. I'm good with that."

"What will you do if he invites you along the next time he sees them?"

"I'm not sure. Meeting the parents brings up too many expectations. His mom will keep glancing down at my finger, like she's expecting to see an engagement ring magically appear on it."

"But no pressure, huh?" I laughed.

"I never know if I'm supposed to lie and say that I'm deeply in love with their son and we're thinking about forming a new life together or if I'm supposed to tell the truth and say that their boy is about the only one I can stand to be with for more than a few dates and he'll do, at least for the time being."

"I could see where that would be a dilemma."

"Yeah, it's pretty much a lose-lose for me. No matter what I say, somebody's feelings will eventually get hurt. I prefer to avoid the situation altogether. Nothing good can come from it."

"But what about Milo? Where does he fall? Have you decided yet? Is he good for the long-term, or is he only your current sex toy?"

"Oh, I don't know when it comes to him," she groaned. "Sometimes, he does the dumbest things, but then he'll turn around and become incredibly sweet."

"Men are like that," I laughed. "But who knows, maybe he's the one?"

Sophie only looked at me and shrugged her shoulders.

"Hey," I said. "Debbie's good for lunch today. Are you interested?"

"Yeah, lunch sounds great, but don't make it too soon. I'm going to go back to meditating."

"Meditating? You mean doing another one of your power naps, right?"

"Nope, no more power naps for me. I was meditating. I'm trying to achieve the *Samadhi* state of consciousness."

I looked at my best friend, completely confused.

"I was reading through our employee handbook," she said. "The one Lenny had me buy when Amber first came to work for us. It says that for peak performance, employees should take occasional brief breaks to recharge their mental energy."

"Okay, but what does that have to do with sleeping at your desk?"

"According to the handbook, reading something inspirational or meditating are effective ways for employees to refocus. That's what I'm going to do from now on. I'll follow the handbook. Whenever I can't focus, I'll simply close my eyes and meditate. It's not my fault that I meditate so deeply that I enter a Zen-like state that the uninitiated can confuse with sleep."

I gave her my best *Are you kidding me?* look, and I may have rolled my eyes.

"Hey, don't give me that look," she said, sounding annoyed. "I don't make the rules. I'm only working the system."

Before I started to organize myself for the new assignment, I called Grandma Henderson.

"Hi, Grandma," I said when she answered. "How's

Marlowe doing? He still seemed a little under the weather this morning."

"So far, he's spent the morning sleeping and sneezing. He had a light breakfast over here, but not like he usually does."

"I'm still hoping it's only allergies," I said. "Maybe something's blooming in the desert that doesn't agree with him."

"Well, that could be what's going on," she said somewhat skeptically. "But I'm afraid he's coming down with a cold. At least he doesn't seem overly bothered by it. I was going to suggest we give him a day or two to get over it on his own before taking him in."

Gina came into the back offices a little before eleven. She looked energetic and had rosy cheeks from working on her assignments all morning.

"Hey, Gina," I said as she set her bag on her desk. "It looks like you've been busy."

"Busy and productive," she said with a laugh. "One of the nice things about this job is that you never run out of things to do."

"Oh, hi Gina," Sophie said as she woke up and yawned.

"I was wondering if you'd make it through the day without taking a power nap," Gina said, shaking her head.

"I know," Sophie admitted. "It's my own fault for playing with Milo all night. But on the positive side, now that I've learned to meditate, I'll be more focused and have a brighter disposition at work."

"Meditate?" Gina asked, confused as she looked between

Sophie and me for an explanation.

"Instead of taking power naps, Sophie's switched to meditating at her desk, with her eyes closed," I said.

"Ah," Gina said with a smirk and a knowing nod.

"Hey, don't knock it," Sophie said. "I've been listening to a bunch of TikToks about meditation. I'm learning the importance of self-care. I need to avoid toxic people and situations in order to achieve self-actualization. I've been emotionally triggered in the past here in the office, and I'm working toward making this a safe space and finding deep closure."

"You sound like my freshman psychology class," Gina laughed.

"Are you interested in lunch?" I asked. "Debbie's coming too, but we haven't decided on a place yet."

"Lunch would be great," Gina said. "But I won't have a lot of time. Do you think she'd mind if we walked down the street for tacos?"

"Let's find out," Sophie said.

The three of us walked to the front and found Debbie at her desk, typing on her computer.

"Are you ready for lunch?" Gina asked. "Would tacos be okay?"

"Tacos are perfect," she said. "We haven't been there in a couple of weeks. I'll let Lenny know he'll be manning the fort alone for about an hour."

Debbie pressed the intercom to Lenny's office. "Boss, we're leaving for lunch. I'll forward the phone to my mobile. Should I lock up, or do you mind talking to people if they come in off the street?"

"What?" his voice boomed through the phone, sounding

irritated. "Everyone's going? Even Sophie? You do know I'm trying to run a business here? Right?"

"So, I should lock the front door?" Debbie asked, a playful twinkle in her eye.

"No, leave it open," he grumbled. "I'll take care of *everything* while my entire staff leaves to have a nice lunch. But try not to be gone all day."

"Thanks, Boss," Debbie said in her always cheerful voice.

We left through the front door and headed down the street. Typical of mid-May, the sky was a deep blue, with only a few clouds on the northern horizon.

The temperature was in the low nineties, which was perhaps considered warm in some parts of the country, but it was a pleasant spring day in Scottsdale.

We were about halfway to Dos Gringos, our go-to place for lunch tacos and day drinking, when we heard someone squealing in delight and calling our names. We turned to see a smiling woman in her mid-twenties running down the sidewalk toward us.

She was medium height and relatively thin. Her dark blonde hair hung down to her shoulders. It only took a second for me to recognize her as Susan Monroe.

Susan was a former client, and I'd worked on an assignment with her about six months before. It had involved going into Nevada and breaking into a private casino called the Black Castle so Susan could meet up with her dad, a man named Michael McKinsey.

Things had ultimately worked out well, and I'd hoped to meet her again. It looked like today was the day.

Susan caught up with us, and there were hugs all around. We then introduced her to Debbie. Susan laughed when Sophie said that Debbie had been hired partially to put away the stacks of files that had been accumulating in the office.

"What are you doing here in Old Town?" I asked. "We're going to Dos Gringos for tacos. You should join us."

"I won't be able to today," she said. "But you've got to see this."

She then turned and walked back the way she'd come, stopping at a storefront with windows that had been covered with white paper from the inside. The last time we'd walked by, this had been a small, high-end furniture store in the process of permanently closing.

We stopped next to her, looking for an explanation.

"Come inside and see," she beamed at us.

She opened the door, and we followed her in. The interior had been cleared out, and there were the smells of fresh paint and a recently varnished wood floor.

Susan's mother, Olivia, stood on a tall stepladder, adjusting overhead lights that were illuminating a large and ornate sign on the wall. The sign read *Desert Vistas, Fine Art, Scottsdale*.

"Oh my god," I squealed. "You're reopening the gallery?"

"Laura?" Olivia asked as she looked down at our group. "Is that you?"

"Hi, Olivia," I called out as she climbed down the ladder to give everyone a hug. "When did all this happen?"

"It's our first week of moving in," Susan said. "I was going to head down to your office to say hello, but then I saw everyone walking down the street."

"A friend of Michael's owns the building," Olivia said. "They retired and closed the business last month. I was able to get a ten-year lease. It's a gorgeous space with high ceilings and narrow rooms. It's perfect for a gallery."

"How is Michael?" I asked. "Has he adjusted to life away from the Black Castle?"

"He loves it," Olivia said. "He'd been looking for a way to get out of the casino business for some time. Of course, Katherine kept him on as a consultant, but he goes up there as seldom as possible."

"Honestly, I'm good with never going back to the Black Castle," I said, a small shudder going through me as I briefly relived some frightening memories of the casino.

"Same with me," Susan said quietly, a haunted look on her face. "Once was more than enough."

"How are you doing?" I asked Olivia. "The last time we met, you had some health concerns."

"Yeah, it was touch and go for a while. Fortunately, we found a specialist who was able to diagnose my condition properly. It turns out the previous doctors were treating the wrong disease. I've been on some new medications for several months, and the problems have all but disappeared."

"Well, you look good," I said, and I meant it. Olivia looked like she'd dropped twenty pounds, and her body looked toned and healthy. She'd even started to let her blonde hair grow out, like I'd seen in pictures of her in her twenties.

"I never did get a chance to thank you for rescuing us from that Jonathan LaRose character," Olivia said. "That man was a nightmare."

"It was no problem," I said. "I'm only glad that everything worked out."

"We'll be having our grand opening in a little over a week," Olivia said. "I hope everyone will be able to come by. There'll be drinks and hors d'oeuvres the entire time."

As she spoke, I looked down at her left hand. There was a gold ring with a huge sparkly diamond. Susan saw what I was looking at and giggled.

"Mom and Dad are engaged," she beamed. "Can you believe it?"

"Congratulations," we all sang out in unison.

After the excitement of seeing Susan again, lunch was tame by comparison. Of course, everyone wanted to know what had happened with Olivia, Susan, Jonathon, and the Black Castle.

Gina had heard bits and pieces, while Sophie had already heard most of the story through Milo. But I still went over the entire assignment for Debbie.

I only skipped over the drug operation, the money laundering, the gun battle, the involvement of Max, Gabriella getting shot, Hobbs, the ferryman ramming his barge into the security boat, and Susan almost drowning in the Colorado River. Come to think of it, I suppose I skipped over most of the story.

The one thing I couldn't skip over was that creep Jonathan LaRose, the Vice President of Casino Security. Sophie brought up the fact that he'd placed a bomb on my car's engine. That, combined with Olivia's description of the man, meant that I couldn't pretend he didn't exist.

But I didn't go into any details about how he'd tortured Susan and me by locking us in an actual dungeon and letting us slowly weaken through lack of food and water.

The less I thought about that jerk, the better. I was glad he was gone, likely permanently.

We got back to the office at about twelve forty-five. Lenny

went out for a late lunch, and Gina took off for her next interview. Back at her desk, Sophie yawned, and her eyes started to get the unfocused look that usually happens right before she takes a nap.

"Hey," I said. "Before you start to power meditate, would you start a couple of secret software searches for me?"

"Oh, I already did," she said as she yawned again.

"Really?"

"Yeah, I did it while you were interviewing the client. I knew you'd have me do it at some point today, so I entered everything before I began to meditate."

"Who'd you start searches on?" I asked.

"Um, Valerie Bacchus, William Tillman, Lance Tillman, and Jessica St. James."

"You started a search on the client and his dad?"

"Yeah," she said with a small laugh. "You usually wait a couple of days, then have me do a deep dive on the client, so I thought I'd get a jump on you."

"Fine," I admitted. "You're right."

"Although with Valerie Bacchus and Jessie St. James, I don't know how much information we'll get back. They have weird names, so that will help. But you've got to get me more background information on them. It gives the program something concrete to focus on."

"Okay, what do you need?"

"Just the usual. An accurate age is good. So is the place of birth. But a valid social security number is even better."

"I'll see what I can come up with. Did you happen to search for the wankers? That may have been the name of a group that was searching for Lance's mother."

"Well, I submitted that one as well," she said as she shook her head. "But it seems more like an insult rather than a group name. I'll let you know what I find out."

Chapter Six

I didn't need to be at Lance's house until three-thirty, so I figured I'd use the time to review the journal. Debbie had sent it to me as a digital file, along with copies of the pictures of Valerie, which I now had on both my laptop and my tablet.

As Lance mentioned, most of the journal focused on the day-to-day activities of a woman with a busy husband and an active eight-year-old boy. Overall, I got the impression that Lance's mother was a happy woman with a positive outlook on her future.

Only a few comments were sprinkled throughout the pages concerning the mystery of where she had gone or who had forced her to leave. It was a little like reading a detective novel with the first and last chapters of the story missing.

Whenever I came across a statement that looked relevant, I highlighted it in pink and copied the passage to a separate file. I ended up with ten or fifteen sentences that all seemed to be about her previous life, but nothing stood out.

Every time I encountered an unfamiliar name, I added it to a second column. In addition to Morgan and Jess, I ended up with three extra people: Dalton, Porter, and Mercer. Unfortunately, I had no idea who any of them were or if they were connected to what had happened.

She also had a few scattered references to 'the asshole'

and 'her old life', but I could tell she wasn't spending a lot of time dwelling on the past. Even if she mentioned that something reminded her of the asshole or the wanks, she never followed it up or discussed it further.

That changed after Morgan called her. The last dozen pages were completely taken over by the events that led to her taking off and leaving her family behind.

She was angry and distraught about what was happening, but I also got the feeling that she was resigned to it. It was as if she'd always known that this, or something like it, was going to happen someday.

By the time I'd finished the entire journal, I felt like I had a pretty good idea of who Valerie Bacchus was and how she thought. She struck me as an overall good person who had somehow become caught up in something out of her control.

Unfortunately, I didn't have a clue who Morgan was or why he'd forced her to leave. I could already tell that my new assignment was going to be frustrating.

A little after three, I drove over to Lance's house, an attractive ranch on Orange Blossom Lane. It was a few blocks north of Chaparral Road, with the bulk of Camelback Mountain taking up the horizon to the west.

I entered the circular drive and parked next to a black BMW convertible that I assumed was Lance's. I climbed out and admired the well-maintained landscaping of the homes up and down the quiet street.

When I rang the bell, Lance opened the door and led me into a large living room. "I know it's early," he said. "But could I get you a drink?"

Lance looked somewhat stressed, and he already had a glass of bourbon, or maybe rye, sitting on the counter of a well-stocked wet bar, so I accepted.

"Sure, I'll take a scotch with one ice cube. Whatever you have would be great."

While Lance made the drink, I took some time to look around the living room. Almost a dozen oil paintings, mainly landscapes in gilded frames, hung on the high walls. Colorful glass sculptures sat on the tables and sideboards.

"I love the paintings," I said. "Were these the ones your dad collected?"

"That's right," he said, handing me the drink. "My mom had always been interested in painting and was a bit of an artist herself. That's one of hers," he said, pointing to a gorgeous scene of a mountain sunrise.

I took a step closer to the canvas and gazed at the work. I don't know a lot about art, but the details of the trees were incredible. They had a sort of 3D effect that almost gave them a sense of motion.

"She's really good," I exclaimed. "Did she ever think about selling her work?"

"She sold a few paintings, according to what my dad told me. But she always considered art a hobby rather than something to try to make a living from. But I'm pretty sure it was through her love of art that my dad started collecting. I think he always had a secret hope of finding one of her paintings in a gallery somewhere."

"It looks like the rest of the canvases are from the same three artists," I said as I studied the oil paintings.

"After he started to become successful, my dad started collecting landscapes from an artist out east named Robert Crombie and some from an artist who lives in Maui named

Diane Appler. About two years ago, he began picking up paintings from an artist named Cici."

"Is Cici a first name or a last?" I asked.

"My dad talked about the artist as a woman, so I assume it was a first name."

"Which ones are hers?" I asked as I sipped the scotch, a nice Chivas Regal.

"The three in a row on that wall," he said, pointing to a group of paintings.

Two featured colorful red mountains. I thought I recognized one of them as Cathedral Rock, one of the big red sandstone buttes near Sedona. The third painting was of a town square with a different large red mountain in the background.

"Those are stunning," I said as I stepped closer. "The detail is incredible. They almost look like photographs from a distance, but when you get closer, you can tell they're paintings."

"You can see why my dad liked them so much. I've kept them right where he first hung them."

Lance sat on a black leather sofa, and I took an overstuffed chair. On the coffee table were three folders, each jammed with papers.

"Are those the reports from the other investigators?" I asked, pointing to the files.

"Yeah, I dug them out of Dad's file cabinet in the den. I've been flipping through them since I found the journal. I thought I could maybe make some new connections."

"How old are these reports?"

"My dad hired the first private investigator after the police gave up on finding my mother, so a little over twenty years ago. The second time was about a decade ago, and the last attempt to find her was maybe two and a half years ago."

"Did anything in the reports stand out when you went through them again?"

Lance shook his head slowly. "My dad always hired respectable detective agencies, and they seemed to be serious about finding her. But the only solid thing they all could agree on was that Valerie Bacchus wasn't my mother's real name."

What?

"When we were with Lenny, you mentioned that your mom's name was a tricky issue. Is this what you meant?"

"That's right. Unfortunately, none of the private investigators could discover what her actual name was. She had a driver's license with her photo and the Valerie Bacchus name, but we're not sure how she got it. The same goes for her Social Security number. They traced that back to Valerie Bacchus as well."

"Did they learn anything about it?"

"Oh, sure. The second investigator determined that Val Bacchus was a real person, but she died in a nursing home the year before my mother met my dad. The last investigator thought that my mother had been working at the senior facility while the real Valerie Bacchus was staying there. Unfortunately, the place closed about fifteen years ago, and the employment records from back then were lost."

"Where was the nursing home?"

"It was in the little town of Sycamore Springs. It's up in the mountains, about halfway between Sedona and Cottonwood, along Oak Creek. I went up there to look around a few months ago, and it seemed like a nice place. But I wasn't able to learn anything."

There was a pause while Lance finished his drink and went to the wet bar to make another. He looked at me and pointed to the scotch bottle.

I shook my head and again sensed that he was rather stressed over this.

"Are you doing okay?" I asked.

"To be honest, I'm starting to rethink how deeply I want to look into this," he said as he walked back to the couch, the ice cubes clinking in his new drink as he took a sip. "I've been debating all afternoon if I should tell you to drop this and simply leave well enough alone."

"What do you mean?"

"I've always been curious about why my mother left us, and I'd like to find out what happened to her. You know, is she still alive, and is she happy? Those sorts of things. But it's not like I'm trying for some sort of family reunion or anything like that."

I took another sip of the scotch and thought about what he said. "Look, you came over to the office today and paid Lenny a big retainer. That has to mean something. Why would you be willing to do that if you weren't looking for something more than is she still alive?"

"I've always wanted to know the reason behind why she took off, and finding the journal has only kicked that desire up a notch. If what she wrote was true, then she also went through an emotional rollercoaster over this. But after all this time, I suppose the *why* really doesn't matter all that much anymore. What's done is done."

"But you have to be curious. Why else come to us?"

Lance took a big sip of his drink and shook his head. "Honestly, finding my mother's journal has stirred up a lot of emotions and memories over the last few days. Learning that she was coerced into leaving us is deeply troubling. On top of what happened to my dad last June, it's been hard to think straight about it. Maybe I'm only trying to get some sort of closure."

I finished the drink and set it on the coffee table. "I'll tell you what. We'll start a full digital search for your mom. I'll also interview your grandmother and see what she thinks about everything. If we can find out where your mother ended up, maybe that will be enough information to help you sleep better. Then, if you want me to do more than that, we can discuss it."

Lance shook his head, and I could see he wasn't completely convinced. "I'm still not sure I'm doing the right thing. The more I go over this, the more I get the feeling we'd be poking at a very old hornet's nest. But alright, I've already paid the money. You might as well start to ask around."

"Perfect," I said. "I'll begin the investigation and let you know what I find out."

"Would you like me to go with you when you talk with my grandmother?"

"I'll be okay," I said. "Don't take this the wrong way, but for something like this, I tend to get better answers when I go alone."

Lance called his grandmother to let her know that he'd hired me to investigate his mom's disappearance and that I'd want to talk with her. She said she'd be home all afternoon, and I could stop by anytime.

I drove to the address on East Hazelwood Street and was pleasantly surprised to find that it was across from Navajo Elementary School, about three blocks from where I'd grown up in South Scottsdale. I have a lot of memories of this part of town, and it's always a strange feeling to be back in my old neighborhood.

The houses are smaller than the newer ones in the northern parts of town, but the lots here are much bigger. I guess land was less expensive back then.

I knocked, and a pleasant-looking woman in her early eighties opened the door. She had bright, intelligent eyes and what seemed like a friendly disposition.

She introduced herself as Carol Tillman. As she led me into the living room, she offered me a drink.

"Sure," I said. "Whatever you're having."

Her house had a similar layout to the home I grew up in, I noted as we went into the kitchen. There was already a half-full glass of white wine on the counter.

Carol went to the fridge, poured out a second glass, and handed it to me. We then went into the living room and sat on a black leather couch.

"Lance said you're looking into Valerie's disappearance?" Carol asked. "It was horrible for the family, but that was a long time ago. All Lance has are fuzzy memories of his mother. There have already been three investigators who've looked into it, and they never came up with anything. I've honestly been hoping that he'd leave well enough alone."

"I'm sure you know about this," I said. "But he's gotten ahold of some information recently that sheds some new light on what happened back then."

"Valerie's diary," she said stiffly as she drained the rest of her glass. "Lance had me read it."

At the mention of Valerie's journal, Carol tensed up. I normally hate it when the person I'm interviewing goes stiff, but in this case, I was thrilled.

I could tell that something was going on. Something that perhaps even Lance didn't know.

"Carol," I said. "You found something in the diary that has you concerned, didn't you?"

Carol nodded, and I could see she was deeply troubled. "Perhaps it would help if I had another glass," she said. "Honestly, this entire situation has me questioning what happened."

I followed her into the kitchen and watched as she poured herself another glass. Taking a large sip seemed to steady her nerves, and I let her compose herself.

"Bill told me about something that happened last year," she said slowly. "He asked me to keep it a secret from Lance, at least until he could straighten everything out. He said the situation was complicated."

"What happened?" I asked.

"As you could probably tell from the number of private investigators he hired, Bill never gave up on finding Valerie. Well, late last spring, he located her. I don't have any of the details, but they apparently spent several days together."

Late last spring? Crap.

"That would have put them together right before he was murdered," I said.

Carol nodded and took another long sip of her wine. "I can't be certain, and I've never openly expressed my concerns, but it was only a few days after Bill mentioned being with Valerie that he was murdered."

"Do you think the two events are related?"

"Well, the police don't think Bill was targeted. They concluded that it was a home invasion that had taken a tragic turn."

"But you have your doubts?"

"I've never told Lance or the police. But whatever happened between Bill and Valerie may have resulted in my son being murdered."

"Why not tell them?" I asked. "Maybe the police could catch the killers?"

"The detective let us know that there was no DNA, fingerprints, or physical evidence of any kind other than the doorbell camera video. If I started making accusations against an unknown group of men, I could see them coming back for a second round. I don't want anything to happen to Lance. He's the only family I have left."

"But now that you've read Valerie's journal?"

"It seems like she knew all about these men and how violent they were, even all those years ago. I can guess that they found out about Bill and Valerie being together last spring and decided to take revenge."

"Are you going to tell Lance about it?" I asked. "He should probably know what he's up against."

"You're right, of course. I've needed to tell him ever since I read the damn diary. Now that I've told you, it might make it easier to tell him as well."

I grabbed a carne asada burrito from Filiberto's Mexican and drove back to my place. After dropping off my dinner on my dining room table, I stopped by Grandma Henderson's to see how Marlowe was doing. When the door opened, Grandpa Bob was standing there.

"Hello, cookie," Bob said in his cheerful voice. "How's

the private eye business? From what I see on the news, there's still plenty of criminals out there for you to nab."

"Business has been busy lately," I said.

I've explained to Bob what I actually do several times, but he's never seemed able to grasp the concept.

We walked into the living room, where Marlowe was sound asleep on his chair. Grandma Henderson came out of the bedroom and seemed happy to see me.

"Hello, dear," she said. "It's good to see you,"

"Same here," I said. "How's Marlowe doing?"

"Well, he's been a little restless, and he's had a few sneezes, but so far, he hasn't gotten any worse. His nose has been a little runny, and his sneezing sometimes makes a mess. I had to change my shirt earlier, and I've washed his afghan."

"I'm glad you're here to watch over him," I said. "I'd worry if he was alone in an apartment all day."

"Don't spend a lot of time worrying about that," Grandma said. "I don't mind taking care of Marlowe. I just wish he didn't make such a mess when he sneezes."

I took Marlowe back to my place and set him down on a towel on the couch. I glanced at the clock and thought this might be a good time to catch Max.

"Hey," I said when he answered. "How have you been? I've been thinking about you all day."

"I'm doing good," he said. "Tell me about your new assignment at work. Hopefully, it's something without cheating spouses or international terrorists."

"It's more of a missing person. The only problem is that it's from a long time ago. I'll likely be running around and chasing down a lot of dead-end leads."

"Well, good luck in solving the mystery quickly," he said. "But keep me in mind whenever you have a free evening or even a free weekend. I hate going more than a few days without seeing you."

"You think I like not seeing you?" I laughed. "Trust me, I go a little bonkers when I don't get to kiss you every day. We'll get together as soon as I can. I promise."

Chapter Seven

A little after seven the next morning, I was swiping on mascara and getting ready to go down to the office. Marlowe was still asleep on the bed.

This had me somewhat concerned, especially since he'd been sneezing off and on the entire night. His usual routine was to dash into the kitchen at the first signs of me waking up. He'd then sit in front of his food bowl and remind me that he was nearly dead from starvation until I fed him.

My phone rang, and I picked it up. Looking at the readout, I recognized the number as Lance's.

That was quick.

"Good morning," I said as I went out to my living room, grabbed a notepad, and sat on the couch. "I didn't expect you to call me back so soon."

"Honestly, neither did I. But I ended up having a long conversation with my grandmother last night, and she shed some new light on things. From what she said, she'd already told you what she'd learned."

"What did she tell you?" I asked. "We had a long conversation yesterday afternoon, but I'd like to compare notes."

"She said that late last spring, Dad had found my mother,

and he spent several days with her."

"Did she have any information on where your mom was living or anything else that could help us find her?"

"I pressed her on it, but that was all my dad shared with her. He'd found my mother and spent time with her."

"Okay, that tracks with what she told me," I said. "I was thinking that your dad finding her might have accounted for the mood swings you said he was having. I find it especially troubling that your father was killed only a few weeks after he was with your mom."

"Those were my thoughts as well," Lance said. "I'm not a big believer in coincidence. I'm starting to think that when my dad was attacked, it wasn't simply a random burglary gone wrong. My grandmother shares those thoughts as well."

"Honestly, in my line of work, I don't believe in coincidence either," I said. "Do I take it you'd like me to continue the investigation?"

"Please do. I don't know how my dad being murdered last June ties into him locating my mother or even to what happened twenty-five years ago, but we'll need to find out."

As I was talking with Lance, Marlowe sauntered into the living room. He saw me on the couch and hopped onto my lap, wanting to be petted.

"Did your grandmother say why she waited until now to tell you about this?" I asked while stroking my purring cat.

"I asked her about that," Lance said. "It seems that when Dad told her about finding my mom last year, he swore her to secrecy. He told her that things with my mother were complicated and that he would need to work out some details before he could openly talk about her. My grandmother said she put the timeline together after the murder and didn't want me to get involved in something that may have killed her son."

"I'll get going on this right away. I'll go over the reports from the other investigators again, especially the last one. There must have been enough information in those for your dad to piece together where your mom was living."

"Let me know how I can help."

"I might need you to come with me when I interview my leads. Will you have any free time over the next few days?"

"I've already let my senior managers know I may need to take some time off. I should be good this afternoon and pretty much for the rest of the week."

"Alright, let me set things up, and I'll give you a call."

I petted Marlowe for another few seconds. He seemed tired, and his eyes were a little watery. "How are you feeling?" I asked.

Marlowe looked up at me and sneezed. To my horror, globs of green gunk sprayed all over my navy blue shorts.

Oh, yuck!

Marlowe seemed surprised that he'd made such a mess. He looked up at me and squeaked, his version of a meow.

"It's okay," I said as I put him on the floor. "I know you don't feel good."

I went into the bedroom and changed outfits, then went back to the kitchen and plopped a spoonful of Ocean Delight in Marlowe's bowl. Instead of his usual inhaling the food, he only lightly picked at it.

I walked over to Grandma's apartment and knocked on the door. I knew that by now, she would have had her morning walk and would be fixing breakfast for Grandpa Bob.

"Why, Laura," Grandma said in her bright voice. "It's good to see you. How's Marlowe today?"

"He's not getting any better," I said. "Would you mind keeping an eye on him today? If his cold doesn't start to clear up, I'll need to take him to the vet."

"Of course," she said. "If you'd like, I could take him down. I still have the cat carrier from the last time we had to take him in. Do you still use my old vet?"

"That's right, Doctor Dusty. Let's see how Marlowe does today, but I may take you up on the offer."

Still thinking about Marlowe, I stopped by Dunkin' and got a box of doughnuts before heading to the office. I wanted to thank Sophie for running the searches the day before using the secret software.

After talking with the client and his grandmother the previous afternoon, I knew the Valerie Bacchus name would likely go nowhere. Fresh doughnuts with chocolate icing and rainbow sprinkles would be a great way to apologize for that.

When I parked and went into the back offices, Gina and Sophie were both drinking coffee and chatting away. Sophie saw the box of doughnuts, and her eyes got big.

"You know, I was telling Gina this would be a good day for you to bring in doughnuts," Sophie said as she made urgent hand motions for me to bring her the box.

"Yeah," I said as I opened the lid and presented it to my co-worker. "Thanks for starting the searches for me yesterday."

"It's no problem," she said with a chuckle as she plucked out a doughnut from the box. "Although I don't think you're going to be overly thrilled with the results. The folders are on your desk."

I then pressed the intercom button for Debbie's phone in reception. *"Dough-nuts!"* I sang out.

"Sophie was telling me more about your twenty-five-year-old kidnapping case," Gina said as she pulled out a Boston Cream. "Those are tough. Even if there'd been some solid leads at one point, I'm sure they've mostly evaporated over time."

"Yeah," I agreed. "When it happened, no one knew why the client's mother took off and left her family. But it now appears that someone from her past had found her and threatened to kill her fiancée and child unless she went with him."

"It's well past the seven-year statute of limitations," Gina said. "But make sure to keep the police informed if you learn who was involved. It might help them with other cold kidnapping cases."

"That's not all. I learned that the client's dad had managed to locate his mother and had apparently spent some time with her late last spring. He was then killed a few weeks later in what appeared to be a random home invasion and burglary gone wrong."

"It sounds like your assignment got complicated faster than usual," Gina said with a smile. "Let me know if I can help you with anything. But look at it this way, at least you won't need to take pictures of naked people having sex."

"Yeah," Sophie agreed as she took a bite of her doughnut. "That's what I told her. You'll only need to deal with kidnappers and murderers this time around. That beats hiding out in closets listening to skanky women and sleazy men moan with pleasure."

The door to the front offices opened, and Debbie came hurrying in. She held a mug of coffee and had a huge smile on her face. "Did somebody say doughnuts?" she laughed.

After several minutes of chatting and munching on pastries, Debbie went back to reception, and Gina started to type up some notes. I picked up the first folder and began to flip through the twenty or thirty pages of information.

Rather than spending the next hour trying to learn what was in each file, I looked at Sophie. "What did the secret software find?"

"The client came back okay, and so did Jessie St. James," she said as she took a bite of her second doughnut. "They both led relatively normal lives, and neither one ever got into serious trouble with the law. Lance spent most of his life here in Scottsdale. He went to Coronado High and ASU. Never been arrested, and his credit is over eight hundred."

"What about Jessie St. James?" I asked.

"Her dad was a cowboy up in the mountains, and she lived at whatever ranch her dad worked at. After college, she worked on a ranch outside of Kingman and eventually saved up enough money to make a down payment on a small plot of open land outside of Payson. That was more than thirty years ago, and she named it 'Moonlight Ranch'. It's been steadily growing, and now it's one of the bigger ones along the Mogollon Rim."

"That makes sense from what our client's mom wrote in her journal," I said. "It looks like I'll need to go up to Payson and talk with her. What about the dad, William Tillman?"

"Pretty much the same," Sophie said. "Bill Tillman had a wild streak in his youth. He served two hitches in the Army, rose to staff sergeant, and was honorably discharged. After he got out, he was arrested a few times for fighting, resisting arrest, and being intoxicated in public. But it was never for anything serious."

"Okay, what else?"

"He went to ASU, got a business degree, and started a financial services company here in town. It steadily grew, and by the time of his death last June, it was quite valuable. Lance is currently running it, but I don't think he'd need to work another day in his life if he ever decided to sell it."

"Did anything come back on the mom?" I asked. "I picked up some interesting information on her yesterday."

"Valerie Bacchus was the weird one," Sophie said. "I figured with a name that unusual, there couldn't be too many people to sort through. Unfortunately, when I filtered the names with people who lived in Arizona, I came up with two hits."

"Well, that should have made it easy," I said.

"Yeah, you'd think," Sophie said. "But the first one died roughly thirty-five years ago when she was ninety-six years old."

"Okay," I said, somewhat confused. "But wouldn't that make the other one Lance's mother?"

"Um, not exactly. It's more like Valerie Bacchus came back to life. Same name, same social security number. Only this time, she was in her early twenties and had curly blonde hair. Here, look at this," Sophie said as she turned her monitor towards me.

On the screen was a photo that likely came off a driver's license. Behind her was the typical neutral blue background of the Arizona MVD.

It showed a thin, pretty woman in her early twenties with medium-length hair looking blankly into the camera. From the pictures Lance had shown us, the woman on the monitor was his mother.

"Okay," I said. "That actually makes sense. According to the private investigators who looked into her background,

Valerie Bacchus wasn't her real name. Lance's mother must have lifted the name and social security number from the real Valerie."

"If the original Valerie died and the client's mother took over the name, they likely knew each other ahead of time," Gina said without looking up. "Where did Valerie pass away?"

"Um," Sophie said as she looked through the report on her monitor. "Hold on. I know it's here somewhere."

"The previous investigators think it was in a little town in the mountains called Sycamore Springs," I said.

"Oh, really?" Gina asked. "I've been there a couple of times. It's on the banks of Oak Creek, about ten miles downstream from Sedona. It's at about four thousand feet of elevation, so they have nice weather pretty much all year round. The mountains are lovely up there, and they have some great hiking trails."

"Here it is," Sophie said as she nodded her head and pointed to the monitor. "Valerie Bacchus died at the Briarwood Manor in Sycamore Springs. It sounds like an extended care facility for seniors."

She then typed some information into her computer. "Hmm," she said. "I looked it up on the internet, and it's not listed. It might not be operating anymore."

"That tracks with what the other investigators found," I said. "It apparently closed about fifteen years ago. They thought Lance's mother might have worked there, but the employment records were lost when the facility shut down."

"So, the last time we know our client's mother went under her real name was at least thirty-five years ago, before she met Valerie Bacchus," Gina pondered. "That's a long time to try to piece together what happened. But her living in Sycamore Springs back then sounds like the only solid lead you have.

Fortunately, in a town that small, somebody might still remember her."

"I was thinking the same thing," I said. "It looks like I'll also be heading up to Sycamore Springs."

"Road trips?" Sophie perked up. "Would the client come too?"

"Maybe," I said. "It depends on what I find. Do you think you could behave?"

"Hey, I have a boyfriend," she said, acting as if she'd been insulted.

Of course, as she said this, her cheeks were already turning slightly pink. I knew I'd need to keep an eye on her for the client's sake, if nothing else.

I spent the next hour flipping through the reports of the three previous private detectives. I was getting to the point where I had each one, more or less, memorized.

Although each of them had found a few clues to the puzzle of what had happened to our client's mother, none of them could add the final piece and give a definitive answer as to where she was living. Sycamore Springs was mentioned in the last two reports, but mainly as a dead-end lead in the search for Valerie Bacchus.

After going over everything one more time, I leaned back in my chair and stretched. I'd hoped that something obvious would have popped out of one of the reports, but the answer was still eluding me.

"Hey," Sophie said as she motioned me over to her desk. "I've got something for you."

"Great," I said, happy for the distraction. "What is it?"

"Well, I punched the words Porter, Dalton, Mercer, Morgan, Wanker, and Sycamore Springs into the secret software. I thought maybe we'd get lucky, and something would pop out."

"Okay, that's clever. What happened?"

"According to the software, there's a prominent family called the Mercers who live in Sycamore Springs. Porter Mercer runs it. He's eighty-four years old. His sons are Dalton, age sixty-two, and Morgan, age sixty."

"Well, I'd say those names are too big of a coincidence to ignore. Did the software have anything else on them?"

"Apparently, they're loosely involved in organized crime. According to the software, almost everyone in the family has been arrested at one time or another for drugs, illegal gambling, wire fraud, or simple bar fights. Dalton has spent the most time in prison at almost two years, but Morgan also served over a year."

"Sophie, you're amazing."

"I know," she said with a giggle. "Remind our cheapskate boss of that fact the next time he chews me out about something."

"Was there any connection between the Mercers and the Wankers?"

"Not a thing. I think we can assume it was only our client's mother slinging insults around."

From Sophie's research into Jessie St. James, Sycamore Springs, and the Mercer family, we were starting to put together the outlines of an investigation.

Jessie St. James struck me as an independent woman who had been the head of a successful ranch for many years. Rather than trying to do anything over the phone, I got the feeling that talking face-to-face with her would be the best way to learn anything.

When it came to the Mercers, I hoped to get some background information ahead of time. Knowing they were involved in crime, even if only in the past, opened up a new avenue of investigation.

I picked up the phone and called my boyfriend.

"Hey," I said when Max answered. "Do you know anything about a family that lives up in the mountains southwest of Sedona called the Mercers?"

"Hello to you, too," he laughed. "You're super sexy when you're hot on an investigation. Do you know that?"

"We definitely need to work on me showing you how super sexy I can be," I giggled. "It's already been too long since we've been together. But, in the meantime, do you know anything about the Mercers? They're a family of ranchers near the town of Sycamore Springs."

"That name sounds vaguely familiar, but I don't know anything about them. I assume it's related to your assignments?"

"It's the new one where I'm looking for the client's mother. We've picked up some information that they're possibly involved in some low-level organized crime. I thought you might have possibly run across them during your time in Arizona."

"I haven't, but Tony's in the office today. I'll ask him and see what he knows. He was here in the thick of it when Arizona was still the Wild West, and he's a walking encyclopedia when it comes to these sorts of things. By the time I joined the group, things like turf wars had pretty much calmed down."

Chapter Eight

I called Lance, and he picked up right away. From the background noises, it sounded like he was in his office.

"Hey," I said. "We've started searching through your mom's background, and it looks like there are two leads I'd like to track down. The first is Jessica St. James, the rancher that your mother called when she was looking for someplace to hide. I thought we could get some additional history, and maybe Jessica knows where your mother ended up."

"It's great that you were able to locate her. Before finding the journal, I'd never connected anyone else with the disappearance. I don't believe that the other private eyes even knew to look for her."

"The second lead is Sycamore Springs. A lot of the assignment seems to revolve around the town. I'd like to go up and at least look around."

"That seems reasonable," he said. "I've been meaning to go back to Sycamore Springs in any case. The one time I was there, I didn't do a lot more than walk through the town square. Which one would you like to do first?"

"Let's do Jessica. I'll give her a call and see if she'll talk with us. I normally do these interviews by myself, but in this case, I may get better answers if you're there as well. Once she sees that you're Valerie's kid, she may open up. If she's agreeable, would you have any time this afternoon to head up? It'll take us about two hours to drive there."

"I can have the entire afternoon off. If you can reach her, let's talk with her today. We'll then have the rest of the week to go up to Sycamore Springs."

I called Jessie St. James at the number in the secret software report. When she picked up, she seemed somewhat surprised at my call.

"Hello?" she answered. "Who is this?"

"Ms. St. James, I'm Laura Black, an investigator for a law firm in Scottsdale. I'm looking into the disappearance of a woman named Valerie. I have her last name as Bacchus, but it could be something else."

"How did you get this number?" she asked, sounding annoyed. "It's an unlisted number I've kept for family emergencies and the like."

"Um, I found the number in a report I have," I said evasively. "I'm actually the fourth investigator who's tried to find Valerie over the years."

"Well, you're resourceful, I'll give you that. Why do you want to know about her?"

"I know that at one time she was a close friend of yours, but she disappeared almost twenty-five years ago. Like I said, I'm trying to track her down. Would you mind if I came up and asked you a couple of questions about what you remember from back then? I promise I won't need more than a few minutes of your time."

"Well, I haven't chatted with her in years, but it's news to me that she's disappeared. I'll talk with you, but I won't make any promises. Plus, you'd better have a good reason for asking. I won't dish the dirt on my friend unless you can explain to me why I should."

I let her know that I'd be up to her ranch around two o'clock. She said she'd be there.

Sophie had been in reception with Debbie while I'd been talking with Jessie. She came back in time to hear me making the final arrangements. When I disconnected, Sophie cocked her head to the side and looked at me with a puzzled expression.

"I'm heading up to Payson after lunch with Lance to talk with Jessica St. James," I said. "Hopefully, it will give us some insight into why Valerie took off."

"You and the cute client are going on a road trip?" Sophie asked. "Do you want some extra company?"

"I don't think I'll need it this time. Besides, between you, me, and the client, nobody has a car that will hold more than two people. Well, unless somebody sits in the back of your Volkswagen."

"My back seat is hardly big enough to put groceries in, and you don't even have a back seat. What about your old Accord? You know, the crap-mobile. We could take that."

"I can only use that car to drive around town. The last time I took it on the highway, it started to backfire. It sounded like the thing was about to blow up."

"Really?" Sophie asked. "That sucks. I'm not sure why, but you always seemed to love that car. I wonder what happened to it?"

"Do you remember that time we removed the hose from the motor to make it misfire while we were trying to get a video of Rudy Realto? I'm beginning to think it somehow permanently damaged my engine."

"Alright, fine," Sophie grumbled. "I'm sorry about your car. Go have fun with the sexy client. But you owe me. Next time you go on a road trip, we'll have Lenny rent us a big SUV."

Lance met me at the office a little before noon and offered to drive. Fortunately, it was another beautiful day, and within a few minutes, we were headed up the Beeline Highway to Payson.

Lance turned out to be a good conversationalist. He'd led an interesting, if traditional, life and had some fascinating stories to tell.

Most of his tales seemed to come back to the events surrounding his mom's disappearance and the murder of his dad. I could tell how much both events had affected him.

From Payson, we drove east for several miles until we reached Star Valley, a wide, flat basin between two mountain ridges. From the highway, we turned down Moonlight Drive. This winding country road eventually led to a vast area of low, rolling hills with pretty clusters of mountain mahogany, cottonwoods, sycamores, and junipers.

We turned onto a dirt road and drove beneath a ranch entry arch supported by three brick pillars. *Moonlight Ranch* was inscribed across the top of the arch in wrought iron letters.

After passing under the arch, we drove through nearly a mile of open rangeland. Along the way, we spotted dozens of cows grazing peacefully in the distance.

The main ranch house was easy to identify among the outbuildings. It was massive and likely had six or eight bedrooms.

It was built on top of a sloping hill overlooking the valley, with the front of the house facing southwest. The sides were painted maroon-red, while the roof appeared to be made of sheets of green metal.

The house had a deep front porch with half a dozen white rocking chairs scattered along it. I could only imagine how gorgeous the summer sunsets would be from there.

As we parked in an open area in front of the house, we saw a woman who I assumed was Jessie St. James on the porch. She was sitting on one of the rocking chairs, drinking a tall boy Coors, and tapping on a laptop.

Climbing out of Lance's BMW, I could feel the cooler temperatures of the mountains and smell the pine trees. It was always a nice change from Scottsdale.

As we reached the porch, the woman rose to meet us. She was athletic-looking and somewhere in her late fifties or early sixties. She wore cowboy boots, blue jeans, and a pastel pink button-down blouse with pearl-snap closures, which seemed to fit in well with the outdoor ranch setting.

"Jessie St. James," she said as she stuck out her hand and gave me a firm shake. "You must be Laura."

Jessie had a wide smile and sharp, intelligent eyes. Her long blonde hair, with a few notable gray strands, hung in a thick braid down her back.

"Laura Black," I said as we shook. "Like I said when we spoke on the phone, I'm an investigator for a law firm in Scottsdale."

"Lance Tillman," my client said as he shook Jessie's hand as well.

Upon hearing his name, Jessie looked mildly surprised. "When you called, you said you wanted to ask me about Val."

"That's right," I said. "According to what we've learned, about twenty-five years ago, a woman, perhaps named Valerie Bacchus, called you and said she needed to hide somewhere for a while. Does that ring a bell?"

"Well, sure," Jessie said with a nod. "But why do you want to know about Val? I don't simply give out information about my friends, even if it was a long time ago. Does she owe you money or something?"

"Not at all," Lance said. "She's my mother."

On hearing this, Jessie looked Lance up and down and nodded. "Okay, I thought you might be Val's boy. Your age is about right, and I can see her features in your face. You were still in diapers the last time I saw you. But that must have been thirty or thirty-five years ago."

"I recently learned that my mother came to you for help, and we're trying to piece together what happened back then," he said. "Anything you can tell us might be useful."

"Why not ask your mom?" Jessie asked, taking a sip of her beer. She'd asked the question casually enough, but I could tell that she would need a legitimate reason before revealing anything to us.

"I can't ask her," Lance said. "I have no idea where she is."

"What? Are you saying you haven't heard from your mom in over *twenty-five years*?"

"That's right," Lance said. "She took off when I was in the third grade, and I haven't seen her since."

The look on Jessie's face was somewhat hard to read. It seemed to be anger mixed with sorrow. "Well, alright then. It sounds like I'll be telling you some stories about my past. But this might take a while. You'd better grab yourselves something cold to drink."

Jessie pointed to a huge white Yeti cooler sitting on the back of the porch, and we both dug around in the water and ice. Not finding a Diet Pepsi, I pulled out a Coke, and Lance grabbed a tall boy Coors Banquet. After that, we each took a rocking chair on either side of her.

"Although," Jessie continued. "I'm not sure how you could know about that phone call from back then. Your mom sounded like she was in a pretty desperate situation and was frightened out of her wits."

"Did she say what was going on?" Lance asked.

"She said a guy from her past had caught up with her, and she needed somewhere to stay where he couldn't find her. I said she could stay with me as long as she needed to."

"Did she ever come up here to hide out at your ranch?" I asked as I looked around at all the places someone up here could go.

"Well, back then, my 'ranch' was nothing more than forty acres of open rangeland and some cattle pens," she said. "I was still sharing an apartment with some girlfriends in Payson. But, no, I didn't hear from Val for several months after that phone call."

"Really?" Lance asked. "Did you see that as unusual?"

"Damn right, I did," Jessie laughed. "It seemed totally out of character for her, and I was worried about what had happened. I kept checking the Phoenix and Scottsdale newspapers, but there wasn't anything in either of them. You'll have to remember this was before the internet had fully got going, so I couldn't simply Google her."

"Did you ever talk with her again?" Lance asked.

"Val called back five or six months later. She apologized for the hysterics and said everything had been resolved."

"Did she say what happened or where she ended up?" I

asked.

Jessie shook her head. "We chatted for several minutes, but I could tell she was reluctant to talk about what had happened. But Val seemed to be okay, so I didn't press her on it."

"Did you ever see her again after the phone calls?" Lance asked.

"No, she didn't give me her phone number, and I knew there was no way I could simply look her up. Until you called yesterday, I'd pretty much pushed the possibility of ever seeing Val again out of my mind."

Jessie then looked at me, a touch of annoyance on her face. "You still didn't tell me how you knew about what happened all those years ago. It's not like I ever told anyone about the phone call, and I'm pretty sure Val didn't either."

"I found her journal from back then a couple of weeks ago, Lance said. "She wrote about someone named Morgan finding her. He threatened to kill both my dad and me if she didn't willingly go with him. That's when she called you. She was looking for somewhere to hide while everything calmed down."

"Do you know anything about Val and this Morgan?" I asked. "It could be anything. They must have had some prior history together."

"I remember hearing she was dating someone for a while, maybe the summer after her sophomore or junior year of college. The name might have been Morgan, but I'm not sure. Honestly, we'd pretty much lost track of each other by the time we'd both finished college. When she called me that day, it was the first time I'd heard from her in years."

"Do you know where she was living when she dated Morgan?"

"I'm not sure. It could have been someone she'd met at college or someone from her hometown. She grew up in the little town of Sycamore Springs."

"You were close friends with my mother until you both went away to college?" Lance asked. "How long did you know her?"

At that, Jessie laughed again. "We met at summer art camp back in about the second or third grade. But, if I'm being totally honest, at first, I didn't think much of your mom."

Lance started at this, but Jessie held up her hand to calm him.

"Sorry to talk about your mom that way, but at the time, it was true. She thought she was the most beautiful girl in camp with her big blue eyes and her long, curly blonde hair. But we kept meeting every year, and by the last time we spent the summer together, we were good friends. We were pen pals for three or four years after we stopped going to camp."

"What was the name of the art camp?" I asked.

"Whispering Pines," she laughed. "It was about five miles south of Prescott. I never really had a mother, and my dad was a working cowboy. Summer was his busiest time of the year. He'd put me in camp for the entire school break, so I'd have something fun to keep me occupied while he was out working on the range."

"Was that difficult? I asked. "Being away from home like that every summer?"

"Not at all," she said with a shake of her head. "Dad would come out to visit me every couple of weeks, and Whispering Pines had an outstanding teacher, Miss Costello. She was a working artist with a commercial studio and gallery in Prescott, and I think she was part-owner of the camp. Over the years, she taught Val and me how to paint with acrylics and oils. I felt a little like her apprentice, and I know Val loved it as well. It's ultimately the thing that brought us together as friends.

Jessie stood, walked over to the cooler, and pulled out another Coors Banquet. "Come on into the great room," she said. "I'll show you something I did."

Jessie led us into the house and a huge living room. The exposed beam ceiling must have been twenty feet above our heads. A broad, curving staircase led up to the second level, where a balcony surrounded the entire room.

"That's one of mine," she said as she pointed to a beautiful landscape painting in a gilded frame. The piece depicted a mountain viewed through a grove of juniper trees. It was mounted on the wall behind the wet bar and was the centerpiece of the room.

"That was the last one I did, and I spent over three months on it between my junior and senior years in college. I sort of looked at it as my magnum opus."

"That's gorgeous," I said as I stepped closer. "From a distance, it almost looks like a photograph."

Lance and I walked to the painting and spent several moments admiring it. The details were incredible, reminding me of the Cici paintings at Lance's house.

"Is that how Miss Costello taught you to paint?" I asked.

"Yup," Jessie nodded. "That's all her influence. She taught us several techniques, such as glazing, scumbling, and sgraffito. Those help to add depth and bring out details through brushwork, perceived lighting, and layering."

"You probably could've done that for a living," I said, being totally sincere.

Jessie shook her head. "Maybe, but I wanted to start a ranch. My dad always talked about ranchers as being at the top of his profession. He thought they were honorable men and something worthy to strive for."

"Well, you certainly have built a great place," Lance said.

We were all chatting away like old friends, so I asked one of the main things I wanted to get from Jessie. "What was Val's last name? We have it as Bacchus."

"When we were growing up, her name was Val Johnson," she said with a shrug. "Maybe Bacchus was her married name?"

"We have Valerie Bacchus as the name of an elderly woman who died in an extended care facility in Sycamore Springs about thirty-five years ago," I said. "We think Val might've taken the identity of the woman and used that to live in Scottsdale for about ten years before Morgan caught up with her."

"If that's true, Val probably got the idea since they both had the same first name," Jessie said. "I don't know anything about the Bacchus part, but she's always been Valerie."

Chapter Nine

I'd hoped that talking with Jessie would have made the situation with Lance's mother clearer. Instead, I now only had more questions.

According to Jess, Val Johnson grew up in Sycamore Springs and attended college at NAU in Flagstaff. We'd need to confirm that this was indeed Lance's mom, but I suspected that she was.

Morgan was also an unknown. Val may have dated someone with that name while in college, but even so, it was still a mystery why he'd want to track her down ten years later.

Once we got into Payson and had a strong cell signal, I called Sophie back at the office.

"Hey, chica," I said when she answered. "I have some new information. It looks like Valerie Bacchus's real last name was Johnson. She grew up in Sycamore Springs and would now be in her late fifties."

"Johnson?" Sophie asked, sounding a little annoyed. "You do know that Johnson is the second most common name in the U.S., only behind Smith, right? Do you know how many Valerie Johnsons I'll have to go through to find the right one?"

"I know, it's a common name. Try to concentrate on the Sycamore Springs connection. That should cut down the list a bit."

"Fine, but I still think you'll end up owing me lunch for this one. I'm talking Friday tacos with a couple of Coronas."

"Alright," I said. "But only two beers. The last time we started day drinking, you had an entire bucket and were pretty much useless for the rest of the day."

"You're not lying about that," she laughed. "I went home after work that day and crashed hard. I had plans for going out with the Cougars that night. Instead, I woke up at three in the morning and couldn't get back to sleep. Do you know how much it sucks to watch the sun come up when you're alone and in your own apartment?"

"So, call me when you get something back?" I asked.

"Yeah, yeah. You'll be the first to know."

As Lance and I drove back to Scottsdale, I couldn't get Jessie's painting out of my head. I rolled it around and around in my mind until I had to talk about it.

"I've been thinking about the landscape that Jessie hung in her living room. There was something odd about it. Did it remind you of the Cici paintings?"

"It's funny you say that," Lance said. "I was thinking the same thing. When Jessie first showed us the painting, I assumed it was another one by Cici. I was a little surprised when she said she'd painted it herself. I went so far as to look at the signature, but it was clearly *Jessie St. James*."

"I don't know a lot about art, but if Jessie didn't do the Cici paintings, they were done by someone who uses the same techniques."

"Maybe by someone who also attended summer art classes at Camp Whispering Pines?" Lance pondered, a questioning look on his face.

"Maybe," I said. "But I don't want to read too much into it, at least not yet. At the moment, it seems like Jessie, your mother, and Cici all have similar styles. I think we should try to find out more about who this Cici is. I get the feeling it will help clear up whatever's been going on."

When we got back to the law office, it was a few minutes after five. Lance found a spot in front of the office and had planned on dropping me off. But on the drive down from Payson, I had an idea on how we could learn more about Cici.

"If you still have a few minutes, I think I know someone who can help us."

"Sure," he said as he turned off the car. I then led him down the street to the new art gallery being opened by Olivia and Susan Monroe.

The white paper had been taken down from the windows, allowing people on the street to see inside. The interior was brightly lit, and it appeared that they were about halfway finished setting up the gallery.

The top facade of the storefront now displayed *Desert Vistas* spelled out in large and ornate gold letters. A professionally printed poster was attached to the inside of the window, calling out to passersby:

Desert Vistas
Fine Art Gallery
Grand Reopening
May 24th – 31st

Olivia was sitting at a desk in the back of the shop, working at a computer. On the walls behind and next to her were roughly two dozen brightly colored oil paintings with room for many more. She'd also added a couple of shelving units that were about halfway full of colorful glass and ceramic sculptures.

I knocked on the glass, and Olivia looked up. She smiled when she saw it was me, walked over, and unlocked the front door.

"Hey, Olivia," I said as I took in the room. "It's looking great in here."

"We're getting there," she beamed as she glanced around at her work. "It'll be tight getting everything finished on time, but I think we'll make it. I even heard today that a reporter from the Scottsdale Progress will stop by during the opening."

"It's terrific that you've been able to fill the gallery so quickly."

"I called the artists I represented at the last shop, and many of them are still around. I was grateful that most of them were willing to come back. Michael also called in some of his artist friends from Las Vegas. Most of them were willing to display a few pieces here to help broaden their sales footprint."

"We'll all be sure to stop by," I said. "It'll be fun to have a new art gallery on the block."

I introduced Lance as a client, and they shook hands. "I have a question for you," I said. "I'm working on an assignment and came across an artist named Cici. Judging by her paintings, it looks like she lives in Arizona or at least somewhere in the Southwest. Would you know where I could get more information on her?"

"I could give it a shot," Olivia said. "Unfortunately, there's no universal database that tracks artists or art sales. I've often wished for something like that whenever someone came in asking for a particular artist."

"You'd think there'd be something," Lance said. "How can people find information on an artist if they find a painting they like?"

"Well, there's Artsy, Artnet, and the Fine Art Dealers Association database," Olivia said as she counted off on her fingers. "All of those are good. But most private galleries aren't required to disclose what art they sell. It makes it frustrating when you're looking for someone specific, but let me see what I can come up with."

Olivia typed into her computer for several minutes, shook her head slowly, and sighed in frustration. Lance and I used the time to walk around the gallery and admire the paintings.

Much of the colorful artwork touched an emotional nerve, and some of the pieces seemed to actively call out to me. Unfortunately, I didn't have a spare five or ten thousand dollars to spend on any of them.

"There are a lot of artists named Cici," Olivia eventually said. "But most of them also use their last names. Did you say that you think she only goes by her first name, like Cher or Beyoncé?"

"It seems like it," I said. "At least that's how she signs her paintings."

"That should narrow it down a little," she said. There was then another five or six minutes of typing and head shaking.

"Oh, I think I found her," Olivia finally said as she brightened. "This Cici has three listed shows. The first was two years ago, the second one was last year, and the third one opened this week. Her new show is titled 'Mountain Splendor', and it looks like it'll be going on until the end of the summer."

"Wow, that's great," I said. "Where is it?"

"Everything's been at The Art Loft. That's a gallery in the little mountain town of Sycamore Springs. It's about halfway between Sedona and Cottonwood."

"Sycamore Springs?" I laughed. "It figures. I've been running across the town a lot so far."

"Does it have any information on the artist?" Lance asked. "I'd be interested in her age."

I looked at him, knowing what he was getting at. "Sorry," he said. "I can't shake this feeling I've been getting about Cici."

"Unfortunately, the database doesn't have that type of information," Olivia said. "Have you tried to Google her?"

"Well, I've tried," he said with a nod. "And I always run into the same problem as you did. A lot of artists around the world have Cici as a first name, but I couldn't find anyone who lives near Arizona."

"Do you know anything about the art gallery up there?" I asked.

"I've been up there a couple of times over the years," Olivia said. "It's run by a woman I used to hang out with named Evelyn something. The last time I was there must have been ten or fifteen years ago, but it sounds like she still has the gallery open. If you go up to Sycamore Springs, tell her 'Hello' from me. It's been a while, but she might still remember me."

After promising to return for the gallery's opening, Lance and I walked back towards the office. We stopped at his convertible and made plans.

"I'd like to head up to Sycamore Springs as soon as possible," I said. "Do you still have time to go up tomorrow morning? We could meet back here about nine?"

"That would work out well," Lance said, seemingly pleased that we'd made so much progress. "I'm curious what we'll be able to learn up there."

"It will probably only be a day trip, but to be on the safe side, make sure to bring an overnight bag."

"Good idea," Lance said. "I've let my office manager know that I might take a few days off. Fortunately, the business more or less runs itself. They won't have any trouble handling things until I come back."

As Lance got in his car and drove down the street, I used my key to get into the front office door. Given that it was after six o'clock, the office was empty. I went to the back cubicles and grabbed my things for the night.

I was about to head out the rear door when my phone rang. I was surprised to see that it was Tony DiCenzo.

"Hello, Tony," I said when I answered.

"Laura Black," he said in his familiar gruff tone. "It's good to hear your voice. I trust you're doing well?"

"I've been busy lately, but I'm doing great. It's good to hear from you."

"Max tells me that there's some information you wish to know."

"There is. I'm looking for the mother of a client who was kidnapped a number of years ago. It appears that the man who took her is named Morgan Mercer. He seems to be part of a larger family living in the mountains near Sedona. Max thought you might have some information on them."

"I may know a few things," Tony said with a chuckle.

"The family is led by an old acquaintance of mine, Porter Mercer."

"What do you know about him?"

"There's quite a bit I could tell you, but such things are best done in person. Would you have any time tonight to stop by the Tropical Paradise?"

"Sure," I said, happy for the opportunity to see my friend again. "I'm free now. Where should I meet you?"

"Let's get together at the Headhunter Lounge. It's a familiar setting, and we should be able to have a quiet conversation there."

"That sounds perfect. I'll be there in about half an hour."

Thinking about Marlowe, I called Grandma Henderson as I drove up Scottsdale Road to the Tropical Paradise.

"Hi, Grandma," I said. "How's he doing?"

"He's still sneezing and seems a little more lethargic than usual. I scheduled an appointment for him in the morning with Doctor Dusty."

"Thank you so much for doing that," I said. "I've been worried about Marlowe, and I'm going to be stuck with this assignment all day tomorrow. Let me know what I owe you?"

"Oh, don't worry about that," she said. "I still think it's only a cold, but I want our little guy to get better. I spent most of the day cleaning cat boogers off his chair."

Eeewww.

As we chatted, Grandma told me that Marlowe would likely stay with her overnight. He looked comfortable on his afghan, and she doubted that he would want to go anywhere for a while.

I disconnected from my neighbor and pulled into the resort's main drive. I drove around until I found an open space toward the back of the lower visitors' lot at the bottom of the hill.

It's time for some exercise.

The walk up the peaceful, winding path both calmed and relaxed me. It happened every time I was here, and I always looked forward to strolling through the trees, shrubs, and flowers.

Chapter Ten

After making my way up the hill, I entered the enormous tropical-themed lobby and made my way to the Headhunter Lounge. I found Tony at a table off to the side in the rear of the bar, near where they had a lifelike display of cannibals cooking some jungle explorers in a large iron pot.

Tony was flanked by two waitresses and a younger man in a suit. They were all laughing at some story Tony was sharing.

"Ah, Laura Black," Tony said as he saw me enter the bar. "Please join me."

The other people scattered as I walked up to the table and gave Tony a hug. He then ordered two 21-year-old Glenlivet scotches from the remaining server, one ice cube in each.

"Hi, Tony. How's Celeste?" I asked. "It was great meeting her at Gabriella's party."

"She's doing well. Now that I'm fully retired, I've been able to have a more open relationship with her, much like what you're experiencing with Max. The constant need to be guarded about my personal life was one aspect of my old position that I didn't enjoy."

"I'm glad you have someone like that in your life," I said. "It'll keep you from being lonely."

"As a matter of fact, Celeste and I will be hosting a get-together here in a few weeks. I'll be sure to send you an invitation."

"Thanks, Tony. I look forward to that."

The waitress brought over the drinks, and I picked up one of the bulb-shaped Glencairn glasses. I gently swirled the drink to warm the scotch and melt the ice cube. At the same time, I held the glass to my nose and breathed in the delicious aroma of a 21-year-old spirit.

I took a sip and felt a wave of intense pleasure as the scotch seemingly evaporated on my tongue, and a warm feeling passed through my body.

"Wow," I breathed out. "That's delicious. I love how these old scotches make you feel. Thank you, Tony."

Tony was finishing his first sip and had a similar reaction. "That is remarkable," he said. "Being the malt master at a fine old scotch distillery must be one of the most satisfying jobs there is."

"Yeah," I had to agree. "Although if I were surrounded by barrels of scotch all day, I'd probably be smashed a lot of the time."

"I won't keep you here all night, Laura Black," Tony said. "You were looking for information on Porter Mercer. I'll tell you what I know, but you'll need to keep in mind that the last time I saw the man must have been twenty years ago. Circumstances may have changed since then."

"I understand," I said as I held the glass to my nose once more, inhaling the aroma of the scotch. "Anything you know could be helpful. I hate going into a situation completely blind."

"Very well. At the time, Porter Mercer owned a sizeable cattle ranch outside of Sycamore Springs called the Laughing Armadillo. It's comprised of several thousand acres on top of

The Rim, about halfway between Sedona and Cottonwood."

"Why would anyone name a ranch something like that?" I asked.

"It was named by Porter's uncle, a man named Homer Mercer. According to their family legend, when Homer first went up to buy the property, an armadillo saw him walking around and started chirping at him. Homer thought it sounded like the little guy was laughing at him for buying a dry ranch so far from anything."

"I'm surprised that someone could simply buy up so much land, even back then."

"Homer bought the bulk of the property soon after the war, long before Sedona became a tourist magnet. Open land was cheap back then."

"Tell me more about the town," I said. "It sounds like you've been up there before."

"Oh, many times. Sycamore Springs is in the valley formed by Oak Creek. The little town grew until it butted up against the ranch, so Homer Mercer began to rent out tracts of land to expand the village in fifty-year leases. Because of that, he pretty much runs the town as well."

"What can you tell me about the family? I've heard they're into organized crime."

"Well, I wouldn't go as far as calling them a crime syndicate," Tony chuckled. "Their main business is raising cattle. They've been known to dabble in drugs, and they were involved in gambling for many years."

"They aren't anymore?"

"Like many of us, they were gradually forced out of the gambling business by the tribal casinos that came into being about thirty years ago. The thing that took him out of the gambling trade completely was when they opened the Cliff

Castle Casino in Camp Verde. It's an easy twenty-five-minute drive from Sycamore Springs, and they've made it an enjoyable place to visit."

"Doesn't having an independent family operating in the mountains cause some friction with the more established groups, like Johnny's?"

"Not really," Tony said with a slight shake of his head. "They're a relatively small group a long way from anyone else, and they've never tried to expand their territory. They pretty much keep to themselves, and the other factions in the state leave them alone. That way, the overall peace is maintained."

"What else can you tell me about the Mercer family?"

"The father, Porter, is tough but honorable. He took over as family patriarch after his uncle died. As I remember, Porter had two boys. One was named Morgan. Although I don't remember the name of the oldest."

"Dalton, perhaps?" I asked.

"That could be it, but it was a long time ago. I'm not sure where Porter went wrong with his kids. Maybe it was because his wife died soon after the youngest was born, and the boys were basically raised by ranch hands, but as I recall, each one was a handful."

"Really? How so?"

"It's something I've often seen with the children of wealthy men, especially boys. They grew up lacking a strong female presence and experienced no real hardship or challenge. It not only made them mentally weak, but it established a mindset that they were destined to live a life of privilege. The boys were constantly in barroom fights, and they assumed that women were simply there for their pleasure."

"That seems to fit in well with what I've learned about the

family so far."

"After Max mentioned that you wished to know about the Mercers, I dug around in my closet a bit. If you think you might run into Porter Mercer, let me give you something that should make things go a little smoother."

Tony opened a black velvet bag that had been sitting on the table and brought out a jeweler's box. Inside was a gorgeous gold watch with a gold mesh wristband.

He pulled it out and held it up so I could see it. He slowly turned it back and forth so it sparkled in the lights of the lounge. I'm not much of a watch person, but I could see that it was beautifully made and obviously expensive.

"This is a Patek Philippe Moon Phase watch, and it once belonged to Porter Mercer. From the inscription on the back, he got it from his Uncle Homer when he turned twenty-one."

Tony handed it over. In addition to the standard watch hands, it had a small dial that showed the phase of the moon.

"This looks like a remarkable watch," I said. "How'd you get it?"

"I won it in a poker game," Tony said with a chuckle. "Porter had the game up at his ranch house, a real fortress of a place overlooking both Oak Creek and the town of Sycamore Springs. My old pals Vince Sanders and Roger Wade were there, along with a few other guys I've known and done business with for a long time."

"Seriously? Porter bet his uncle's watch over a hand of cards. Why would he do something like that?"

"He had four jacks and assumed he could win the hand," Tony said with a shrug. "When he slid the watch off his wrist and tossed it into the pot, the only thing I had on me that could match it was my old convertible."

"You mean the silver Mercedes?"

"The very same vehicle I gave to you last year. I tossed the keys into the pot to call his bet."

"What happened?"

"Unfortunately, for him, I had four queens and took it all."

"He must have been upset," I said.

"You bet he was," Tony said with a wicked smile and a chuckle. "Porter was livid. For a second, I thought there might be some trouble. But like I said, he was an honorable man. He handed over the watch and never said another word about it."

"Okay, but why are you giving it to me?"

"Oh, I figured that one day my path would again cross with his. It's the way these things happen. I wanted to be prepared in case I ever needed some extra leverage over him to make a deal go through. I had his watch cleaned, polished, and put in a new Patek Philippe box."

Tony put the shining gold watch back in the box, closed it, and slid it across the table to me. "Here, you take it and use it if you need to. If not, bring it back."

"You'd be okay giving it back to him? From what I understand, these are pricey watches."

"I've simply been keeping it in storage, and I now doubt that I'll ever have an occasion to do business with Porter Mercer again. Besides, if he gets his watch back, he'll know you're a friend of mine. He'll also know he owes me, and by extension, you, some goodwill for bringing it back to him."

"Thanks, Tony. I appreciate it. How are things going over here with you? I heard a rumor that Las Vegas is thinking about trying to move into Scottsdale?"

"I think at this point it's more than a rumor," he said with a slow shake of his head. "However, the problem is Johnny's to deal with. I won't be involved other than to give advice if he asks for it."

"I can't imagine how frustrating something like that would be to work through. In a way, I imagine you're glad to be out of it."

"I'll be honest. I will miss the feeling of fulfillment I experienced while holding the position. But I am thankful I was able to exit the business cleanly without leaving a lot of loose ends. This way, Johnny will only have Las Vegas to deal with. He won't need to take on the Black Death at the same time. Thank you again for your assistance in helping to solve that problem."

"I was glad I could help," I said. "Before I go, do you mind if I ask you about something else? It's been weighing on my mind a lot lately."

"Of course," he said with a serious look on his face. "What would you ask of me?"

"It's not a favor," I said quickly. "It's more about philosophy."

"Alright, Laura Black," Tony said with a grin. "What's been troubling you?"

"The things I do in my line of work have a direct impact on the people I investigate. If someone comes in to have us prove that something happened, that means that someone else will suffer some consequences. Sometimes it's financial, and sometimes it will send them to prison. I usually know what I'm *supposed* to do, but I'm not sure if it's always the *right* thing to do."

Tony looked at me for a moment, then nodded his head as if this were an obvious question for someone to ask. "I won't presume to give you advice on how you run your life," he said. "But I will share how I've always made these types of decisions. First, gather all of the information you can on a problem. Then, be open and honest with yourself, and look at the problem from every angle you can, especially from the viewpoint of the person it most affects. After you've done that, you simply go with your heart. Don't worry about whether it's legal or if it's what others expect from you. If you go with your heart, then you'll be able to sleep at night even if your decision causes others frustration or pain."

"Thanks, Tony," I said. "I'll try to keep that in mind."

I spent the next twenty minutes chatting with my friend, and we each had another tasting of the wonderful scotch. Finally, I noticed that several people had begun to gather casually at the end of the bar. They weren't being pushy about it, but I could tell that they were all waiting to speak with Tony.

"Laura Black, this has been very enjoyable," he said. "Unfortunately, I have some additional obligations tonight, and I must cut our conversation short."

"That's okay, Tony. It's been great seeing you. Thank you again for the advice and the delicious scotch. I look forward to seeing Celeste again."

"The night is early. Perhaps you should call Max? He should have some time before the wrap-up meeting, and I'm sure he'd enjoy seeing you."

"Actually," I said with a grin. "I was thinking about doing just that."

After saying goodnight to Tony and giving him a hug, I went to the lobby and called Max. When he answered, he said he was in his office and that I should come up and see him.

I went up the stairs to the mezzanine level, but since it was almost seven-thirty, the outer doors to the offices were locked. I dug out the keycard from my bag and pressed it against a black plastic square next to the entrance. There was a gentle click, and the doors unlocked.

I buzzed myself through the inner turnstiles and walked through the nearly empty halls until I reached the executive offices. Since no one was at the admin desk, I called Max on the phone.

"I'm here," I said when he answered. The door to Max's office buzzed, and I walked in.

Reminding me of the many times I'd seen Tony in this same office, Max sat behind his large desk. In addition to a computer monitor, several piles of papers and reports were scattered across it.

On the coffee table in front of the black leather couch sat a delicious-looking meat and cheese tray that I recognized as coming from Anthony's Prime Steakhouse. It seemed untouched, reminding me that I hadn't eaten anything for some time.

"I'm glad you're here," he said as he stood and walked over to give me a hug. "It's been a long day."

With his arms wrapped around me, he leaned down and kissed me softly. His lips barely brushed against mine, but, as always, it had the effect of igniting every nerve in my body.

How can he do that to me?

Max must have also felt the desire building as his kisses gradually grew more intense. I found myself running my hands over his hard body and moaning with desire.

After almost two minutes of kissing, I knew we needed to decide between eating and taking things further. Not wanting to seem like a sex maniac, I went to the refrigerator and grabbed a bottle of San Pellegrino and two glasses. I then sat down on the couch.

"Are you hungry?" I asked innocently. "This looks wonderful."

Max smirked like he knew exactly what I'd been thinking.

Rather than comment on my obvious needs, he sat beside me.

"I'm glad you're here to help me with this," he said. "They size this tray as an appetizer for four. I always feel a little guilty when I don't finish it."

For the next ten minutes, we dug into the meat and cheese. It came with clusters of red and green grapes and a basket of warm bread and butter.

The food was incredible, but once the edge of my hunger was taken care of, thoughts of Max's lips on mine started to take over again. I sat my glass of sparkling water down on the coffee table and looked at my boyfriend.

"What?" he asked playfully.

I leaned forward and started kissing him again. Within a minute, my body was again awake and wanting more.

I would have felt somewhat bad about getting turned on in Max's office on a Wednesday night, but I could feel that he was ready and having similar thoughts.

"Um, how much time do we have before your nine o'clock meeting?" I asked.

Max glanced at his watch. "Long enough," he said with a grin.

I stopped by Grandma Henderson's the following morning before leaving for work. When she answered the door, she was holding Marlowe in her arms.

"Good morning, dear," she said, sounding tired.

"How's he doing?" I asked as I scratched him behind his ear.

Marlowe looked up at me and gave me one of his squeaky meows, then sneezed.

Eeewww.

"He's still not feeling his best," Grandma said. "But I'll let you know what the vet says."

After thanking Grandma again for taking care of Marlowe, I drove to the office. I got there a little before nine. Gina wasn't there, and Sophie was still getting organized for the day.

"Hey, Laura," she said. "I entered your request yesterday afternoon and should get back something on Valerie Johnson this morning. I'll give you whatever comes back, but don't be surprised if a common name like that confuses the database."

"She's in her late fifties," I said. "So if she grew up in Sycamore Springs, she should be in the high school yearbook from around thirty years ago. Maybe you can use that as something solid to build on."

Debbie buzzed me to let me know that Lance had arrived in reception. When I went up to get him, he'd taken my advice and brought a small duffle with a change of clothes. My overnight essentials bag was already in my car, and I offered to drive.

We headed into the northern mountains and drove up to the top of The Rim. When we got to the town of Camp Verde, we turned off Interstate-17 and started up the winding two-lane road that led into Sycamore Springs.

It was a beautiful day, with fluffy white clouds dotting the deep blue sky all the way to the horizon. I'd taken the top of the Miata down when we'd gotten off the Interstate. It had been an unusually wet spring, and we were enjoying the casual drive through the lush green mountains.

After twenty minutes, we were maybe three or four miles from Sycamore Springs when I came around a curve and saw several twisted, metallic-looking objects scattered on the road, each about the size of a shoe.

"Watch out," Lance called. "Those look sharp."

I tried to thread my way through them, but a vehicle was passing in the opposite lane, which limited my swerving options. I ended up nicking one of the shards of metal with my front driver's tire. As I feared, there was a soft hissing noise, and then the steering started to go mushy as the tire gradually went flat.

Chapter Eleven

"Damn it," I cursed as I pulled the Miata off to the side of the road.

We got out and looked down at the flat tire, as if we could fix it simply by staring at it.

"At least it's only flat on the bottom," Lance said, then looked at me with a pathetic grin.

"Dad jokes?" I asked. "Really? And it wasn't even funny."

"Fine," he said. "Although it was pretty funny. My grandfather would always tell that joke whenever he got a flat. Let's put on the spare."

I opened the trunk and removed the jack from its holder while Lance reached in and started digging around.

"I don't see a tire," he said as he picked up our overnight bags to look underneath. "But I honestly don't see how one could even fit in here. Your trunk's pretty small. There was barely room for our little bags. Maybe it's under the car?"

"Miata's don't have a spare," I said, remembering the odd fact about the car as I sighed and shook my head.

"Seriously?" Lance asked. "What *do* they have?"

"Well, they have a tire repair kit. It's in that pouch," I said, pointing to a small black nylon bag with a bright blue zipper.

Lance and I were somewhat skeptical as we pulled out the repair kit and looked through its contents. There was a mini air compressor, a can of Mazda fix-a-flat gel, and an instruction sheet with pictures that looked more like hieroglyphics than useful information.

"Well, it's a new car, and I have roadside assistance," I said. "But I can't imagine a Mazda dealer being anywhere near here."

"You're probably right," Lance said. "Fortunately, it's only a tire. Calling for someone local to come out still might be the better alternative rather than trying to repair it on the side of the road."

I pulled out my phone to call the roadside assistance number, but I didn't have cell service. "I'm not getting a signal in this valley," I said. "It looks like we'll either have to fix the tire ourselves or walk into Sycamore Springs and hope that someone there can come out and repair it."

"I'll give repairing it a shot, but I'm not sure this will work," he said, holding the air compressor in one hand and the instructions in the other. "But maybe it will fix the tire enough to let us limp into town."

We were about halfway through jacking up the car when a black sheriff's SUV came down the road from the direction of Sycamore Springs. He flipped on his emergency roof lights, made a U-turn on the road, and pulled in behind us.

After a few moments, a man in a uniform, maybe forty-five years of age, got out of the vehicle. He settled a black cowboy hat on his head and slowly walked up to us.

The deputy resembled a small-town sheriff from the Old West. Tall and lean, with a gunfighter's black mustache, he appeared friendly, but there was a look of hardness in his eyes. He carried what seemed to be an old ivory-gripped Colt Peacemaker in a tooled black leather gun belt holster, the kind with bullets stuck in loops on the belt.

"I'm Deputy McGill," he said as he took in our situation. "Looks like you folks ran into a spot of trouble."

"I'm Laura Black, and this is Lance Tillman," I said, trying not to sound as annoyed as I felt. "It's not a big deal. I ran over something back there, and it punctured my tire."

The deputy held his hand to the brim of his hat as he looked down the road. "Yup, I see it. It looks like someone spilled part of a load when they took the turn. I'd better clear it off before someone else hits it."

While the deputy walked back to pick up the pieces of scrap metal, Lance finished jacking up the car. He then spun the tire around until he found the puncture. It was a ragged hole about an inch and a half long.

"I don't know if the can of tire repair goo is going to work on a hole this big," he said. "We may need to get it towed to a proper repair shop."

The deputy came back, and we explained our situation. He squatted down, examined the tire, and reached the same conclusion.

"If you want to take it to a Mazda shop, the nearest dealership is in Prescott. But it will take a while to get a tow truck to Sycamore Springs. It's a good hour from here, and that's assuming they leave right away."

All I could do was sigh and shake my head. It looked like we were going to waste the entire day fixing my car.

"I tell you what, folks," the deputy said. "Since it only looks like a bad tire, we have a guy in town named Hank Purcell who runs an auto repair shop out of his garage. It's not fancy, but everyone in town uses him, and his rates are reasonable. If you'd like, we can talk with him about getting your car and looking at the tire. If he can't repair it, I imagine he can have a new one up here by tomorrow afternoon at the latest."

That sounded like the best alternative we could come up with, so I told the deputy we'd go with his suggestion.

After stowing the jack and grabbing our overnight bags from the trunk, I put the top up and locked my car. We then climbed into the back of the deputy's cruiser, and he drove us to Sycamore Springs.

It was a little creepy sitting on the hard plastic seat in the back of a county sheriff's cruiser. There was a thick metal grate between us and the front seats, with similar mesh on the side windows. We were locked in and couldn't get out until the deputy opened the door.

I hope we don't get into an accident.

I looked over at Lance. He gave me a slight grimace, and I knew he was likely thinking the same thing.

We made it to Hank Purcell's house and saw that the deputy had understated the size of the auto repair shop. Instead of a simple garage, it was more like a huge metal building with room for four cars to be worked on at once.

Three cars were being serviced, one of which was on a hydraulic lift. Classic rock was blaring out from an ancient boombox sitting on a side shelf. I recognized the song as *Don't Fear the Reaper* by Blue Oyster Cult

As the cruiser pulled into the gravel driveway, a man with a weathered face, a short gray beard, and long salt-and-pepper hair straightened up from underneath the hood of a white Jeep Cherokee. He wore a stained one-piece blue overall with the name *Hank* embossed over the right breast pocket.

"Hank," Deputy McGill called out. "These two ended up with a flat out by Javier Miller's place. Do you think you could pick up the car and get them back on the road?"

"Sure," Hank said as he pointed to the Cherokee. His voice had the roughness I've come to expect in a person with a two-pack-a-day habit. "I'll need to finish Maggie's Jeep first so she can get her kids after school lets out. But I'll be able to go down and get it in about an hour."

He then looked between Lance and me. "What kind of car do you folks have?"

"It's mine," I said. "It's a new Miata."

"A Miata?" he repeated with a laugh. "Yeah, that's a nice car, but they never bothered to add a spare tire to those. Do you know what trim package you have on it?"

"Not really," I said. "Does it make a difference?"

"Well, the base version and the two nicer trims each take a different tire. Unfortunately, I only have tires in stock for the Sport model. If you have the Club or Grand Touring models, we're out of luck."

"I think it's the Grand Touring package," I said.

"If that's the case and I can't fix your tire so it will last, I'll need to get a new one up here. It'll come out of the Cottonwood warehouse, and they make morning deliveries around eleven-thirty. Worst case, I should be able to get you on the road again by late afternoon tomorrow."

I thanked Hank and gave him my keys and contact information. We then walked out to the parking lot in front of Hank's garage.

"Alright, deputy," I said. "Thanks for getting us set up. Is there a hotel or somewhere we can stay for the night?"

"I'll drive you folks down to the Starlite Motel," the deputy said. "It's not the Ritz, but Sally keeps it clean. It's right off the town square, so that'll give you some dinner options. Of course, there's also Sedona and Cottonwood. They have some nice rooms in either town, but those'll cost you about three times what Sally will charge."

"Thanks, but staying in Sycamore Springs works better for us," I said. "Can you tell us about The Art Loft gallery? Is it in the town, or will it be a drive somewhere?"

"The gallery's about two blocks past the town square, maybe three or four blocks from your motel. Did you folks come up here to look at some paintings?"

"That's our goal," Lance said. "My dad had bought some pieces from a local artist named Cici, and we read that she's having a new show at the gallery in town. We came up here to check it out."

Realizing we were simple tourists, the deputy nodded. I thought this would be a good time to ask him about the names from Valerie's journal. "Can you tell me anything about the Laughing Armadillo Ranch? I heard it's somewhere around here."

"Well, sure," he said as he swept his arm out to the horizon. "You're looking at it. Matter of fact, almost everything you see to the north and east from here is the Laughing Armadillo. It goes most of the way to Sedona and Red Rock State Park. Parts of the eastern side of the town are actually built on ranch property."

"I'd heard it was big," I said. "Who owns it?"

"The Mercer family runs it," Deputy McGill said. "They've had it for almost eighty years. The boys will likely inherit it after Porter Mercer passes."

"Thanks," I said.

The deputy seemed talkative enough, and I was going to ask if he remembered a woman named Val or Valerie Johnson who lived in the area thirty-five years ago. Instead, he asked me a question.

"Is there any particular reason you're asking about the

Mercer family?" His voice had shifted from friendly to politely inquisitive.

Unfortunately, I was all too familiar with the voice inflections. Jackson Reno, my detective ex-boyfriend, always used the same tone whenever he wanted to pull information from a suspect.

"Oh, no," I quickly said. "I was reading about the area before we came up here and was curious."

The deputy looked at me for a moment without saying anything, then nodded his head slightly. "Alright, let me get you both over to the Starlite. It's not too far. I'll then need to get down to Camp Verde. That's where I was originally headed when I found you two."

The Starlite Motel turned out to be a cute one-story courtyard motor lodge on the banks of Oak Creek. It had a dozen single-room cottages set up in a row, a separate office, and a large neon sign out front.

The top of the sign had two colorful round spheres with long metal spikes coming out of them. I assumed these were the "stars," and I was looking forward to seeing the sign when it was lit up after dark.

The door to the motel office had been propped open with a basket of colorful desert four o'clock flowers, and we walked in. After two steps, we were met with the not-so-subtle scent of patchouli incense. Several glass crystals hung in the window in the direct light of the afternoon sun, creating thousands of bright rainbows that shimmered throughout the room.

The Grateful Dead were singing *Sugar Magnolia* from a vintage stereo system on a shelf. Next to this was a lava lamp, where a glowing glob of fluorescent pink goo slowly floated up and down in a clear orange liquid.

I immediately felt at home in the office, and when I looked over at Lance, he was smiling and nodding in time to the music.

Behind the counter, a woman, whom I assumed was Sally, was engrossed in a paperback romance novel. From the tattered state of the cover, which featured a rather explicit photo of a sweaty, half-naked man, it looked like one she'd read a few times before.

The muscular man wore only a Marine Corps desert camouflage hat and a pair of overly tight combat pants. He held a leather strap with a black handle and had a wicked grin on his handsome face. *Corporal Punishment* was plastered across the cover in colorful pink letters.

Sally was maybe forty years old, with a thin, pretty face and long, flowing, dark hair. Reminding me of pictures I'd seen of the original Woodstock concert from the sixties, she wore a bright floral-patterned scoop-neck top with fringe on the sleeves.

She wore a necklace with a peace symbol medallion resting above her ample cleavage, along with several piercings, rings, bracelets, and tattoos. But all these seemed to add to her character rather than detract from it.

When she noticed the sheriff's SUV in the parking lot, Sally stood and gazed out at Deputy McGill, a look of longing on her face. He was still sitting in his cruiser with the window open and his arm hanging out.

"Oh, I'd let that man handcuff me anytime he wanted," she said half to herself as she let out a sigh of desire and waved. The deputy nodded, flashed her a grin, and tapped twice on his horn before taking off.

"Hello, folks," she said after watching the deputy leave the parking lot and head down the main road. "Welcome to the Starlite Motel. I'm Sally Montgomery, the owner, manager, and head landscaper. I'm even the maid when Virginia's fighting with her boyfriend and is too upset to come in. Are you two having some car trouble?"

"How did you know about my tire?" I asked.

"It's not magic or ESP," she said with a laugh. "Whenever Deputy Dan drops off someone during the day, nine times out of ten, it's due to car trouble."

"Well, you've got us pegged," Lance said. "We ended up with a flat tire out by what the deputy called the Javier Miller place."

"Oh, sure," Sally said with a nod. "Is your car over at Hank's shop?"

"Not yet," I said. "He'll get it after he finishes up with a white Cherokee."

"That would be Maggie Conrad's car," Sally said with a knowing nod. "And, yeah. If Hank doesn't have it fixed before she has to pick up her kids from the elementary school at three-thirty, there'll be hell to pay. Maggie's a sweet woman, but she does have a bit of a temper."

"We'd like a couple of rooms," I said. "I think we'll only be here for one night."

Sally glanced back and forth between Lance and me. I noticed her looking at our left hands, and she gave us a small grin.

"Oh, I won't make you get two rooms," she said. "I believe in free love. I don't make judgments on who's married and who's not, and I certainly don't care whose room you'll end up in tonight."

At this, I felt my cheeks grow hot, which only made Sally's grin wider. "No, really," I said. "We'd like two rooms."

"Oh, okay, sure. Here you go," Sally said with an

exaggerated nod as she slid two keys attached to red plastic handles across the counter. "I do cash in advance, so you don't have any paperwork when you check out."

"Thank you," Lance said as he grabbed the keys and handed one to me. He then pulled out his wallet and slid a few bills over the counter.

"Do you want me to pay for it?" I asked. "We can put it on the tab."

"I know how lawyers work," he laughed. "When you add the time for you to copy the receipts, for Lenny to review it, and for Debbie to bill me for it, the cost of the room will have doubled."

I could only smile and shrug my shoulders. After all, he was right. Knowing Lenny, the ultimate cost for the rooms would likely triple.

"I put you two in eleven and twelve," Sally said with a mischievous grin. "Those are adjacent cottages at the very end of the courtyard. There'll probably be three or four rooms between you and the next guest. You can make as much noise as you want."

Her voice then dropped to a whisper. "That way, nobody needs to know."

"What? No, you've got it all wrong," I protested.

"Nobody needs to know," Sally softly repeated while holding up her hand and shaking her head.

I looked over at Lance, expecting him to back up my version of events. Instead, he leaned over the counter and looked at Sally. "That's probably a good idea. She gets pretty loud at times. Thank you for your discretion."

"What the hell was that for?" I asked Lance as we walked to our rooms. "She already thinks we're going to spend the night together, and you confirmed it."

"She's going to think we're sleeping together no matter what we say," Lance said with a laugh. "You saw what she was reading. This way, it'll give her something fun to think about."

Chapter Twelve

After we dropped off our bags, we headed out to find the art gallery. Fortunately, the afternoon was still gorgeous. The mountain temperatures were in the lower eighties, with a light breeze that smelled faintly of campfires and pine trees.

We walked up the gently sloping street to the town square, a pretty park-like area with flowers, trees, and a white gazebo in the center. Like a smaller version of Whiskey Row in Prescott, the square was ringed on two sides with shops, restaurants, and a saloon.

Lance went over to look at a flowerbed of Mexican gold poppies while I checked out the pavilion. As we took in the sights of the park, Lance suddenly stopped.

He gazed into the distance for maybe a minute, and I went over to stand next to him. He was holding his hands in front of his face, making a frame with his thumbs and forefingers, like a director on a movie set.

"Did you find something?" I asked.

"Yeah, look at that mountain through these trees," he said. "See the buildings on either side? Does it look familiar?"

I stared in the direction Lance was looking and saw a large red mountain taking up the entire horizon. We were at a high enough elevation that it was covered in mountain mahogany, piñon pines, and juniper trees. Between the red shades of the mountain rock and the bright greens of the vegetation, it was very pretty.

Suddenly, things came into focus, and I knew what Lance was seeing. I quickly found myself doing the same thumb-and-forefinger director's thing as I looked at the mountain.

"This is the Cici painting you have hanging on the wall in your living room," I exclaimed.

"She must have set up her easel right here when she painted the picture of the mountain and the town square. Not only that but after seeing it in person, I'm pretty sure the mountains in the other two paintings are also from around here. Maybe from Red Rock State Park or Sedona."

"Whoever Cici is, it's a safe bet she either lives nearby or she often comes to Sycamore Springs for inspiration."

"Let's head over to the gallery," he said. "There must be someone there who knows who she is."

We walked down a sloping street to *The Art Loft*, a stand-alone gallery on the main road a little beyond the town square. A gravel parking lot was off to the side, and a split-rail fence surrounded the mountain landscaping in front of the building.

Through the gallery's large windows, we could see dozens of colorful paintings, glass sculptures, and vibrant art objects. A bright neon sign proclaimed the business to be *Open*, so we walked in.

As we entered the shop, a bell on a spring hanging over the door softly jingled. Hearing the friendly ring made me smile.

Maybe we should get a bell for our office?

The building was divided into several sections, and we slowly strolled from one room to another until we found the gallery where Cici's paintings were on display.

The exhibit consisted of almost a dozen works. Each was a beautiful landscape of what appeared to be the red sandstone mountains around Sycamore Springs and Sedona.

The only exceptions were three paintings depicting scenes of iridescent sunsets over a distant range of mountains, as seen from the top of a low hill. Each twilight landscape was similar but different enough to make a nice set.

Like the paintings in Lance's and Jessie's houses, each was full of depth and incredible detail. Again, they gave the odd impression of being halfway between an oil painting and a photograph.

As we were admiring the works, a woman in her early thirties walked up to us. She was slim, slightly taller than me, and had a pretty smile. According to her badge, her name was Gwendolyn.

Her long, dark hair was parted in the middle, beautifully framing her face. She wore oversized black glasses, a navy blue scoop-neck dress accentuated with a single strand of pearls, and medium-heeled strappy sandals. The classy outfit was sexy and slightly revealing without being slutty.

"Hello," she said. "Welcome to The Art Loft. Let me know if I can help you with anything."

Lance's eyes flicked over her body, and then he glanced down at her unadorned left hand. "Gwendolyn," he mused. "That's a beautiful name."

"Oh, it's Gwen. Gwen Tasker," she said as her cheeks flushed pink. "The only person who still calls me Gwendolyn is my mom, and that's when she's upset with me. But she likes it when I wear the name badge."

"I'm Laura Black," I said. "We heard Cici was having a show up here again this summer."

"That's right," Gwen said, sounding professional.

"Everything from Cici is in this room. The only exception is a new piece she brought in a few days ago, which is currently on display in the front window. There's also one she did of Bell Rock that's currently in the back."

"I'm Lance Tillman," my client said as he held out his hand.

As they shook, I noticed Gwen quickly checking him out, her eyes flicking over his body. It was subtle, but I could see the interest in her eyes.

"What can you tell me about Cici?" he asked.

"Well, she's one of our newer artists," Gwen beamed. "This is only her third exhibition. As you can see, she excels in the hyperrealism style of painting. She captures incredible levels of detail and depth, letting you experience the beauty of the natural scene on an emotional level. Her current works mainly focus on the red rock buttes that surround Sedona and Sycamore Springs, but she also has three paintings here from her new *Sunset* series."

"We're also looking for the woman who runs the gallery," I said. "We heard her name was Evelyn. We wanted to ask her some questions about Cici."

"Oh, that's my mom," Gwen said. "She's managed The Art Loft ever since she and my dad opened the shop, twenty-five years ago. She's in the back, unboxing some new paintings that came in this morning. I'll let her know you'd like to see her."

A few minutes later, a pleasant-looking woman in her late fifties, dressed in a light blue blouse and a black skirt, entered the gallery, accompanied by Gwen. Her dark hair was styled in a soft pixie cut.

"Evelyn Tasker," she said as she shook our hands, and we made introductions. She seemed friendly enough, but you could tell that she was the no-nonsense person who ran the place.

"It's good to meet you," I said. "We heard about your gallery from a friend of ours in Scottsdale, Olivia Monroe. She said to tell you 'Hello' if we got a chance to see you."

"Liv Monroe?" Evelyn asked, a look of pleased surprise on her face. "I remember her as well. We would hang out at the art dealers' conferences, maybe ten or fifteen years ago. There are four or five major events a year, and we seemed to travel the same circuit for a while. She ran a gallery in Scottsdale called Desert Vistas, if I recall. How's she doing?"

"She ended up closing that one down for a few years, but she's about to reopen it," I said. "She has a new fiancé and seems happy."

"That's wonderful," Evelyn reminisced. "Liv was a bright spot at those conferences. They were always informative but dreadfully dull. My daughter says you have some questions about one of our artists?"

"Right," Lance said. "My dad, Bill Tillman, was up here at least twice over the last few years to buy some of the Cici paintings. We're here to check out her new work, and we'd like to know more about the artist."

"Oh, sure," Evelyn said, softening slightly. "I remember your dad. He first came in here a little over two years ago. As I recall, he became rather captivated by a small exhibit of paintings by Cici. She's one of our local artists and is growing in popularity. Your dad caught her first show a few days after it opened."

"Other than the fact that Cici's paintings are stunning, did Bill give any reason for liking them so much?" I asked.

"I'm not sure if it was anything specific," Evelyn said. "At first, he seemed to come in only to browse through the shop.

128

But when he saw Cici's landscapes, they seemed to call out to him. Art often has a way of doing that to people."

"Is that when he bought the first painting?" Lance asked.

"That's right," Evelyn said. "He ended up buying one of them during that show, a landscape of Courthouse Butte. He then acquired two more at the follow-up show we had last summer. After he had bought those paintings, I arranged for him to meet the artist. By the way, how is your dad? I've been halfway expecting him to return to see Cici's new works."

"Unfortunately, my dad passed away almost a year ago," Lance said. His voice had tightened as he held back emotions.

"Oh no," Evelyn said as her face fell. "I'm so sorry."

"Thank you," Lance said. "Over the last few years, fine art had become a true passion for him. He liked to spend his free time traveling around the state and exploring the local galleries. He seemed to be particularly fond of the three paintings by Cici. They held a place of prominence in his home."

"I'm glad we got a chance to know him," Evelyn said. "He seemed to be a wonderful person and a true art lover."

"Let me ask you about Cici," Lance said, a touch of nervous anxiety in his voice. "How old is she? Is she around fifty-seven or fifty-eight?"

The question seemed to catch Evelyn off guard, and she shook her head. "No, sorry, you aren't even close. Cici's in her early twenties. I've known her and her family for many years and have been following her artistic progress ever since high school."

Disappointment washed over Lance's face, and I knew what he'd been thinking. After learning from Jessie St. James about the painting techniques of Miss Costello, he'd been hoping that Cici and his mom were the same person.

Unfortunately, it was now evident that they weren't.

"Would you happen to know if Cici was ever a student of Miss Costello?" I asked. "Perhaps she spent her summers at Camp Whispering Pines."

"I'm surprised you know about Miss Costello," Evelyn laughed. "But her style is rather recognizable, isn't it? She was always the area's best art teacher. She retired and sold Whispering Pines some time ago, but she continues to teach classes at her studio in Prescott. I believe Cici was one of her students. Her son, Ron Jr., is now running her gallery."

"Would it be possible to meet the artist?" Lance asked. "I very much enjoy her work and would love to get to know who's hanging in my living room."

"For that, you're in luck," Evelyn said. "This morning, we noticed that Cici didn't sign one of her paintings. She'll be in later today to do that."

"How can an artist forget to sign a painting?" I asked. "That seems like a basic thing."

"Oh, it happens more often than you'd think," Evelyn said. "Most artists won't sign a piece until they're finished with it. For many artists, it's difficult for them to view a work as truly complete."

"Do you know when Cici will be here?" Lance asked. "I'd hate to miss her."

"She said she'd be here around five," Gwen replied. "She's usually fairly prompt. But if you're planning on sticking around town, give me your number, and I'll call you if she arrives early."

"Sure," Lance said, a hint of a grin on his face. "Give me your number, and I'll text you mine back."

As they exchanged numbers, I glanced down at my phone. I was a bit surprised to see that it was only three-thirty. It had been a busy day so far.

"Okay," I said. "We'll head out and be back a little before Cici arrives."

Lance and I walked back to the town square and eventually found ourselves at the white gazebo.

"For a moment, I thought we were about to find out what had happened with my mom," Lance said. "But it seems we've only discovered someone with a similar painting style."

"Don't be hard on yourself," I replied, shaking my head. "I've been half-wondering the same thing since we talked with Jessie St. James yesterday. There have been a lot of strange coincidences happening here."

"It's crazy that they all paint so much alike. But if Miss Costello taught art classes in this part of the state for thirty or forty years, I guess it's not too much of a leap to find others here who paint the same way."

"What do you want to learn when we talk with Cici?" I asked.

"I'm not sure," Lance said, shaking his head slowly. "But we now know that Dad met with her about a month before he died. Maybe they discussed something that led him to find Mom. I realize that basing a connection on painting styles is pretty flimsy, but hopefully, something will come of it."

"So, what do you think of Gwen?" I asked. "I've noticed you sneaking glances at her when she isn't looking."

"Jeez, am I really that obvious?" he chuckled. "I guess I should probably work on my subtlety. But she's very pretty, and you can tell how smart she is just by talking to her."

Lance glanced down at his watch. "We have an hour or so until we're due to go back. What would you like to do?"

"Well, there are half a dozen cute shops along the square.

Would you mind if we did a little shopping?"

As we were strolling through a store that sold Christmas ornaments, Hank, the mechanic, called about the tire. He said that the puncture had occurred on the side rather than in the tread. Apparently, this meant he couldn't patch it.

He let me know he'd already called the warehouse in Cottonwood to have another one shipped out in the morning. Unfortunately, this meant that my car wouldn't be ready until sometime in the late afternoon.

Chapter Thirteen

We arrived back at The Art Loft a little before five. Evelyn was hanging a painting in one of the rooms. She saw us come in and let us know that Cici hadn't arrived yet.

We then spent the next twenty minutes meandering from room to room. As always happens when I visit an art gallery, I completely fell in love with several of the paintings.

Not for the first time, I was a little bummed that I wasn't extremely wealthy. It would be a real kick to be able to buy high-end artwork on a whim.

Around a quarter past five, the bell above the front door jingled, and a woman in her early twenties walked in. She carried a small canvas tote with *Art Supplies* written on the side in sparkly purple letters.

She was of medium height, pale, and thin. Her large, light blue eyes were complemented by long, curly blonde hair that appeared mostly natural, with only a few noticeable darker highlights.

Or are they called lowlights on a blonde?

"Hi, Gwen. Hi, Evelyn," she said, flashing a broad grin at both women. "Sorry about the painting. Which one did I forget to sign?"

"It was the one you did of Bell Rock," Evelyn said. "But

don't worry about it. It makes things so much easier if you come in to sign it *before* someone tries to buy it. That way, I won't have to call you down here as a last-minute thing."

"Thanks for not being too annoyed with me," the artist said. "I'll check them better the next time we do this."

"Cici," Gwen said as we stepped up beside her. "There are two people who'd like to meet you. This is Lance Tillman and Laura Black. Lance's dad was Bill Tillman, the man who bought three of your works."

"Oh, sure," Cici said, giving Lance a curious smile. "Bill Tillman's your dad? It's nice to meet you. I hope you find something in this year's exhibition that you like."

"Would you mind if we watched you sign the painting?" I asked.

"Of course," Cici said. "Evelyn, is it in the back?"

"It's all set up," the gallery owner said. "Let me know if you need anything."

We followed Gwen and Cici into the back room and found a gorgeous landscape sitting on a paint-splattered wooden easel.

"Um, do you have a number two round sable brush?" Cici asked Gwen as she searched through her bag. "It looks like I didn't bring one."

"Oh, sure," Gwen said as she went over to a workbench full of supplies to find a brush.

Cici took out a small palette from her bag and started squirting dabs of paint on it from some half-empty tubes. She then used a flat metal tool to swirl the colors together.

"It looks like you're making black," I said to Cici as I watched the process. "Why wouldn't you simply use black paint?"

"Well, if I only used a tubed black, the signature wouldn't be as vibrant or pop off the canvas as nicely," Cici said. "I'm mixing ultramarine blue and burnt sienna. Those are complementary colors that will create a rich, dark gray with warm undertones. It'll give the signature some additional depth without making the brushstrokes overly thick or wide."

As the artist got ready to sign her work, I became rather lost in the painting. It was a landscape of Bell Rock, one of the huge red sandstone buttes outside of Sedona. The mountain was depicted as if viewed through a grove of pine trees, which added even more depth to the scene.

The picture on the canvas was so realistic that it briefly transported me back to last summer when Sophie, Suzi Lu, and I hiked around the base of the mountain searching for the Bell Rock vortex. According to the locals we spoke with, the vortex was said to be a place where concentrated spiritual energy flowed up from the earth, providing physical healing and a positive mental feeling.

"I absolutely love the look on your face," Cici beamed at me. "Should I take that to mean you like my painting?"

"It's incredible," I said, still halfway mesmerized by the landscape. "I spent the afternoon at Bell Rock with some friends last August. We were looking for the vortex that was supposedly there. It was a beautiful day, and your painting brought back the emotions of the experience."

"Did you ever find it?" she asked.

"The vortex? Well, we hiked around and eventually ended up standing on a rock near where it was supposed to be. I'm not sure if we ever found a gateway to the supernatural, but standing on that rock with my friends was definitely the best part of that entire two-week assignment."

"I've often heard about the vortexes of Sedona," Lance said. "Where was the one you were looking for?"

I gazed at the painting and pointed to an area to the left of the massive red mountain. "If you could see through the trees, it would be about there, right at the base of the cliffs on the west side."

"You mean the part of the painting that looks a little fuzzy?" he asked as he leaned in closer for a better look.

"Fuzzy?" I replied, glancing back at the landscape. Sure enough, the sky above where I'd pointed seemed slightly off, as if there was a faint smoke rising from a campfire.

I looked at Cici. "Did you purposefully make the sky in that part of the painting different?"

"Huh. Until you pointed it out, I never noticed it," she said, now staring at the spot Lance had noted. "The sky in that part of the painting looks a little distorted."

Everyone gathered around the easel and looked at the painting. After a moment, Cici sighed and shook her head. "Oh well, it's too late to redo that part. It'll need to stay fuzzy."

"No, it looks perfect like that," I said.

After Cici signed the painting, we drifted out to her exhibition. "It's wonderful that you could come up here," the artist said as she talked about her landscapes. "I know it's a long drive from Scottsdale. I love getting to know the people who have my paintings. Do you know if your dad will be coming up here? I'm working on a new landscape that I think he'll like."

"Unfortunately, my dad passed away about a year ago, shortly after he got the last painting from you," Lance said. "It was, um, very sudden."

Cici's eyes widened, and an expression of grief swept across her face. "That's so terrible," she said in a small voice. "I got to know him a little bit last spring, and he seemed like a good man. He said a lot of nice things about my artwork, and

I could tell he was sincere."

"Thanks," Lance said. "The three paintings he bought are on the main wall in the living room. I know how much he loved them."

"Do you have plans for dinner?" I asked the artist, wanting to switch to something happier. "We'd love to get to know you better."

"Yes, I hope you can," Lance agreed. "We're spending the night here and would enjoy getting a chance to learn about you. Drinks, coffee, or dinner. Whatever you have time for."

"Um, sure," Cici said. "That would be great. I didn't have lunch today, and I'm starving. Unless you have a preference, the Crazy Cowgirl Café on the square has some of the best food in town. I'd planned on heading over there after this in any case."

As Lance and I were chatting with Cici, it was clear that Gwen was keeping track of our conversation. As a spur-of-the-moment thing, I turned to her. "Gwen, we're heading over to the café for a bite to eat. Would you like to come along as well?"

She'd been giving Lance quick glances whenever she thought I wasn't paying attention, and it seemed her interest in him was growing. For a moment, she appeared somewhat conflicted about my invitation.

It was clear Gwen wanted to go out to dinner with us. But she also didn't want to be overly obvious about her attraction to Lance since she was mainly trying to sell us artwork.

"That's a great idea," Lance said, flashing her a broad smile. "I hope you don't already have plans."

Gwen looked over at her mom, who had also been listening to the conversation. From the look on her face, I got the feeling that Evelyn wasn't too keen on one of her younger artists going to dinner with two strangers from out of town.

"Go ahead," Evelyn said to her daughter. "I'll take care of things here."

We made it to the Crazy Cowgirl, a noisy diner on the town square that was almost full. Most of the people there seemed to be locals, with only a few tables occupied by obvious tourists.

One of the passing servers directed us to a booth in the corner. I slid in next to Cici while Lance and Gwen took the other side.

"Do you live in the area?" I asked Cici. "We've noticed that most of your paintings are from this part of the state."

"I live with my family over at the Laughing Armadillo," she said. "That's the cattle ranch outside of town. The place is huge, and my whole family lives there."

Cici lives at the Laughing Armadillo?

"Everyone in your family?" Lance asked.

"Well, almost. My parents, my granddad, and my uncle live there. His wife used to be with us as well, but they got divorced, and she moved out. I also have an older cousin named Jeannie who lives there. She's about the best friend I have."

"Have you always lived at the ranch?" I asked.

"Pretty much. Except for a few years when I went to college and lived in Flagstaff, it's all I've ever known."

"What's that like, living somewhere so open?" I asked. "I've always lived in the suburbs or in the city."

"Honestly, it would seem a little strange to live close to other people. I sometimes visit friends who live in town, and the houses there feel crammed together."

"I've lived in the suburbs ever since I moved away for college, and that was like fifteen years ago," Gwen said. "I remember that having neighbors who lived so close seemed a little strange at first. But after a while, I think you simply learn to ignore it."

"Your painting style is incredible," Lance said. "How did you learn to do it?"

"Well, several people in my family paint," Cici said, blushing slightly. "I guess it started with my great-granduncle Homer. He died before I was born, but he has several oils hanging throughout Longview."

"Longview?" I asked. "What's that?"

"That's the name of the main house at the Laughing Armadillo. My uncle and my mom both know how to paint. But I mainly learned my technique from an artist my family knows in Prescott. She owns a gallery, and I took lessons from her for several years."

"Miss Costello?" I asked.

"Yeah," Cici laughed. "How'd you know?"

"She has a distinctive painting style and seems to be rather famous in this part of the state," I said.

"Mom said if I was going to paint with oils, I needed to learn to do it properly. Unfortunately, Dad never thought much about my artwork. He thinks it's a waste of my time and says I should learn to do something useful. But Gwen and Evelyn think I could make a go of it as a professional artist."

"Oh, definitely," Gwen said. "Mom's already working with some gallery owners she knows in Las Vegas to have Cici's work shown there."

"Tell me about when you met with my dad," Lance said. "I'd love to hear the story."

"There's not much to tell," Cici said. "I met him last summer when he came up to see the exhibit. After Evelyn called and told me your dad had bought two additional paintings, I invited him up to my studio in Longview to see my other work."

"Do you often invite people to your home?" I asked.

"Oh, almost never," Cici said with a quick shake of her head. "But your dad was the first person to buy a painting from my first show, and he'd bought two more from my second exhibition. I guess you could say he was my first fan, well, other than Gwen and Evelyn."

"Dad called me the day after he met you," Lance said. "It was all he could talk about, and it seemed to affect him deeply. He spoke about you and your work until the very end."

"I'm finishing up a painting I've been doing with him in mind," Cici said. "It would have given him a set of the major mountains around here."

"I'd love to see it," Lance said. "Is it at the gallery?"

"It's in my studio in Longview. But why don't you and Laura come over tomorrow and see how it looks? Gwen, if you have the time, why don't you come over as well? I'm not sure if it'll be ready for this year's exhibition, but you can tell me what you think about it."

"Oh, definitely," Gwen said. From the smile on her face and her sideways glance at my client, I got the feeling that she was looking forward to being with Lance as much as she was to seeing the new painting.

"You said you're only here in the summer?" Lance asked Gwen. "What do you do the rest of the year?"

He was looking at her intently. His deep, steady gaze gave

him a handsome and somewhat commanding appearance.

Gwen became lost in his eyes and quickly looked my client up and down. She then gave him a slightly awkward smile and reached up to fiddle with a strand of her hair.

After a moment, she blinked rapidly a few times as she recovered her equilibrium. Her eyes then flicked quickly to me to see if I'd caught her checking him out.

It made me feel a little better to see she had a slight look of shame as she searched my face, looking for my reaction. After all, as far as she knew, Lance and I were a romantic couple.

"I teach second grade down in Tempe," she said quietly with a small shrug. "I typically have several kids who are at risk, and it can be a stressful job at times. Being up here with Mom for summers and the Christmas rush helps me to decompress. The spring semester finished last Friday, so I'm still getting back into the swing of things here."

Upon learning that Gwen worked less than five miles from his home, Lance broke into a thoughtful grin. "I'm glad you have a beautiful place like this to retreat to," he said. "I can see how it would help you relax after a long school year."

Gwen agreed, and I could see her getting lost in Lance's eyes again. Honestly, it was kind of sweet to see.

After dinner, coffee, and some delicious cherry pie, we strolled through the town. The sun had dipped below the distant range of mountains, lighting up the clouds in the west with the vibrant oranges, yellows, and reds that make Arizona sunsets so spectacular.

It had been a fun evening, and we wandered into the town square as a group. We ended up at the gazebo and chatted for several minutes, with no one wanting to be the first to leave.

Lance and I agreed to meet Gwen at the art gallery parking

lot the next morning at nine-thirty. She'd then drive us to the Laughing Armadillo, and we'd be at Cici's studio in Longview by ten o'clock.

As our group walked back down the street towards the art gallery, Lance started chatting with Cici, which put me several paces back, talking with Gwen. She was helpful and friendly, but I could tell that she was still in her professional saleswoman persona.

She answered all of my questions with a quick sentence or two. I could sense she was still a little unsure of how things were coming together with our group, so I thought I'd help her out.

"Gwen," I said softly so Lance and Cici couldn't hear. "Just so you know, Lance and I aren't together. He asked my company to look into some things for him, which makes him a client. I've only known him for a few days, but I think he's completely single."

"Really?" she asked, a hopeful spark of interest in her eyes.

"I've seen the way you two keep sneaking glances at each other, and there seems to be some mutual chemistry. Perhaps you should think about pursuing it?"

"Oh, okay then," she stammered as she relaxed and let out a nervous giggle of relief. "God, I thought I was being completely subtle, but I guess not."

"Don't worry about it," I said. "From what I can tell, Lance is a good guy. You could do worse."

With that settled, we escorted Cici and Gwen to their cars at The Art Loft. Once they took off, Lance and I walked back to the Starlite Motel.

Chapter Fourteen

I wasn't disappointed when I saw the big motel sign in the parking lot. It was brightly lit in colorful neon with dozens of sparkling lights.

The two metal spheres on top of the sign were also brilliantly illuminated, and the spikes on the spheres each had rows of flashing lights. These "stars" slowly rotated, giving the parking lot a fun and peaceful atmosphere.

We walked by the office, where Sally was once again behind the desk. She waved and yelled out, "Hello, you two."

Lance and I glanced at each other. Then, by mutual agreement, we went in.

The room still had the strong scent of patchouli, but the music had switched to Jefferson Airplane. Grace Slick was singing about Alice and the pills she would take to make her small.

"I hope you both had a good day in Sycamore Springs," Sally said, a broad smile on her face.

"We did," Lance said. "We ended up at The Art Loft and got a chance to meet one of my dad's favorite artists, a local woman named Cici."

"Oh, sure," Sally said. "Cici Mercer is nice, and she's very active in the community. Her cousin Jeannie and her mom are great, too. Whenever there's a charity event, you can always expect all three of them to be there."

"What about the Mercer men?" I asked. "Are they nice as well?"

"Um, I don't know any of the guys over there very well, at least not any of the family," she said, becoming somewhat evasive. "But I do know some of the ranch hands, and they're all great."

We wished Sally a goodnight and took off. As she had predicted, the four rooms closest to ours were dark, and none had cars parked in front of them.

"Let's meet for breakfast at eight," I said when we got to our rooms. "That should give us enough time to meet Gwen at nine-thirty."

"Alright," he said, with a small chuckle as he looked at our two rooms, no doubt thinking of Sally. "I'll see you tomorrow morning."

I unpacked my overnight bag and hung the next day's clothes in the closet, hoping some of the wrinkles would fall out by morning. I then slipped on an oversized Vail T-shirt, propped up some pillows, and lay back on the bed with my back against the headboard.

I glanced at my watch and noted it was only eight thirty. Hoping I could catch Max, I spent a few moments organizing my thoughts and then called.

"Hey, you," I said when he answered. "Do you have time to talk before your nine o'clock meeting?"

"Your timing is perfect," he said. "I'm glad you called. I

was hoping to hear your voice tonight. What's going on with your case? Have you been able to track down your client's mother?"

"Not yet, although we've picked up a pretty strong lead. We've met a woman named Cici, who appears to be part of the Mercer family. It's possible that our client's dad used information from Cici to locate his mom last year, about a month before he was murdered. We're meeting with Cici tomorrow at the main house at the Laughing Armadillo Ranch to look at some of her artwork. I'm hoping to get a chance to ask questions and maybe poke around a little."

"You're still looking into the Mercer family?" Max asked. "Tony said he talked with you about them. From what I understand, they aren't very active outside of the Sycamore Springs area, but that doesn't mean that they're nice people. Please keep that in mind as you investigate."

"I will," I assured him. "If everything goes well, I'll be back later tomorrow. If I'm early enough, I'll stop by."

After I'd finished talking with Max, I brushed my teeth and then glanced at the time. Since it was only a few minutes after nine, I called Sophie. She almost never goes to bed before eleven, so I knew I wouldn't wake her.

"Hey," I said as she answered. "I hope I didn't catch you at a bad time."

"Nah," she said. "I'm on the couch, flipping through the TV. I've got over three hundred channels and can't find a fricking thing to watch. For the last ten minutes, I've been watching one of those reality survival shows where the contestants are nude the entire time. This one's called *Naked and Scared in Texas*."

"Really? How does that one work?"

"They dropped off a bare-naked man and woman down

the road from a small farming community outside of Lubbock. They then have to survive completely nude for twenty-one days."

"Seriously?" I asked. "It sounds like they're starting to run out of ideas for these reality shows."

"Yeah, especially since they blur out the good stuff and mostly only show their butts."

"I guess cable reality shows aren't the place for full frontal. Is the show any good?"

"It's alright. So far, the guy's been tossed into jail as some sort of hippie pervert. His cellmate, a guy called Big Willie, thinks he's cute, so that's causing some awkward situations. Plus, the guards made him put on prison clothes, so he's pretty much blown his chances of winning."

"What about the woman?"

"She became the den mother of a senior citizen biker gang. She's been walking around the clubhouse naked, cooking, and cleaning for the guys. From what she says, the gang treats her better than her own family does, and she's thinking about moving there permanently when the season's over."

"I hate to tell you, but that show sounds terrible."

"Oh, I know," Sophie said with a laugh. "Hey, I just sent you pictures of Porter, Dalton, and Morgan Mercer. Porter only looks like a mean grandfather, but Morgan and Dalton both look like people you'd see in a prison gang."

"Thanks," I said as I heard my phone buzz with the incoming texts. Looking at the pictures, I had to agree with Sophie's assessment of the Mercer men.

"I've got some new information for you," I said. "Cici, the woman who painted the pictures in Lance's house, is also part of the Mercer family. She's in her early twenties, but I don't know a lot about her other than that. Could you expand the search to cover her as well? Everything seems to be converging on the family and what's going on in Sycamore Springs."

"Okay, I can do that. I'll have the secret software search for everyone at the house. Have you seen any evidence that connects Cici to our client's mother?"

"No, at least not yet. All I have is that both Cici and Valerie Bacchus learned how to paint from Miss Costello. She's a local art teacher who also taught Jessie St. James at her summer camp."

"Well, that's a good connection, but probably not enough to find the client's mother."

"I know. Did you ever get anything back on Valerie Johnson?"

"Jeez, I sure did," Sophie laughed. "Using the Johnson name, I got over three hundred hits, even when I filtered the results for Arizona and Sycamore Springs. I added a few more filters to the results, and that knocked it down to eight women. I should get the final reports by tomorrow."

"That works. We're going up to the main house at the ranch tomorrow morning. Hopefully, we'll get a chance to look around and find out more about her."

"Well, okay. But be careful. These Mercers sound like a bunch of wankers, and there's already been one murder in this assignment, even if it isn't directly related."

Sophie said she'd modify her secret software search as soon as she got back into the office. Before I disconnected, I wished her luck in finding something good to watch as she flipped through her channels.

I knocked on Lance's door at eight the following morning. He seemed eager to get started but looked like he hadn't slept a lot the night before.

As we walked into the office, Sally was again behind the counter. Like the day before, she was dressed in clothes that gave off a sixties flower-child hippy vibe.

In addition to a flowing purple blouse, she wore a leather vest trimmed in fringe, decorated with several colorful buttons. One had a peace sign on it, one proclaimed *"Down with Pants,"* and the biggest one said, *"Make Love, Not War."*

Sally didn't seem to be a morning person. She'd turned down the stereo to the point I could barely make out that the band playing was Crosby, Stills, Nash, and Young. Her eyes were slightly unfocused, and she was barely able to mumble out a "good morning" as she sipped an earthenware mug of what smelled like jasmine tea.

"Hi Sally," I said. "If it's possible, we'd like to extend our stay another night. Hank let me know that the car wouldn't be fixed until later in the afternoon. Plus, we're heading up to Longview today to see some of Cici's paintings, and I don't know how long that will take."

"Oh, um, sure," Sally said as she took a noisy sip of her tea and glanced at her computer monitor. "Um, I have three checkouts today and only have two new reservations coming in. You can keep the same rooms, no problem."

"Thank you, Sally," Lance said as he slid a few bills across the counter. "We appreciate how accommodating you've been."

We then strolled up the gently sloping street to the Crazy Cowgirl Café. As the small town gradually came to life, it felt quite peaceful.

Given the time of day, I was a little surprised at how

crowded the restaurant was. The night before, most of the people there had been families and couples. Today, the tables were filled with groups of seniors and people dressed to work outside.

We each got a cup of strong coffee while we looked over our menus. I eventually chose the *Rootin' Tootin' Rodeo Round-Up,* while Lance decided on the *Arizona Sunrise Supreme* with a side of bacon.

"How'd you sleep?" I asked after we ordered breakfasts from a cheerful server.

"Um, I didn't get to sleep until late," he said, sounding slightly embarrassed as he sipped his coffee.

"I'm surprised. It was dead quiet last night. The only sounds I heard were the splashing sounds from the river. After living in a loud apartment building for so many years, being in the country put me right to sleep."

"It wasn't that," he said with a chuckle. "Gwen texted me about twenty minutes after we got back, and we ended up texting for quite a while."

"Oh really?" I asked with a laugh. "That seems like a good sign. Or was she only trying to figure out the real reason why you were up here?"

"No, nothing like that. We mainly talked about our jobs and the places we both like to eat in Tempe and Scottsdale. It turns out we have a lot in common."

"Well, if nothing else, it sounds like you've found a new friend. Speaking of friends, I have pictures of the Mercers."

I then pulled up the three images that Sophie had texted the night before. "Do any of them look familiar?"

Lance took the phone and scrolled through the photos. "No, I've never seen any of them before."

"I had a thought this morning," I said. "Evelyn is about the same age as your mom. If they both grew up here, they likely knew each other. Let's stop by after we visit with Cici and see if we can learn anything new."

"That's a great idea," he said, nodding thoughtfully.

Chapter Fifteen

At nine-thirty, we met Gwen at The Art Loft. She drove a red Toyota Highlander, and I hopped in the back, letting Lance take shotgun. From the broad smile on Gwen's face as he climbed in, I didn't think she would mind.

"How far is it to Cici's house, Longview?" I asked as Gwen pulled out of the parking lot.

"Maybe three or four miles as the crow flies. But since we're in a valley and there are steep cliffs on the east side of the river, the only way to cross Oak Creek is over the Laughing Armadillo bridge. Unfortunately, it's about two miles the other way from where we want to end up."

Gwen drove us northeast along a peaceful, tree-lined road that followed the banks of the river on the west side. After maybe five or six minutes, a beautiful silver bridge came into view.

It was one of those old-fashioned truss bridges that you often see crossing rivers in Arizona. An open metal framework of steel beams formed a series of triangular shapes that supported its structure. From the side, the open metalwork had a distinctive "crisscross" look.

When we reached the bridge, I was surprised to see a substantial black gate blocking the way. A large sign read, *Laughing Armadillo Ranch. No Trespassing.*

"There's a gate?" I asked. "It's not a public bridge?"

"The Mercers built this back in the forties when they were first getting the ranch going and building Longview," Gwen said with a shake of her head. "The main house is at the top of a low mesa about two miles east of Oak Creek. Between the cliffs on the east side of the river and only having the one bridge, I guess it gives them plenty of privacy."

"If it's so hard to get across the river, how do they move the cattle around?" Lance asked.

"Oh, further south of town, the cliffs on the east side drop away, and the valley widens out. That's mainly where the Mercers winter their cattle. After another three or four miles, Oak Creek merges with the Verde River. There are tons of roads and bridges down there."

We pulled onto the bridge and stopped in front of the gate. A black box mounted on a pole on the driver's side had a camera, a keycard pad, and a speaker. It also had a red button that Gwen reached out and pushed.

"Yes?" a gruff male voice asked from the speaker after a delay of maybe thirty seconds.

"It's Gwen Tasker and two guests. We're here to see Cici and her studio. She's expecting us."

"Hold on," the voice told us, then clicked off.

We waited in front of the gate for four or five minutes. I studied the bridge and noted a sidewalk on the right side of the metal decking. A fence and a sturdy-looking gate efficiently blocked it. I also noticed a keycard pad next to the person-sized entryway.

Gwen was getting a little fidgety and was thinking about pushing the button again when there was a mechanical whirring noise, and the big gate swung open. We drove onto the bridge and quickly passed over the river.

From there, it was a pleasant ten-minute drive up a well-maintained paved road. It made several broad switchback turns as it wound its way up the low hill.

Along the way, we drove by at least a hundred head of cattle that were peacefully grazing on the open pasture. The scene was so pretty that I had Gwen stop so I could take pictures of the livestock with a range of high mountains in the background. We then passed by several ranch buildings that seemed to be workshops, bunkhouses, and storage sheds.

After passing a dozen of the outbuildings, we pulled up in front of the main house. It was huge and sat at the summit of the wide, flat-topped ridge.

The brown two-story home, which looked like something from an old cowboy movie, had a wide wrap-around porch that surrounded the entire structure. *Longview* was carved into a wooden sign attached above the main doors. The house appeared to be well-kept, and the surrounding grounds looked pristine.

There was an old-fashioned wooden hitching post along the side of the wide gravel driveway where two horses were tied. Each one was peacefully munching on some hay that was in a trough in front of them.

As we parked in front of the ranch house, we saw Deputy McGill standing next to his SUV, talking with a man of maybe eighty-five years. Four other vehicles, two sports cars and two pick-up trucks, were parked in front of the house, none of which were more than three or four years old.

On the doors of each truck was a cute cartoon picture of a smiling armadillo. *Laughing Armadillo Ranch, Sycamore Springs, Arizona*, was written in flowing letters in a circle around the animal.

Recalling the photos Sophie had sent over, I knew that the older man was Porter Mercer, the family patriarch. He stood ramrod straight at about five feet eleven inches tall and had a bit of a belly. His salt-and-pepper hair was longer than most men wear but combed straight back.

Reminding me of Tony DiCenzo, Porter had an unmistakable air of command about him. From his body language and forceful gestures, it was clear that Porter was giving the deputy instructions about how he wanted something done.

The most striking feature about Porter was his eyes. They seemed to bore intently into the lawman as they spoke.

Gwen had stopped her Toyota near the stairs leading up to the porch. Both Deputy McGill and Porter Mercer then watched as we climbed out.

"Hi, Mr. Mercer," Gwen said in her cheerful voice. "We're here to see Cici. She has some new paintings she wants to show off."

"Hello, Gwen," Porter said in a deep, raspy voice. "It's good to see you back in town. How's your mother? I haven't talked with her in several weeks."

"She's doing great," Gwen said. "It's the start of the tourist season, and I came up last weekend."

"I'm glad you've returned to help at the gallery. I know your mother appreciates having you here. Introduce me to your friends," he said in a tone that was more of a command than a question.

"Lance Tillman," my client said as he stepped forward and shook the older man's hand.

"I'm Porter Mercer," he said. "Tillman? That's a rather storied name. It's of Old English origin, if I recall correctly. One who tills the earth, a farmer."

"You're spot on about the name," Lance said. "Although there haven't been any farmers in my family for quite some time. I run a financial services firm down in Scottsdale."

"I'm Laura Black," I said as I stepped forward to shake his hand. "Cici's working on some new paintings, and she's meeting us in her studio to show them off."

"Painting has always been something of a family tradition here, starting with my uncle," Porter said. "I'm glad my granddaughter has taken up the hobby to carry on his legacy. Although she perhaps spends a little too much time on her art. She needs to start thinking about what she wants to do with the rest of her life."

As we were talking, I noticed that Deputy McGill was silently watching our group, listening to every word. With a brief flick of his fingers, Porter wordlessly dismissed the deputy, who climbed into his cruiser and pulled away slowly.

"Gwen, I believe you know the way to Cici's studio?" Porter asked.

"I do," Gwen said. "It was good seeing you again, Mr. Mercer."

Gwen led us into the house. We entered a huge, atrium-style main living room with an open-hearth fireplace and a floor-to-ceiling river rock chimney.

The room had high picture windows that looked out over the mountains, allowing in a lot of natural light. Several stuffed animal heads and seven or eight oil paintings were mounted on the walls. She then led us down a hallway toward the back of the home.

We soon came to Cici's studio, a large, high-ceilinged room with picture windows facing south and west. We glanced around, but Cici wasn't there yet.

"I guess we know where she gets the inspiration for her sunset paintings," Lance said as he gazed out the west-facing windows.

From the ranch house, it was a long, gradual slope down to the high riverbanks on the east side of Oak Creek and then to Sycamore Springs beyond. The stunning vista continued unobstructed to a range of high mountains that must have been ten or fifteen miles away.

"Longview is certainly the right name for this house," I mused. "I'd love to be here for one of the sunsets. I imagine they're pretty spectacular."

"Longview sits at almost six thousand feet," Gwen said. "In December and January, they get some cold winds blowing up here, and they can even see some snow. But the rest of the year, the weather's beautiful, and you can't beat the view."

"Hello, everybody," Cici's voice called out from the door to the hallway. "I'm glad you could make it."

We spent the next twenty minutes letting Cici show us her latest paintings. The one she was doing with Lance's dad in mind was Capitol Butte, a large orange-red sandstone mountain outside of Sedona.

Lance seemed pleased that Cici had painted a landscape specifically for his dad and offered to buy it when it was finished. Everybody then grabbed something to drink from a refrigerator in the corner.

We opened a door that led out to the big wraparound porch and stepped outside. As we went to the railing, the view opened up further. The vista was gorgeous, and with the cattle grazing on the slight downward slope of the hill, it was a very peaceful scene.

"This may seem like a weird question," Lance said as he sipped on a Coke. "But when my dad was here last year, did anything strange or unusual happen?"

"Like what?" Cici asked, looking back and forth between us.

"Oh, it could have been anything," Lance said. "After he came back to Scottsdale, you and the paintings were all he wanted to talk about. I could never figure out why he was so excited about meeting you."

"Did you ever ask him about it?" Gwen asked.

"Unfortunately, my dad died about a month after he was up here. I was living in an apartment at the time and only talked with him on the phone once or twice a week. I wish I'd known how short his time was. I would have been with him more."

"Wow," Cici said. "That's so sad. But no, he came up here, and we looked around the studio for almost an hour. He liked several of my paintings but said that after buying the two new ones from the gallery, he was going to need to find some space on his walls before he could get anything else."

"So, nothing else happened while he was here?" Lance asked.

"Not really. After going through my studio, I gave him a quick tour of the house. He wanted to see some of the original paintings that my great-granduncle had done. He chatted with Mom in the living room for a few minutes and later with Uncle Dalton."

"Did they talk about anything unusual?"

"I don't think so. But from the way they talked, I could tell that your dad and my mom had gone to high school or maybe college together. Your dad said it was great to see her again, and they'd need to keep in touch. I remember that he asked Mom for her email."

"Did she give it to him?"

"She wasn't going to at first, but he kept asking nicely, and she eventually gave in."

"Do you remember what my dad and your uncle spoke about?" Lance asked.

"Some. Your dad talked about running a financial services company in Scottsdale. My uncle said they already had a finance guy for the ranch, but he'd keep him in mind in case anything came up, something like that."

"And that was everything they talked about?" he asked. "Did you ever see my dad again?"

"That one time was it," she said with a slight shrug. "I'd been hoping he'd come up for the exhibition again this year. I was looking forward to showing him my new work. I'm sorry that I won't be able to meet him again. I know I only met him one time, but I really liked your dad."

"Cici?" I asked. Something had been bugging me, and I suddenly had to find out. "This will also seem like a weird question, but how old are you?"

"I'm twenty-three and a half," she said, giving me a slightly puzzled look.

"When's your birthday?"

"November 23rd. It was the day before Thanksgiving that year." She then looked back and forth between us. "Why do you want to know my birthday?"

"Was there anything unusual about your birth, or are there any family stories surrounding it?" I asked.

"Not really, other than I was about six weeks premature."

"Wow, that must have been hard on your mom," I said. "But they could do remarkable things with babies, even back then. How much did you weigh?"

"That's a funny question," she said. "I once asked Mom about it, and she said she didn't remember. But I needed my birth certificate to register for college, and it was there. I was a little under seven pounds."

"Huh," I said. "That's not so bad for a preemie."

"You all have to stay for lunch," Cici said as we walked back into her studio. "Then I'll show you both around the place. Most of my family likes to paint, and there are about a dozen works on display. They go back to my great-granduncle Homer almost a hundred years ago."

"We'd love that," Lance said.

"Let me go down to the kitchen and let them know," Cici said. "Feel free to look around, but don't forget that the paint is still soft on most of the canvases here. I'd avoid touching anything."

"While you're doing that, I'll head back out to the porch and make a couple of phone calls," Gwen said.

Cici took off, and we slowly went from easel to easel, looking at works ranging from rough pencil sketches to what appeared to be finished paintings.

A few minutes later, the door to the studio opened, and a woman in her late fifties walked in. She looked at the two of us and then quickly glanced around the room.

"Do you know where Cici is?" the woman asked. "Her grandfather's looking for her."

"She went to talk with someone in the kitchen about us staying for lunch," I said.

"Oh, okay..." the woman said, but her voice trailed away. She stared at Lance with the strangest expression in her eyes. Her mouth slowly dropped open, and she began to tremble.

"Lance?" she asked. "Is that you?"

Oh crap, I thought, recognizing who she was.

Lance stared at the woman for several moments. Then, recognition flooded onto his face.

Chapter Sixteen

"Mom?" Lance asked.

I looked at the woman, who had already started to cry. Her hair was shorter, and she'd had it styled, but her face closely resembled the pictures Lance had shown us of Valerie when she was much younger.

She ran over to Lance and threw her arms around him. Still looking shocked, Lance hugged her back.

"What are you doing at Longview?" she asked several moments later as she stepped back, her voice a mix of fear and anger. "Son, of all places, you can't be here."

"What do you mean, of all places?" Lance replied.

Valerie took a deep breath as if trying to compose her thoughts. "If Morgan or Dalton discover that you're here, there'll be trouble," she warned, fear evident in her eyes. "You need to leave Longview as quickly as possible."

"Mom, what are you talking about? Morgan forced you to come here. We need to get you away from this place."

"No, I have to stay here. Son, it's a long story, but as long as I'm here at the ranch, everything will be fine."

"What are you talking about?" he asked.

Valerie looked embarrassed and ashamed. "If you know

about Morgan finding me, then I'm guessing you found my old journal. Even after all these years, I'm still upset that I left it back at the house. But if you did read my diary, then you know why I had to leave."

"Morgan was blackmailing you to leave Dad and be with him," Lance said.

"Son, you're completely wrong. I had to come back home. That was all."

"Mom, that makes no sense. What do you mean about coming home?"

"The truth is, I was married to Morgan, and I had been since I graduated from college."

"Married?" Lance asked, now sounding mad. "You mean you were married to him the entire time you were with Dad? How could you do that to him?"

"Look, I'm not proud of what I did," Valerie said. "But I was in a tight spot. I never meant to hurt either you or your father. But after Morgan found me living in Scottsdale, he threatened to hurt both Bill and you. I had to go back home with him."

"That man sounds like a nightmare," Lance spat out, now sounding angry and hurt. "How could you have married him?"

"Morgan was handsome and charming, at least at first. He made it easy to fall in love with him. Of course, after we were married, he started drinking and whoring, pretty much full-time. It didn't take long for me to get sick of him and his antics. Within the first year of our marriage, well, some other things happened that would have made my situation here even worse. I ran away to Scottsdale, cut my hair, changed my name, and got a job as a barista at the Daily Drip."

"Dad said he met you at the coffee shop," Lance said.

"I met Bill on my first day on the job, and it was love at

first sight for both of us. Your dad was a remarkable man. I, um, became pregnant with you right away, but it didn't bother Bill. It only seemed to make our love stronger."

"But you never mentioned that you were already married? Didn't you think that was something he should have known?"

She again looked ashamed and shook her head. "I never told Bill about my marriage to Morgan, even though it upset your dad when I said I didn't want to marry him. But I couldn't file for divorce. Once Morgan found out where I was living, he'd take me back home. I also knew he'd hurt anyone who stood in his way."

"But your husband found you anyway," Lance said, putting everything together in his head.

"I'm not sure how, but Morgan eventually located me. I'd been gone for over ten years by then. I figured he would have stopped looking for me and moved on to some other sucker with a pretty face, but I was wrong."

"It's still not too late to have a decent life," Lance said. "Come back to Scottsdale, then file for divorce. I'm still at the house, and you can stay there too. I know my grandmother would be thrilled to have you back with us."

"No, I can't. I know too much about what's been going on up here. I'll never be able to leave."

"Mom, what are you talking about?"

"Son, I made a mistake last year. Your dad found me, and I spent a weekend at a hotel in Sedona with him. I should never have done it. It was stupid and impulsive of me. But you have to understand, I'd never stopped loving your dad."

"But why was it a mistake?" Lance asked. "If you still loved him, I don't see why you thought it was wrong."

"Morgan and Dalton discovered what I had done, and they went nuts. They learned where Bill lived in Scottsdale. They

162

went down there to confront him, and there was a fight. They shot and killed Bill in his living room."

"My god. Mom, are you serious?" Lance asked. "You know who killed Dad? Why haven't you told the police about it? They both need to be in prison."

"Morgan and Dalton know that you are Bill's son, which puts you in danger as well. I found out what they did to your dad, and I threatened to go to the police. But Morgan is using the fact that you're my son to keep me in line."

"What do you mean?" Lance asked.

"Son, they've promised that the same thing that happened to Bill will happen to you if I talk to the authorities or even if I simply take off again."

"But that's crazy," Lance said. "You need to come back to Scottsdale and tell the detectives what you know. They need to be arrested for what they did."

"You don't know Morgan and Dalton," Valerie said as she shook her head slowly. "They're both extremely violent, they have fierce tempers, and it never takes much to set them off."

Lance looked at his mother, and I could see the gears turning in his head. "Mom, the way I see it, Morgan and Dalton are vicious killers. They're still threatening you and, to a lesser extent, me. But if we can ensure that they're held accountable for their crimes, you'll be safe."

"Son, I've been thinking about how to work with the Scottsdale authorities ever since I found out they murdered Bill. But that's easier said than done. I don't have keys to any of the vehicles, and they'd never let me over the bridge alone. Whenever I go into town, Morgan or Dalton always goes with me to make sure I don't try to escape. There's no way I could make it down to Scottsdale."

"Could you call or maybe even email the detectives?" I

asked. "I know they'd love to hear your story."

"I've thought about calling, but I'm pretty sure they'd want to talk with me in person before they took any action. Unfortunately, nobody goes over the bridge without Porter's approval. There's no way he'd allow detectives from Scottsdale to come up here and interview me. It would only serve to alert Morgan and Dalton that I'm talking with the police."

"You'd think there'd be some legal way for them to come up here to find out what you know," Lance said.

"It might be a challenge," I admitted. "Longview is outside their jurisdiction. Plus, I don't think they'd have any luck trying to go through the local sheriff's office."

Lance nodded. "You're right. After seeing how chummy Deputy McGill is with Porter, I don't think we'll be able to bring the homicide detectives up here. We need to get you down to Scottsdale. You need to tell the police what happened."

"But what about Deputy McGill?" Valerie asked. "He'll still run interference for the Mercers."

"Once the detectives in Scottsdale get arrest warrants, I don't think the local sheriff will have a lot of say over it," Lance said. "The men who killed my father must be brought to justice. Otherwise, this will continue to hang over our heads for the rest of our lives."

Valerie thought about what Lance had said and then seemed to come to a decision. "It's true. My silence will ultimately do more harm than good, not only for me but for you and Cici as well."

"Are you willing to try to make things right?" Lance asked.

His mother nodded. "If you can figure out a way for me to

get to Scottsdale before anyone here finds out I'm gone, I'll do it. But we can't mess this up. Once Dalton and Morgan discover I'm missing, they'll know what I'm doing. If they can find out where we are before they're arrested, they'll come after us."

"I'll come up with a plan," Lance said. "What's your phone number? I'll text you later this afternoon, and we can figure out what to do."

"Okay," she said as she gave him her number, which Lance typed into his phone. "But remember, it's not only you and me who are at risk. Your sister has no idea of the danger she could be in if I make another mistake. So far, I've kept her out of this, but with you here, it could pull her into the middle of it."

Lance stopped as his mother's words started to sink in. "Sister? Cici's my sister?"

"Well, half-sister. But she can never know what happened back then. Her entire world is up here. Promise me you won't do anything to upset her."

Gwen came back into the room and saw Valerie talking with Lance. Fortunately, Lance's mom had stopped crying, and her eyes hadn't gotten too red.

"Hi, Mrs. Mercer," she said with a wave. "It's good to see you again. Cici has really outdone herself this year. We're hoping we can sell several of her works."

"Hello, Gwen," Valerie said a little stiffly as she turned to leave. "That's wonderful. I appreciate how much work you and Evelyn have put into selling Cici's paintings."

Valerie took off as Cici came back in. "I see you both met my mom," she said, looking at Lance. "Are you alright? You look a little upset."

"Um, I got a text from my office," Lance said. "A

problem's come up, and I'm afraid we'll need to leave right away."

Gwen looked at Lance, and her face fell. "Oh no. Does that mean you need to head back to Scottsdale?"

"I'm afraid so," Lance said.

"Oh, that's a shame," Cici said, also disappointed. "I hope you both can come up to Sycamore Springs again sometime soon. I had a great time at dinner last night. We'll need to plan on doing that again."

"Absolutely," Lance said, looking at his sister. "I'll be up again as soon as I can arrange it. Maybe you could head down to Scottsdale sometime soon? I'd love to show you around."

As Gwen drove us back to Sycamore Springs, Lance remained silent. I could tell that meeting his mom, learning the truth about his dad's murder, and realizing Cici was his half-sister had a profound effect on him.

Gwen attempted to start a conversation with Lance a couple of times, but he was so distracted that his brief responses seemed almost rude. I noticed Gwen's confusion as she glanced back at me, searching for an explanation. All I could do was smile and mouth, "It's okay."

From the backseat, I found that I had a good cell signal, so I called Hank about my Miata. He confirmed that my car would be ready by three o'clock. I thanked him and said we'd be there.

When we made it back to the Starlite Motel, Deputy McGill's cruiser was parked outside the office. Lance and I exchanged glances, hoping the deputy wasn't there for us.

Gwen pulled in next to the office and stopped the car. "Well, if you're heading back to Scottsdale today, I guess this is it," she said to Lance. "It's been great meeting you. Maybe we can get together sometime when I'm back in Tempe?"

"Yes, I'd like that," Lance said, coming out of his funk. "Sorry, I know I've been distracted. I suddenly have a lot on my plate, and I'll need to focus on that, at least for the next few days. But let's keep talking and texting. Hopefully, I can make it back up here again before the summer ends."

I could tell that Gwen had hoped to hear something more positive, but she gave him a small smile and nodded. "It's okay," she said. "I understand. Sure, let's keep texting. You know where I'll be, at least until the start of the fall semester back home."

We both climbed out and gave Gwen a final wave as she drove away. Through the open office doorway, we could see that Sally was behind the desk, talking with the deputy. From the way she was batting her eyes, giggling, and twirling her hair, it was pretty obvious that she had feelings for the man.

Not wanting to look suspicious, we waved at Sally and the deputy as we walked by the office.

"Afternoon, folks," Deputy McGill said as he touched the brim of his cowboy hat. He then stared at Lance for four or five seconds, perhaps sensing his distress over the events of the morning. "I hope you found something you liked up at Longview."

"Actually, I did," Lance said with a tight smile as we stepped into the office. "Cici was finishing up a landscape of Capitol Butte, and I let her know I'd buy it when she was done with it."

"I'm glad to hear that," the deputy said. "A lot of us here in Sycamore Springs think that Cici Mercer has the makings of a real artist."

In a way, I was grateful that the deputy was there. With him distracting Sally, I didn't need to have another discussion with her about the night's sleeping arrangements.

"How are you doing?" I asked Lance as we walked toward the end of the cottages. "We've taken in a lot today. I'm not sure about you, but I'm still trying to make sense of everything."

"I'm completely overwhelmed," he admitted. "Not only did I find out that my mom is still alive, but I also discovered that I have a half-sister. Then, I learned that my mom is basically under house arrest because she discovered that her husband murdered my father. This is the same husband she was married to the entire time while she was living with my dad and me."

"Talking with your mom has brought up a lot of issues. How would you like to handle them?"

"We'll need to come up with a game plan before I text my mom back. But first, I'll need to calm down and collect my thoughts. Give me an hour or so, and I'll meet you in your room.

I went into my room and considered collapsing on the bed. A nap sounded like a good idea, but before I could lay on the bed, I got a text from Sophie.

Hey, I got the report back for the people living at Longview. One was Jeannie Mercer, age twenty-five, and one was a woman named Clarice, age twenty-three. That name is pretty close to Cici, so she might be the same person. There's also a woman listed as Valerie Mercer, age fifty-eight. I don't have a lot of information on her yet, but she could be our client's mom. I thought you'd want to know right away.

I went outside to a bench next to my door and called Sophie back. "Thanks for the text. We met Valerie Mercer while we were there today, and she is Lance's mom."

"So, does that mean you're done with the assignment? Are you coming home?"

"Not yet. It turns out that Morgan and Dalton Mercer are the ones who murdered Lance's dad last summer. Valerie knows all about it, and they're keeping her a prisoner at the ranch so she won't talk to the police. Lance wants to get her out of there so she can talk to the detectives in Scottsdale."

"Jeez," she said, laughing. "How do you always end up in the middle of these things? Well, let me know how I can help."

Chapter Seventeen

After disconnecting with Sophie, I texted Max, asking if he was busy.

He called back almost immediately. From the background sounds of steel drums, squealing kids, and water splashing, he was outside by one of the resort's pools.

"Hello, beautiful," he said as I answered. "How's your investigation going?"

"We've definitely had some movement. We found the client's mother today."

"That's great," he said. "So why do you sound so bummed about it?"

"It turns out that Lance's mom is Valerie Mercer, and she's married to Morgan Mercer. They got married right after she graduated from college. That was nearly forty years ago."

"Really?" Max asked with a chuckle. "So, the entire time she was living in Scottsdale with another man and having a kid with him, she was already married to one of the Mercers? That's one of those things you normally wouldn't believe if you heard it."

"That's not the half of it. Lance's dad, Bill Tillman, found Valerie last year, and they had a romantic tryst at a place in Sedona. Morgan and his brother Dalton found out about it and went down to Scottsdale to threaten Bill. During the confrontation, they apparently shot and killed him."

"Who else knows that Morgan and Dalton committed the murder?" Max asked, now sounding concerned.

"So far, only Valerie and now Lance. But last summer, when she hinted that she might go to the police, they put her under house arrest at the main home, Longview. Now, she can't leave the ranch without an escort by one of the Mercer brothers."

"I can see how that puts both your client and his mother in a difficult position."

"We're trying to find a way to bring Lance's mom down to Scottsdale. With her as a witness and the circumstantial evidence the detectives already have, it should be straightforward to secure an arrest for both brothers."

Max let out a soft chuckle, and I could tell he was shaking his head. "How do you always end up in the middle of these situations?"

"Hey," I blurted out. "That's what Sophie said. But I *hate* finding myself in the middle. It just sometimes happens."

"Sometimes?"

"Shut up," I said. "It's seriously not my fault this time. I get assigned to these things at work."

"Well, after discussing the Mercers with Tony, I suggest you tread carefully. They're an old-school family, and they aren't the kind of people you should get too entangled with."

"Trust me. My goal is to never talk with any of the Mercer men for as long as I live. I've already met Porter, and that was more than enough."

"When you come back to Scottsdale, we can discuss the best ways to extract a hostage from a hostile environment. I couldn't go up there personally without it causing a scene, but perhaps we could find somebody trained to go with you."

"Unfortunately, I think we'll need to get her out sooner rather than later. There seems to be something off about the situation at the ranch. I'm starting to get a bad feeling about Valerie if we let this drag on."

"When do you plan on getting her?"

"Um, I'm not sure, but it will likely be soon, within a few days at most. We're currently figuring out the best way to get up there without being spotted."

The phone went silent for a moment, and I could tell that Max was having an inner debate. He was probably asking himself if it was worth it to have someone like me as a girlfriend.

"Well, use your best judgment," he said. "Let me know if you need any help. You know I'll support you all the way."

"Got any advice for me? My goal is to do a quick in and out."

"I agree with your strategy. For something like this, you're going to need to rely more on stealth than on strength. Use darkness to hide your movements, and be sure you approach any building or structure from an unexpected direction. My suggestion would be to plan it so that nobody knows you have your client's mom until you're halfway back to Scottsdale. Let me know if you need a place to hide her until things are sorted out. I couldn't keep her at the resorts without looking like I'm interfering, but I'm sure we can find her a safe place."

"That sounds reasonable. I'll let you know if it comes to that. Anything else?"

"Try not to get into a situation. But if you need me, call me. I'll come right up."

"Hey, you know me. I should be okay doing this myself,

and I don't want you to get into trouble with anyone. I'll do my best not to get in too deep."

"I do know you," Max chuckled. "That's what I'm worried about."

While I chatted with my boyfriend, I watched as Deputy McGill climbed into his cruiser and took off. A few minutes later, Sally appeared and began strolling down the row of cottages. She carried a large watering can and methodically paused at the flower boxes outside each of the rooms.

Now that the desk didn't hide her, I could see she wore a yellow paisley skirt and leather strappy sandals. They nicely complemented her sixties flower-child hippie personality.

Sally eventually stopped and watered the colorful display of flowers in the box next to my bench. "Hello, Miss Black," she said in her cheerful voice. "Sorry, I couldn't talk earlier."

"It's no problem, and call me Laura. You have such a beautiful place here. How long have you run it?"

"I started working here as a housekeeper when I was in high school and found that I liked the motel business. My dad was a semi-famous working musician back in the day, and he passed away about twenty years ago. Fortunately, he left both my brother and me with a nice chunk of change. My brother started a business in Flagstaff, and I used mine to buy this place. I love the feeling of running a motel in a quiet mountain town."

"I couldn't help but notice who you were chatting with a few minutes ago. Am I wrong, or are you a little sweet on Deputy McGill?"

Sally breathed out a sigh and rolled her eyes. "Well, I'm trying. I even convinced him to go out a couple of times about a month ago."

"That's a good sign. How'd it go?"

"It was a disaster," she moaned. "I thought everything was going great. I even found out that Dan's a great kisser. But that's all he'd do with me."

"Well, maybe he thought that's all you wanted and was being a gentleman about it?"

"I don't think so," she said, her frustration evident. "I've seen the look he gets in his eyes when we're together. I'm pretty sure he wants me as more than a friend."

"Men are pretty stupid when it comes to relationships. Sometimes you have to be direct. Have you come out and told him how you feel?"

"Jeez, are you kidding?" she asked with a snort of laughter. "I've done everything short of stripping naked and offering him my body on the desk in the office. But he won't take it further, no matter how obvious I am. What do you think, Laura? Is there something wrong with me?"

"There's nothing wrong with you. Like I said, some men are idiots when it comes to dating. Tell me about the deputy. Was he ever married, or do you know if he sees other women?"

"He was married years ago and has a son who's in high school. He's a good kid and one of the better athletes in this part of the state. Everyone likes him. As far as other women, I don't think so. No one's ever seen him out with anyone other than the people he works with from the county."

"What happened with the wife?" I asked.

"Well, she was never the most attractive woman, and having her son only added another twenty pounds to her fat ass," Sally said with some snark. "But she went on a diet and exercise spree about ten years ago. She slimmed down and built up some muscle. She started to pay attention to her hair, and I think she even had her boobs done."

"What happened then?"

"She was working here as a real estate agent and started dating an older guy from Los Angeles. He'd been in the area a few times to buy a block of condos in Sedona. She took off with him in the middle of the day and only left a *Dear John* letter for her husband to find when he came home. I heard she had someone serve the divorce papers about a week later."

"That's rough," I said, thinking back to the similar situation with Lance and his dad. "But I wouldn't give up on the deputy just yet. I'm sure you'll get his attention sometime soon."

"I hope so," she said with a sigh. "Is everything okay with the rooms?"

"So far, everything's perfect."

"Just so you know," Sally said softly as she looked both ways. "Nobody's complained about the noise or anything like that. You're both still doing alright."

"We didn't sleep together," I said, perhaps a little louder than I meant to.

Sally held up a hand to stop me. "Laura, it's okay. Nobody knows," she said as she shook her head and leaned closer to me. "Trust me, nobody here knows a thing."

Lance appeared at the door to his room, holding his laptop. He seemed to be in a better mood and grinned slightly as he heard the motel manager talking with me.

"Hello, Sally," he said as he walked to my bench. "You have a great place here. Thanks for putting us at the end of the row. It was really quiet last night. The only sound at all was the water going over the rocks in Oak Creek. I'm glad we didn't disturb anyone."

"No problem," she said with a knowing grin as she glanced between us. Then she heard something and stopped talking. I was about to ask her what was going on when she again held up her hand to stop us.

"Suush," she said quietly, a broad grin on her face. "Do you hear that?"

"Hear what?" Lance asked.

"The wind," she said, a huge grin on her face. "It's been blowing from the south all day and is starting to pick up. Can't you hear it blowing through the trees?"

Lance and I stopped, and we could hear the gentle, *whooshing* sound of the spring breeze through the trees. As I concentrated, I could smell the faint aromas of juniper and sage carried by the wind.

"I can hear it," I said, glad that Sally had pointed it out. "I can also smell it."

"It's the music of the forest," she laughed. "It's one of the reasons I love Sycamore Springs so much. The south wind is carrying the scents of the desert from down the Rim and Mexico. I'd say we're going to be due for some rain tomorrow."

Sally took off, and we stepped into my room and closed the door. "Are you doing okay?" I asked.

"I think so," he said. "I've been going over a dozen different scenarios in my head. Unfortunately, each one will involve a great deal of risk. About the only thing I know for certain is that once we set things in motion, we'll need to go all the way. I don't think we'll be able to stop halfway through if it starts looking bad."

"You're right," I agreed. "We'll need to make sure we don't screw it up."

Lance nodded, then texted his mother to check if she was doing okay. His mom must have been waiting for the message because she replied within about three minutes.

Son, you need to leave Sycamore Springs right away. Dalton and Morgan know who you are and that you were at the house today. Although Deputy McGill doesn't know about their involvement in the murder, I think they somehow learned you were here from him. They'll assume you're here to investigate the murder of your dad. If they find you, they'll likely try to kill you as well. Please don't underestimate them. Cici should be safe since they know she's not part of this. Besides, between the two grandkids, she's Porter's favorite. He'd go nuts if anything happened to his youngest granddaughter.

"Shit," Lance spat out after he read the message and turned the phone so I could read it as well. "We've got to get her out of there and back to Scottsdale. I thought we could wait a few days before we made an attempt, but if they decide that she knows too much, she could be in real danger."

"Yeah," I agreed. "It'll need to be as soon as we can arrange it. Once she tells the detectives what she knows about the murder, Dalton and Morgan will be arrested, and everyone should be safe."

"Now, all we need to do is figure out how we're going to get her out. Longview's set up like a fortress. It's so open around the house that they'll spot us coming from half a mile away. If we want to have any chance of getting her out of there in one piece, it'll have to be tonight. The hard part will be getting across Oak Creek."

"Well, that's one of the hard parts," I said with a small chuckle. "You're right that we won't be able to use the bridge. But, there must be another way across the river."

Lance opened his laptop, pulled up a topographical map of the area, and we both leaned in to stare at it. Unfortunately, we both quickly came to the same conclusion.

"The only direct way to Longview is over the Laughing

Armadillo bridge," I said. "And we've seen there's no easy way to climb over the gates. There were lights and cameras all over it, likely motion detectors as well."

"From the map, it appears Gwen was right," Lance said as he pointed to the screen. "There are several other bridges over Oak Creek, but the closest ones are either three miles to the south or four miles to the north. Even if we cross over at one of those points, there's still no direct way to get to the house. No matter which way we approach Longview, we'd need to cross over at least one steep canyon."

"We might be able to do that during the day," I said. "But at night, with your mom? I can see that ending badly."

Lance let out a sigh. "After looking at the map, I think you're right. We'll need to figure out a direct way in, then a direct way out."

"Alright," I said. "One step at a time. I need to get my car from Hank's garage. It'll be interesting trying to cram all three of us in it on the drive back, but I see that as the easiest of our problems to deal with."

I pulled up Hank's Auto Repair Service on my phone, and the navigator said it was only a twenty-minute walk. We took off, and the phone routed us down several smaller side streets, eventually ending back on the main road, where Hank's garage was visible in the distance.

When we arrived, our mechanic was under the hood of a black Dodge Durango. As before, classic rock was pounding out of the boombox. This time, it was the Steve Miller Band singing *Take the Money and Run*.

Hank straightened up when we called out to him and pulled a red rag from his back pocket to wipe his hands. He then pointed to my car, which was sitting off to the side in the gravel parking lot. The front tire looked perfect.

"Fortunately, your car's almost new, so I only needed to replace the one tire," Hank said in his gruff voice. "I was able to get an original equipment tire from Mazda, so you won't even notice it's been swapped out. Plus, only needing to replace the one saved you a few dollars."

He went to a computer that was sitting on a counter and called up my invoice. I was pleasantly surprised when it was about half of what I'd expected. I've never felt that my mechanic in Scottsdale, Butch Carbone, has ever tried to cheat me, but there seemed to be advantages in overhead costs when working out of your home.

After thanking Hank for his work, we took off. I'd only been without my car for a day, but it felt great to be back behind the wheel.

Chapter Eighteen

"Okay, let's think this through," I said as we drove back to the motel. We need to find a way across the river and then to Longview. With Morgan and Dalton possibly out looking for us, we'll need to lay low until it gets dark."

"We can't stay in our rooms," Lance said. "It's the one place we're known to be. Let's go to the town square. There are shops and restaurants where we can hang out until it's time to head up to the ranch."

"We should be safe enough in public," I agreed. "But first, let's go back to the Starlite, pack up, and toss everything in the trunk. After we get your mom, we may not be able to go back to the rooms before we skip town."

"Good idea," he said. "I'll turn on my bedside light and set the TV to a network with a lot of talking, like the news. You do the same in your room. It might fool someone into thinking that we're still there. Then maybe they won't look for us as we're driving to Scottsdale."

We got to the Starlite, and I did a casual drive-by of the motel parking lot. I'd tried to memorize all of the cars before we left, and nothing stood out as being new.

"I don't see any vehicles here that were parked in front of Longview," Lance said. "I think we're good."

We went to our rooms and quickly packed. I closed the curtains, turned on a couple of lights, and set the TV to the local weather channel. To someone making a cursory observation from the parking lot, it would appear that the rooms were occupied.

From there, we next drove towards the town square. Not wanting to park anywhere too open, I swung around to the alley behind the businesses and found a space that was tucked between two enormous trees.

"Alright," I said. "If we're going to do this tonight, you should let your mom know what's happening. She needs to get herself ready."

"Okay, I'll let her know," Lance said as he pulled out his phone and sent a text.

Mom, hang tight. We're making plans to get you out later tonight. I'll let you know the details soon.

While Lance texted his mom, I sent a quick note to Max to let him know that we'd likely make the rescue attempt tonight. He didn't immediately text me back to tell me it was a terrible idea, so I took that as a good sign.

Next, Lance and I needed a safe place to lay low until we figured out how to get Valerie away from the ranch. I looked around and spotted the back door to an ice cream shop.

It was open, and two colorful birthday balloons on strings were attached to the handle. I took that as another good sign.

"Let's head over there," I said. "I don't know about you, but with everything going on, I could really go for a hot fudge sundae."

We walked to the shop and placed our orders. Along with my sundae, Lance chose a banana split. We then found a quiet table that was more or less out of sight from the street.

"Okay," I said. "Let's go through this. Assuming we can

get your mom out, what then?"

"We should probably drive straight to Scottsdale. If they discover she's gone, the motel would be the first place they'd look. I don't know if Sedona would be far enough away to spend the night."

"I was thinking the same thing," I said. "Taking the two-lane road south would get us to the interstate the fastest. But if Deputy McGill wanted to set up a roadblock, that's where he would do it. Instead, let's go north to either Cottonwood or Sedona and then loop back around. It'll add about half an hour to our drive, but we probably wouldn't be stopped."

"That makes sense," Lance agreed.

"The next part is how to get across the river," I said.

"Sally might have some ideas, but given how close she seems to be with Deputy McGill, I'd rather not risk it."

"What about Gwen?" I asked. "She grew up here and probably knows the area as well as anyone."

"That's not a bad idea," Lance said as he pulled out his phone. From the grin on his face, I could tell he was enjoying the idea of seeing Gwen again.

He texted to let her know that before we took off, we'd head back to the café for dinner and asked if she wanted to join us. Gwen texted back that she could be there by six-thirty. She also said that she'd never turn down the Cowgirl's cherry pie.

We hung out in the back corner of the ice cream parlor until a quarter after six. Keeping an eye out for anything suspicious, we made our way down the square to the Crazy Cowgirl and got a booth in the back corner. A few minutes later, Gwen came in and slid next to Lance.

"Were you able to get your car?" she asked as she "accidentally" pressed her leg and arm against my client.

"Yup," I said. "Hank did a great job. I'm glad we went to him."

"How's your problem at work?" she asked, turning to Lance.

"I've been on the phone most of the afternoon, and I think it's stable. But I'll still need to head back to Scottsdale later tonight."

"Oh, okay," she said, sounding disappointed. "But we still need to get together soon."

"As soon as we can arrange it," Lance agreed. He was also pressing his arm and leg against Gwen.

We ordered our dinners and chatted for about half an hour. Gwen and Lance still seemed to be taken with each other, and I was glad.

As the server cleared our salad plates, I thought it would be a good time to ask Gwen about the river.

"Maybe you can help me with something," I said as casually as I could. "I'm trying to figure out how to get across Oak Creek without drowning."

"There are a lot of bridges," she said, looking back and forth between the two of us. "Can't you use one of those to drive across?"

"Unfortunately, we were hoping to cross over a little north of town," Lance said. "The only bridge along that part of the river is private. Plus, on the far bank, there's a series of cliffs or at least high, steep riverbanks."

"You want to cross over by the Laughing Armadillo bridge?" she asked, sounding a little confused.

"We were hoping to," I said. "Maybe somewhere slightly upriver from there."

"Well," Gwen said, sounding thoughtful. "If you really

need to get across that part of Oak Creek, there's the old construction cable car."

"What's that?" Lance asked.

"It's a cable system they strung across the river, back when they first built the bridge for the ranch in the nineteen forties. It's what they used to shuttle people and supplies across the river before the bridge was finished."

"It's only a cable?" I asked.

"There's a big metal cargo basket hanging from the cable, along with a separate line so you can pull yourself back and forth over Oak Creek. We'd use it to jump off into the river on hot summer days when I was in high school. I think the local kids still use it."

"Is it safe?" I asked.

"Well, it's never exactly been considered safe," she said with a laugh. "But it's been there for about eighty years and hasn't broken yet, at least as far as I know."

I leaned closer to Gwen. "How exactly do you get there?"

Gwen spent several minutes explaining which road to take, where to park, how to find the construction cable car, and what general things to watch out for. Then, she described in vivid detail the fun of jumping into the river with her high school friends.

When she was done, Lance looked at me. I nodded my head and shrugged. It looked like we now had a plausible way to cross Oak Creek.

Our entrees came out, and while we were chatting, Lance texted his mom. This time, he included me so I could see what he wrote.

Mom, meet us on the west porch outside of Cici's studio at midnight. We have a plan for crossing the river and returning to Scottsdale. Only bring the bare minimum you'll need, and be prepared for a long hike.

The rest of dinner was pleasant, and we purposefully took our time. I felt relatively safe in the café, and we were stuck indoors until nightfall in either case.

After the sun went down, we'd have some more freedom to move through the town without being seen. I tried my best not to think of what we'd be doing during the night, and it seemed to help.

Gwen stayed with us the entire time and even had cherry pie and coffee for dessert. I could tell that she wanted to ask Lance why he seemed determined to sneak onto the Laughing Armadillo Ranch and why he had to rush back to Scottsdale, but she never did.

Instead, she spent most of the time looking at Lance with what I could only describe as bedroom eyes. For his part, my client also seemed to be completely taken with her. The more they talked, the more tentative plans they made.

Lance promised to return in a few weeks so she could take him shopping in Sedona. Gwen vowed to head down to Scottsdale before the summer was over so they could go to a restaurant they both really enjoyed.

I had to chuckle when I heard they were talking about Frankie Z's. This was the romantic Italian restaurant where I had spent many nights hanging out with my old boyfriend, Jackson Reno.

Gwen headed out a little before nine, and Lance walked her out to her car. I wasn't all that surprised when they gave each other a long hug, followed by a tentative kiss.

It was honestly rather sweet to see. When Lance returned to the table, his face showed several emotions at once, mainly happiness and a little bit of nervousness.

"Alright," I teased. "Stop thinking about Gwen. Let's figure out what we're doing tonight."

Using Gwen's directions, we drove along the two-lane road that followed the river north from Sycamore Springs. About a half mile past the brightly lit Laughing Armadillo bridge, we turned onto a dirt road that led down to a well-used parking area next to Oak Creek.

We got out and looked around. The clearing was large enough to hold ten or fifteen cars and seemed to be one of the local high school parking places. The ground was littered with old fast-food wrappers, cigarette butts, and crushed beer cans.

Even though the clearing was fairly secluded, I decided to back my car underneath some thick branches. If someone was actively searching for us, this wouldn't fool them for long, but it might prevent someone in a hurry from spotting my vehicle.

After locking my car, we walked down a wide path to Oak Creek. When we reached the water, we took a right and followed the trail downstream.

Not expecting to be going on a night hike along a muddy riverbank, I hadn't thought to bring anything sturdier than my daily cross-trainers. I mentally checked off *hiking boots* as one more thing I'd need to keep in my trunk for these types of situations.

I thought about using the small flashlight I always keep in my bag, but I was worried that somebody might notice random lights around the bridge. I knew for sure that I couldn't use it after we got to the other side of the river.

Fortunately, the moon was about three-quarters full, and there were only a few fluffy clouds floating across the starry sky. This gave us enough light to more or less see where we were stepping and let us avoid the worst of the puddles.

After a five-minute walk along the riverbank, making several detours to avoid patches of mud, reeds, and some loudly croaking frogs, we found the construction cable car exactly where Gwen said it would be. The main cable was strung tightly across the river, supported by two ancient towers made of open-steel beams.

The shorter tower on the far side of Oak Creek rested atop a line of high riverbanks, while the structure on our side had to be at least forty feet tall. Gwen had said that the condition of the cable car was poor. Unfortunately, as we walked closer, the eighty-year-old construction didn't look nearly as sturdy or as well-maintained as even her unfavorable description had implied.

The basket was currently on our side of the river, but the only way to reach it was to climb up to a platform near the top of the tower. As we got closer, we found a metal gate at the entrance to the first flight of stairs.

It had probably worked to keep kids off the platform at one time, but that was likely twenty or thirty years ago. Since then, it appeared that many people had used crowbars or something similar to repeatedly force it open. Now, the rusted and badly bent gate no longer had any way of staying shut.

Yellow and black police *Keep Out* tape had been strung across the opening, seemingly during the previous summer. Now, all that remained were some remnants tied to the support posts, with only a few broken strands of tape fluttering in the night's breeze.

Hoping nothing would collapse, we passed through the gate and cautiously climbed three flights of stairs, ending up at a pitted steel platform. Looking around, the surface was covered in graffiti and crushed beer cans.

A rusty metal basket, maybe eight by ten feet, hung from the thick overhead cable. The light spring breeze caused metallic moaning and popping sounds as the basket gently swayed back and forth on the line.

On a support frame, slightly below the cable, was an official-looking metal sign declaring that the basket had a *maximum working load of 1500 pounds*. The 1500 had a nicely painted line through it, and *750* was neatly stenciled over it in black letters.

Unfortunately, even this modified figure had been scratched out seemingly decades ago. *Good Luck!* was now listed as the system's weight limit.

"Oh, jeez," I said as I saw what we were about to do. "Until we unload on top of the riverbank on the other side, we'll be twenty-five or thirty feet above the river. If the cable breaks or the basket falls off, there's nothing on the other side to land on but a pile of rocks."

"Well, we've talked about it," Lance said as he peered over the edge of the platform to the river below. "Plan B is to wade across Oak Creek. It looks pretty deep along this stretch, but it can't be more than about seventy or eighty feet across."

"No, even if we swam across the river, we'd still need to deal with the steep banks on the other side," I said, knowing that we'd discussed this point several times already. "That might not be so bad if we could see what we were doing, but in the dark, I don't think so."

"Alright," he said as he undid a thin safety chain that was hanging loosely across an opening on the side of the basket. He then bowed and swept his arm towards the cable car. "Ladies first," he said with a chuckle.

"Oh, thanks," I said with as much sarcastic attitude as I could muster. "I'll be sure to let you know if it's safe enough for you."

Even in the pale light of the moon, I could see that Lance had a wide grin on his face. I climbed into the basket through the opening, and Lance hopped in beside me.

With our combined weight, the cable above our heads groaned loudly and creaked ominously. We briefly paused as we waited for something to break.

Lance grabbed a thin metal tow cable that went through a steel eye on the basket. With a hard tug on this line, he began to pull us across the river.

I had visions of both of us tumbling to the ground, the broken basket landing on top of our crushed bodies. Fortunately, luck seemed to be with us, at least for the moment, and everything held together.

Looking at the safety chain as it dangled in the opening on the side of the basket made me think back to when I was a teenager. Traveling pop-up carnivals would sometimes come through Scottsdale, and I'd let myself get talked into going on the scariest rides at the fair. Each of these rides would have a similar chain to keep you in the car, and I was always nervous that it wouldn't be properly fastened.

Knowing that it wouldn't help us in the least if the main cable snapped, I made sure to securely refasten the safety chain across the opening in the basket's side.

I can't help it. I follow the safety rules.

Chapter Nineteen

From the moment we started to move, there was a loud screeching sound of metal rubbing against metal. Looking up, the noise came from four rusty wheels that attached the basket to the main cable. Two of them didn't seem to be turning very well, and we were more or less dragging them down the line.

It honestly didn't sound like the cable car system would last much longer. Even worse, anyone within two or three hundred yards could hear that someone was coming across.

"So much for being stealthy," I said.

I stood behind Lance, grabbed onto the thin tow cable, and helped to pull us across. With the two of us tugging, we made good progress.

Unfortunately, after the ninth or tenth time pulling on the line, my hands started to get sore from the rough metal. I mentally added *work gloves* to my ever-expanding list of things I'd need to start keeping in my trunk.

"If the basket falls off the cable, the river here doesn't look so bad," Lance said with forced bravado when we were about halfway across. "I'm sure we could swim back to shore."

Far from comforting me, Lance's words only chilled me further. He was also thinking that something horrible was about to happen.

The trip across the river only took four or five minutes, but between the noise of the basket, being so high above the river, and the fact that I was waiting for the cable to break at any second, it was rather nerve-racking.

The worst part was right before we got to the far tower. The riverbank on that side of Oak Creek was covered with piles of large, pointed rocks. Looking down, I again had visions of us screaming as we flew through the air and crashed on the rocks below with a wet *splat!*

I sometimes hate being an overthinker.

When we arrived at the far metal tower, I quickly unfastened the safety chain and climbed out. Fortunately, the platform on this side wasn't so high up, and there were only a few wobbly metal stairs to climb down before we were once again on solid ground.

"See," Lance said with a nervous chuckle. "That was a piece of cake."

"Don't celebrate yet," I said. "I somehow get the feeling that was the easy part."

Our first step to getting to Longview was to orient ourselves. We were about four hundred yards from the paved road that wound its way up the hill from the bridge over the river.

"Let's head to the road," I said. "Then we can figure out the best way to get to the house."

We quickly found a well-worn trail from the tower to the main road. The path was partially covered with broken asphalt and must have been heavily used when it was first built.

Walking with care, we made it to the main road in about ten minutes. Even with the help of the moonlight, we both needed to closely watch where we stepped.

"It's eighteen minutes before eleven," Lance said,

glancing at his watch. "Mom should be waiting for us on the back porch at midnight. Longview is about two and a half miles from here, so we'll need to hurry."

Although we'd discussed it at length during the afternoon, we hadn't come to a conclusion on the best way to approach the house. Now that we were here, it looked like the quickest and safest way to get to Longview would be to simply walk up the paved street.

"We'll need to take the road," I said. "I know that sounds a little crazy, but the land around the house is fairly open. We should be able to spot the lights of anyone driving towards us and still have time to hide before they see us. Fortunately, we're both wearing dark colors, so that should help keep us from being seen by anyone at the house."

"I think you're right," Lance replied. "There isn't enough moonlight for us to try to walk across the range. Besides, if we came across any sort of gully, we'd need to backtrack, and that would slow us down even further."

"Okay," I said. "Let's go."

We took off as the road made its way up the sloping east bank of the valley. Lance was in the lead, and we made good time.

After about half a mile, we came around a corner and stopped. Longview had become visible near the top of the ridge.

The house was brightly lit, but the surrounding smaller buildings were dark. With the moon illuminating the nearby mountains, the lights gave the mansion on the hill an almost temple-like feeling.

Knowing that Valerie would be waiting for us at midnight, I took the lead and kept a fast pace as the road made wide loops up the gentle slope to the main compound. When it was apparent that there weren't too many rocks or other obstructions, we were sometimes able to head straight up the hill rather than go with the longer switchbacks, but for the most part, we stayed on the road.

Lance kept up with me, but I could tell that the fast hike was gradually wearing him down. His breath came in gulps, and he had stopped his habit of nervously talking and telling jokes.

I wish I could say I was doing fine, but I was also suffering from a lack of regular exercise. My heart rate had sped up, and I had also started to gulp at the thin mountain air. Although I was struggling with the walk up the hill and starting to get nervous about what we were going to do when we got there, my main thoughts were on my feet.

My cross-trainers were versatile for day-to-day activities, but night hiking didn't seem to be one of their strong points. I was developing several warm spots that I worried would gradually turn into blisters by the time we reached the house. Not for the first time, I thought about the sturdy hiking boots sitting on the floor in the corner of my closet.

When we were maybe half a mile from Longview, we saw the lights of a vehicle starting up in front of the house. Lance and I hurried off the road and found a small ditch about twenty yards away to lie down and disappear in.

I desperately wanted to use the flashlight in my bag to see what we were about to lie on top of. But I knew that if I turned on a light, it would be sure to attract the attention of the driver or anyone on the porch at Longview.

Please don't let there be a sticker bush in here.

From our hiding place, we watched as the lights of the vehicle came hurrying toward us. As it flashed by, I could see it was one of the ranch pick-up trucks we'd seen in front of Longview the previous morning.

As the truck continued down towards the bridge, we got to our feet and hurried back to the road. We quickly crossed the remaining distance to the outbuildings surrounding Longview and swung around so we could approach the house from the west.

"It's twelve minutes to midnight," I whispered after glancing at my watch. "Let's find somewhere to wait."

We went to a small brown building, a maintenance shed of some sort, about sixty yards from the back porch. We squatted behind it and waited.

As my heart rate slowed from the hike and my feet got a chance to relax, I took a few minutes to look around. The view from the top of the long, sloping hill was breathtaking.

The stars of the Milky Way were splashed across the sky in the bright, wide band that you can only see in the mountains or the deep desert. Further out in the valley, the lights of Sycamore Springs twinkled in the distance, and the dark line of Oak Creek was visible in the moonlight.

"Didn't Sally say that we'd have rain tomorrow?" Lance asked in a whisper. "Where are the clouds?"

"Don't complain," I whispered back. "With the change in elevation, it already seems cold up here. I'd rather have a clear sky than get soaked."

Right at midnight, there was a brief flash of light as the door to Cici's studio opened and then closed. We then saw the faint outlines of a person standing in the shadows on the back of the porch.

"She's right on time," I whispered as we both stood and hurried towards the house.

We crossed the final distance and stopped a few paces from the porch. "Mom?" Lance asked in a low voice. "Hurry. We need to go."

When the shadowy figure didn't move, I called out in a slightly louder whisper, "Valerie, it's us. Come on. We need to leave before they find out what we're up to."

"Don't move," a deep male voice called out to us as Morgan Mercer stepped forward so we could see his face in the moonlight. "I have a twelve-gauge shotgun loaded with double-aught buckshot pointed at you. If either of you tries to run, I'll blow both of your heads off."

The lights on the porch flipped on, revealing that Morgan Mercer was indeed brandishing a double-barrel shotgun. It was aimed directly at our faces.

Shit.

The door opened again, and Dalton stepped out, followed by Porter. Dalton was holding a large caliber chrome revolver, while Porter was unarmed.

"You two spies, come into the house," Porter growled as he pointed at us.

I glanced at Lance, but there was nothing we could do. Dalton led the way into Cici's workshop, which was now brightly lit, and we followed.

It was odd to be back in the studio, surrounded by the beautiful artwork. I wished I could stop and look around at the paintings one more time.

We were almost at the doorway to the hall when Porter turned to Morgan. "There's no need to keep pointing that shotgun at them. The damn thing could go off, and we'd have a mess to clean up."

Morgan looked at his father, and I could see the anger in his eyes. I knew he was sorta hoping the gun *would* accidentally fire, mess or not.

"Don't worry, Son," Porter continued in a slightly softer voice. "If they try to take off, they can't outrun a shotgun.

You'll have plenty of time to take them both out."

Dalton let us into the living room, where a bright fire was burning in the river rock fireplace. Valerie was huddled in one of the big leather chairs near the hearth.

Seeing her condition made me gasp. She had a large red mark and a cut under her left eye, while her lower lip was swollen and split. Her face had a vacant expression, and it looked like she'd been crying for some time.

Lance also sucked in his breath, and he started yelling at Morgan. "What the hell did you do to her?" he fumed.

With a roar of anger, Lance took a menacing step towards the younger Mercer brother. It was only when Morgan brought up the shotgun and pointed it at Lance's chest that he stopped.

Anger surged through me, and I desperately wanted to charge at him. If Morgan hadn't been holding the shotgun, I would have gone after him as well.

"I'm so sorry," Valerie said when she saw us, her tears starting again. "Morgan caught me packing a change of clothes in my bag. He made me tell him everything."

"Shut up, bitch," Morgan barked out at her. "I swear to god, if you don't want to taste the back of my hand again, you'll shut your damn mouth."

"I'll have no more of that," Porter growled at his son. "I don't care what your wife did to you. Mercers don't hit women. And keep your voice down. I don't want you to wake up the girls."

Morgan looked like he wanted to say something back to his father, but instead, he went to a wet bar against the far wall and slopped a double shot of a golden tequila into a glass.

He picked up the drink and tossed it back in one gulp. Then, still holding the shotgun, he went to a chair in the corner and glowered over the group.

"Search them," Porter said to Dalton.

The older Mercer brother lumbered over and efficiently went through Lance's pockets. Not finding anything other than his phone, he turned to me. I gave him my purse, and he quickly found the pistol.

After slipping it into his pocket, Dalton tossed my bag and Lance's phone onto a sideboard cabinet. He then searched me in a way that was more groping and fondling my boobs and ass than actually searching for weapons.

Gross.

Porter pulled a pack of Marlboro reds from his pocket and lit one up with a silver lighter. "Take a seat," he said coldly, looking at Lance and me. "We need to have a little talk."

Two small chairs were sitting slightly apart from the rest of the furniture, and Porter pointed to those. We obediently took our seats, and I noted that two living room lights had already been placed near us to keep us fully lit.

"I want to know what's going on, and I mean everything," Porter said. "Odd things have been going on in my house, and it seems like you two may be able to help me figure out what it is."

"You seriously aren't going to listen to them, are you?" Morgan barked out. "All they're going to do is spew lies. Let me get rid of them both."

Porter paused, and I could see he was having some sort of inner debate. "Morgan, Dalton," he quietly said. "I want the two of you to go outside to the porch. I'm going to have a talk with these people, and I don't want to be disturbed."

"No, Pa," Dalton bellowed. "They're dangerous. We can't leave you alone with them."

"Thank you for your concern," Porter said. "Why don't you give me the pistol you took out of this woman's purse?

I'm sure I'll be safe then."

"But, Pa," Dalton objected in a whiny voice. "You shouldn't be alone with them."

"If they try to escape down the hill," Porter continued, "feel free to shoot them as they run past you."

"Dad, you can't do that," Morgan bellowed as he stood up and waved the shotgun in our direction. "They're only here to stir up trouble. They'll say anything at this point to save their skins."

"Son," Porter said in a patient voice. "I think I can tell the difference between lies and the truth. Now, go outside and let me talk with these people."

Still muttering under his breath, Dalton handed my Glock over to his father. The Mercer patriarch took my tiny pistol and turned it over in his large hands several times as if it were a toy.

"Out with the both of you," Porter barked out at his sons, who were still lingering near the fireplace.

"What about Val?" Dalton asked.

"Leave her here," Porter said.

"Dad, you're making a serious mistake," Morgan growled as he stomped out of the living room, still holding the shotgun. Dalton only shook his head as he followed his younger brother.

There was a brief silence as we listened to a grandfather clock in the corner chime that it was twelve-thirty.

Chapter Twenty

"Alright," Porter said as he looked back and forth between Lance and me. "My boys are out of the room. It's only going to be Val, me, and you for a while."

Porter took a deep breath and then slowly let it out. "You're both in serious trouble. I don't take kindly to trespassers and kidnappers. I need to decide what'll happen to you, but first, I need to know some things. I won't lie to you, and I need you to tell me the truth in return. Are you both willing to do that as if your very lives depended on it?"

I glanced at Lance, and we both nodded.

"Very well," Porter continued, now somewhat more relaxed. "I've been getting a sense that there've been secrets going around the ranch since last summer. But as you saw, every time I try to dig into what these mysteries could be, I get shut down by my sons. Who would like to tell me their story first?"

The room went silent as we listened to the grandfather clock ticking off the time. After a few moments, Porter turned to his daughter-in-law. She'd been so quiet that I'd nearly forgotten she was still in the room with us.

"Val?" he asked. "I know this concerns you as well. Is there anything you'd like to say before we start?"

Valerie didn't say anything. She only shook her head and looked miserable as she seemed to shrink further down in her chair.

I suspected that Lance only knew part of the story. If we were going to get out of this in one piece, I knew it was going to be up to me. Exposing secrets to the head of the family would be dangerous and could easily backfire, but I didn't see another way out of it.

"Mr. Mercer, I'll start," I said.

"And who exactly are you?" Porter asked. "You told me your name is Laura Black, but how are you involved in the lives of my family?"

"I'm an investigator for a law firm in Scottsdale. Lance came to us a few days ago looking for information on the whereabouts of his estranged mother."

"And who is his mother?"

"We had her name as Valerie Bacchus, but after some investigation, it turns out that she's your daughter-in-law, Valerie Mercer."

"Val?" Porter asked, seemingly surprised. "Is this true? Is this man your son?"

Valerie still seemed to be distant after suffering the threats and abuse from her husband. All she could do was nod her head.

"I'd put you somewhere in your mid-thirties," Porter said, looking at Lance like he was sizing up a prized steer.

"I'm thirty-four," my client said. "And yes, after everything we've discovered this week, I believe that she is my mother."

Porter nodded. "The timeline seems about right for that," he said as he stared intently at Lance. "My daughter-in-law disappeared thirty-five years ago and was missing for almost a decade. But, unless you tell me differently, that has no relation to what's been going on up here in Longview over the past year."

"I think I can make a connection for you," I said. "But I first need to confirm two more things. Um, Valerie. Cici isn't Morgan's child, is she?"

Porter narrowed his eyes and gave me an angry look that reminded me of Tony DiCenzo. It was upsetting, to say the least. Valerie had told us that Cici was Porter's favorite granddaughter, so I knew I had to choose my words carefully.

Valerie also flashed me a furious glare for spilling her most personal secret, and then the air seemed to go out of her. "I learned that I was pregnant with Bill's baby a week before Morgan found me in Scottsdale," she said, hanging her head in shame.

"I knew I'd need to leave with Morgan, so I didn't tell anyone about the baby until I'd moved back to Longview. You should have seen Morgan's face when I told him I was pregnant. He spent a week strutting around like a stud bull. But how did you know that Cici is Bill's daughter?"

"You left Scottsdale on Saint Patrick's Day and had the baby the day before Thanksgiving," I said. "You told Morgan that Cici was a preemie, but at almost seven pounds, it was pretty obvious what had happened. I'm surprised he didn't pick up on it."

"I had the delivery room nurse fib to Morgan about the baby being premature," Valerie said. "He had no idea how much a baby was supposed to weigh. He was only happy that she was healthy, so we wouldn't get a lot of extra bills from the hospital. Other than that, he wasn't so much concerned about the details."

"But that wasn't the first time this exact thing had

happened to you," I asked. "Was it?"

"Wait a minute," Valerie said, a look of panic settling on her face as her eyes quickly flicked to Lance. "How could you possibly know something like that?"

"When you found out that you were pregnant with Bill's baby, only a few days before you went back home with Morgan, you wrote some interesting things in your diary. *It looks like it'll happen again,* and that *karma was a wheel, and your life keeps repeating.*"

Lance looked at me, not knowing where this was going, but Porter's eyes lit up with concern.

"I didn't understand what you meant when I first read that," I continued. "But this was something that had happened to you before, wasn't it? Thirty-five years ago, you were living here with Morgan. You were miserable and wanted to leave him, but then you found out you were pregnant with his child. You didn't want a baby to tie you to Morgan and the Mercers permanently, so you ran away to Scottsdale."

Valerie nodded. "I didn't want my baby to be anywhere near my husband or the Laughing Armadillo."

"You started working at the Daily Drip coffee shop and met Bill Tillman on your first day there," I said. "You started dating and told him you had gotten pregnant shortly after the first time you'd been intimate with him. He accepted your story and raised Lance as his own."

"Val, is this true?" Porter asked his daughter-in-law while pointing at Lance. I couldn't tell if he was more angry or confused. "You were pregnant with him before you ran away from Morgan and ended up in Scottsdale?"

Valerie's tears were the only confirmation I needed, but Lance and Porter weren't convinced.

"You're saying I'm *Morgan's* son?" Lance asked, looking

disgusted. "Mom, is this true?"

"Son," she said with a weak and shaky voice. "You have no idea what a monster Morgan is. I didn't want you to be raised by him. It was my good fortune to find Bill Tillman. He was a loving dad to you, and we had a good life together. For everyone's safety, I've had to pretend that you were Bill's son and Cici was Morgan's daughter."

This was a lot of new information, and everyone stopped talking while we took in the new situation. After listening to the gentle tick-tock sounds of the grandfather clock for several moments, Porter spoke.

"Again, Miss Black, this is all very interesting," he said with a dismissive wave of his hand. "And it will raise several concerns if it is indeed true. But all of this happened a long time ago. I need to find out what happened last year."

"What do you know about what occurred last summer?" I asked Porter, wondering what he'd already heard.

"I only know that things up here have shifted," Porter grumbled as he lit up another cigarette. "Everyone's been giving each other nasty looks and sideways glances. People talk in whispers, and they stop when I walk into the room. My daughter-in-law doesn't leave the ranch unless she's accompanied by one of my sons. But when I ask anyone in my family about what's happening, their lips stay tightly shut."

"I'll tell you what I know," I said. "But this next part won't be easy to hear. Two years ago, and again last summer, Bill Tillman was in Sycamore Springs."

"Why was he up here?" Porter asked.

"Bill had never given up on the idea of finding Valerie," I said. "Over the past several years, he'd been spending time traveling from gallery to gallery throughout Arizona, looking for paintings that matched her specific style and technique. I believe he thought he could find her simply by recognizing a piece of art as hers."

"Yes," Porter said with a nod, apparently knowing what I was going for. "Miss Costello's teachings are rather pronounced in the artwork of Valerie as well as Cici."

"Two years ago, Bill Tillman bought one of Cici's paintings from The Art Loft here in town. He recognized the style and thought she might have a connection with his fiancée. Last year, he bought two more paintings, and Cici invited him to Longview to see her new works. While here at the house, Bill ran into Valerie. They exchanged emails and later met in person for a weekend in Sedona."

Porter looked at Valerie while I was telling my story. Her only reaction was to stare at the fire and silently cry. "Go on," Porter said.

"Dalton and Morgan found out about the tryst, although I'm not yet sure how," I continued. "They learned where Bill Tillman lived and went down to Scottsdale to confront him. I'm not sure if it was their intention or not, but they apparently shot and killed him. Word of the murder and the events surrounding it have spread throughout Longview. Dalton and Morgan are worried that Valerie will contact the police about their role in the crime, so they've been keeping a close eye on her."

"Val?" Porter asked. "Is what she said true?"

Lance's mother nodded her head. Porter closed his eyes and took a deep breath.

"God damn it," he said with real anger. "I somehow knew my boys were in the thick of things. But I assumed it was some sort of local trouble. Maybe they got the daughter of one of the ranch hands pregnant again or some sort of similar foolishness. I never guessed it was something as serious as murder."

Porter then got up, still holding my Glock, and walked to the wet bar. He grabbed a bottle of Knob Creek 12-year-old bourbon and poured two fingers into a glass.

"Well, Miss Black," he said as he stood next to the bar and swirled the drink. "It seems like I now have a fresh mess to clean up. You know a lot about my family. Maybe you know too much? You know many of our darker secrets and have made accusations that my sons are murderers."

Porter took a long sip of the bourbon, then casually raised my pistol and pointed it at my face. It had been some time since someone had threatened to shoot me with my own gun. I'd forgotten how big the barrel of my Glock looked when it was pointed at my eye.

Shit.

"Tell me why I shouldn't kill you, Laura Black?" Porter asked. "It seems to me that I should shoot you in the face with this little gun, then drop your body into one of the more remote gulleys here on the ranch. That way, only the coyotes would ever find your remains. You could take all of your speculations about my family to the grave, and I'd be done with it."

I thought about pointing out that Lance and Valerie also knew about the murder. But Valerie hadn't spilled the tea in over a year, and I'd just told Porter that Lance was a blood relative. It looked like I'd need to go another way with this.

Crap. It looks like it's time to play my hold card.

"Um, before I came up here, I had a talk with Tony DiCenzo about you," I said, proud that my voice was only shaking a little. "He gave me the history of the ranch, you, and your Uncle Homer."

"Oh? Is that a fact?" Porter asked in a snarky tone, clearly not believing a word I said. "You had a meeting with Tough Tony DiCenzo? And he told you about me? Really? And what exactly did he say?"

"He told me you were a man of honor and someone who would do the right thing, even if it resulted in a personal loss for you."

Porter snorted with disbelief as he took a sip of his bourbon. "Tony DiCenzo is rather infamous in Arizona. People tend to toss his name around when they're trying to impress their friends or scare their children. How can I know what you say is true and not just a load of made-up horse crap?"

"Um, he gave me something to give to you," I said. "It's in my bag. Would you mind if I got it?"

Porter briefly thought about it, then nodded his approval and waved me over with the Glock. I walked over to the sideboard, picked up my bag, and started to dig through it.

Crap, where is it?

My heart seemed to stop as I couldn't find what I was looking for. Maybe in all the excitement, it had fallen out? Could it be lying in the gulley by the side of the road?

Shit.

I finally remembered where I'd put it and unzipped the inside pocket. Before we left Scottsdale, I'd removed the moon-phase watch from the bulky box and put it in a zippered plastic bag.

"Here," I said as I handed him the Patek Philippe timepiece. He took the bag with a look of uncertainty on his face. But as he examined what I'd given him, the look slowly changed to one of wonder.

He unzipped the bag and removed the gold watch. As he read the inscription on the back, his hand began to tremble.

"How in the hell did you get my old watch?" he asked,

tones of wonder and confusion in his voice.

"I told you. I talked with Tony DiCenzo, and he said that if I ran into you, I should give this back. Now that Tony's retired, he didn't think he'd ever need it to sweeten a business deal, so he wanted you to have it."

I could tell that Porter was still a little uncertain of how I'd come into possession of the watch his uncle had given him.

"If you really talked with Tony about the watch, he must have told you the story of how he got it. Right?"

"Look, we just met," I said. "I know that you don't trust me, and I understand. But Tony and I have a close relationship. I'm dating one of the two men who inherited his business, and Tony even gave me his old car, the one he bet you for the watch the night of the poker game up here."

"The silver Mercedes convertible?" Porter asked, a look of shock on his face. "Tony always loved that car. I'm not surprised he still had it, but I am surprised he gave it to you. You must be close indeed."

Porter looked at Lance and me for another few moments, then put the Glock back in his pocket. "It's very late, and this isn't the time to make important decisions," he said. "You two are going to stay here tonight as my guests. Val, given the circumstances, perhaps it's best if you don't stay in your room with Morgan. I'm going to need to think about how I'm going to resolve this muddle."

"You could put us in the cowboy guest room," she said. "It has a strong door and can be locked from the inside."

Porter nodded, then led us to a large bedroom with several bunk beds and a bathroom. Unfortunately, there was no easy-to-break-out window.

"I'll come for you in the morning," Porter said. "Please don't try to escape in the meantime. Morgan will be prowling around tonight, and he's looking for a reason to shoot you. After hearing what you said about him and his brother, I can understand why he feels that way."

"Do you think it will be okay for us to stay here?" Lance asked. "Dalton and Morgan both want to get rid of us."

"Don't worry about my boys," Porter said. "I won't be sleeping tonight either, and I'll have the only other key to your room."

We locked the door, and I was somewhat relieved to see that it seemed rather substantial. Just to be sure, we wedged a chair against the doorknob. The three of us then looked at each other.

"Son, I'm so sorry you had to learn about things this way," Valerie said. "I never wanted you to know who your real father was. He's an absolute wanker, and I knew that nothing good could come from your knowing."

Lance nodded and held his arms out to his mother. She fell against him, and they had a long hug. It was the first time they'd been able to do that in over twenty-five years, and the moment was very emotional for both of them.

"How do you want to play this?" Lance asked me. "I just found out that Morgan Mercer is my dad. I don't know if that means that I'm safe or simply in more danger. I also don't know what all of this means for my mom. What do you think?"

"I've already pulled my only ace out of my sleeve," I said. "It will either work or it won't. We'll find out in the morning."

"This room seems pretty solid," Lance said as he looked around. "I think we're stuck here for the night."

"Honestly, it looks like things are out of our hands, at least for now," I admitted. "Until we get some more information, we'll need to play it by ear. I'm going to try to get some sleep. I'm beat, and it looks like we'll have a busy day tomorrow."

Chapter Twenty-One

Porter unlocked our door a little after seven the next morning. He then led us to the kitchen, where the remains of a substantial ranch breakfast were laid out.

After warning us not to leave the room, Porter disappeared into the main part of the house. Looking out to the porch, I noticed that Morgan and Dalton were standing against the rail, talking with each other in low voices. I didn't see Morgan's shotgun or Dalton's pistol, but I didn't doubt they had them within easy reach.

None of us had been able to do more than catnap during the night, and we were all still exhausted. We each grabbed some coffee and a plate of food and then sat at a small table in the corner. We ate slowly and thoughtfully, still knowing that we were likely in for an eventful day.

Looking out past the porch, it appeared that Sally had been right. The day was overcast, and a light misty rain was falling. The dull gray sky and cooler temperatures only added to our melancholy mood.

We finished breakfast and then sat at the table, drinking coffee and making small talk, complete with inappropriate gallows humor. A clock on the wall showed us that time was passing, although it seemed very slow.

After we'd been there for almost two hours, I began to get

anxious. I looked through the drawers and cabinets for weapons, but other than a few kitchen knives, there wasn't much we'd be able to use.

At three hours, my nervousness had turned to worry and outright dread. Morgan and Dalton stayed on the porch, but I was waiting for them to burst into the kitchen at any moment, shotgun blazing.

What could be happening that is taking so long?

At about ten-fifteen, Porter walked back into the kitchen. "I just got off the phone with Tony DiCenzo," he said, looking at me. "I wanted to thank him for the return of the watch. However, to be completely honest, I also called him to verify your story. But after talking with my old friend, it appears you downplayed the services you've done for his group."

"It's like I told you," I said with a shrug. "Tony and I have grown close over the last couple of years."

"During the call, Tony and I reminisced about some of the adventures we shared when we were younger. This was back when Arizona was a wide-open land, and the authorities were more apt to look the other way when we stepped out of line. He also reminded me that, as leaders, we have obligations, not only to our families but to the community. Men like Tony and me might not always do things in a strictly legal way, but we never do anything that goes contrary to our core beliefs."

"What are you going to do with us?" I asked.

"I want you three to come into the living room," Porter said, avoiding my question. "We need to hash out a few things."

He led us back into the great room where the fire in the hearth was again burning brightly. Morgan and Dalton were seated in two big leather chairs near the fireplace, neither of them looking happy. Fortunately, the younger Mercer brother no longer had the shotgun.

After directing us to our chairs, Porter walked to the wet bar. He poured himself a bourbon and then absentmindedly took a long sip of it.

"I've sent my two granddaughters into Sedona for a day of shopping," Porter said to the group. "I've given each of them enough money for several new outfits and don't expect them to return before nightfall. We aren't going to be interrupted."

He took another sip of the bourbon, walked to the fireplace, and placed the glass on the stone mantle.

"I think I now have a pretty good idea of everything that's happened here over the past year," Porter said in a loud, firm voice, looking at his boys. "I'll tell you the situation as I know it, and you can correct me if I get something wrong."

"What exactly did they tell you last night?" Morgan demanded to know as he leaned forward in his chair. "A bunch of damn lies, most likely."

"If I understand this correctly," Porter began, "Val got pregnant some thirty-five years ago and decided she didn't want my grandchild to be raised at the Laughing Armadillo. She fled the ranch and ended up in Scottsdale, where she moved in with a man named Bill Tillman. Val had my grandson and lived in Scottsdale for almost ten years."

Porter took a sip of his bourbon and looked at Morgan. "Fortunately, you were eventually able to find your wife. You made her come back to the ranch, but you were unaware that your nine-year-old son was living in Scottsdale under the name of Lance Tillman."

"You're saying he's my son?" Morgan barked out, pointing at Lance. "Not likely. He's a punk and doesn't even look like me. More damn lies."

"Trust me," Lance said. "I'm not thrilled at the news either. You honestly seem like a jerk."

Morgan's eyes flared as he stood up and took a step towards Lance. "Morgan, sit down," Porter snapped. "I'm not finished yet."

Morgan stopped and glared at Lance. His face was flushed with anger, and he was breathing hard. But after a moment, he returned to his chair.

"Things in Scottsdale and here at Longview remained stable for over twenty years," Porter continued. "But Bill Tillman found Valerie last summer and convinced her to spend the weekend with him in Sedona for a sex romp. You two found out about this and went to Scottsdale to confront him. During the altercation, shots were exchanged, and Bill Tillman was killed."

"We only went down to Scottsdale to kick his ass and scare him a little," Dalton blurted out. "But he had a gun, and he came at us. Pa, I swear, it was him or us. We didn't have no choice but to shoot him."

"Shut up," Morgan shouted at his older brother. "They have no proof of any of this. Keep your damn mouth shut, or we'll both end up back in prison."

"Unfortunately," Porter continued, "this tragic event has become somewhat common knowledge, at least within the family. Now, my newfound grandson has come up to the ranch to convince my daughter-in-law to leave us and instead live with him."

"Don't let her leave," Morgan said, pointing his finger at Valerie. "She's my wife, and she belongs here at the ranch. Besides, if she takes off again, she'll only make up more of these wild stories to try to get the law on us."

"I agree, Pa," Dalton added. "I say we get rid of the

woman, along with this guy who's claiming to be a blood relative. They're only here to stir things up."

"It's obvious the only reason he's made up such a wild story is because he wants a piece of the ranch," Morgan added, pointing an accusatory finger at Lance. "These two are nothing more than a couple of swindlers and con artists. We need to get rid of both of them before they spread more lies."

Everyone stopped talking and looked expectantly at Porter. I honestly didn't know what he was going to decide to do with us.

I looked around the room for a weapon, but there wasn't a thing I could use to defend myself other than perhaps a fireplace poker that was in a stand on the hearth.

Porter didn't say anything for several moments. Instead, he looked down at the gold watch on his wrist and absentmindedly played with it.

"I'm not sure where I went wrong with you two," Porter began, looking at his sons. "It's true that I've had many obligations in running the ranch, along with trying to build a solid legacy for our family. Perhaps if I'd spent more time with you boys when you were younger, you both would have had better sense than to kill a man in cold blood and then brag about it."

"Dalton already told you, that wasn't our fault," Morgan said in a menacing tone. "We didn't go down there to kill him. We were only going to teach him what happens when you spend the weekend with another man's wife. It was my right as a husband to kick his ass and let him lay in a hospital bed for a few days to think about it. But the bastard ran at us with a gun pointed at my chest. I had no choice but to shoot him. It was merely self-defense."

"You've both gotten into trouble several times before and even spent time in prison," Porter continued, ignoring

Morgan's words. "I understand the circumstances, and your anger at Bill Tillman was certainly justified. But a Mercer doesn't express his rage through murder. There are far better ways to ruin a man than to shoot him. What's worse, after you killed him, you let word get out that you had done the deed. How did you not expect this eventual outcome?"

"What outcome?" Morgan demanded to know.

"Dan?" Porter called out. "Did you get all that?"

We heard the sound of cowboy boots walking toward us on the wooden floor, and Deputy McGill walked into the room. He must have been standing in the back hallway where he could listen to us talk. He had a serious and troubled look on his face.

"Yeah," he said. "I heard everything. You know, I honestly wasn't sure if I believed the story you told me last night, but your boys confirmed it with their own words."

"We didn't confess to anything," Morgan barked out. "You only heard us disputing the damn lies these two strangers were spewing out about us. Don't get taken in by them, you hear me?"

"Morgan and Dalton Mercer," Deputy McGill said in his deep voice. "You're both under arrest for murder. I'll need you both to turn around and let me handcuff you. Until we get this straightened out, we'll need to go to the sheriff's office in town and go through the formalities. I'll arrange to have your attorney present at all times to make sure everything goes by the book."

"Screw you, McGill," Morgan spat out. "You aren't taking us anywhere."

"Now, Morgan," Deputy McGill said calmly but with a scary undertone. "We've known each other for a long time. You're both in serious trouble here, but let's do this the easy way. Don't make me pull iron on you."

By this point, the fire had gone out of Dalton's eyes, and he turned and placed his hands behind his back. The deputy attached a pair of cuffs, and I saw the older brother wince when he heard the clicking of metal against metal.

When the lawman tried to cuff Morgan, the younger brother took a step forward and swung his huge fist in a roundhouse blow. It was surprisingly fast, and even though the deputy seemed to be expecting the attempt, Morgan's fist still caught him squarely on the jaw.

The deputy's eyes rolled up into his head, and he dropped like a sack of potatoes. After two or three seconds, he shook his head to clear it, then managed to get to his hands and knees and started to cough.

Porter took a step toward his son. "Morgan, stop it," he demanded. "You damn jackass. All you're doing is making it worse for yourself."

Ignoring his father, Morgan turned to the three of us. *"You're dead. All of you!"* he shouted.

From the cruel-eyed look on his nasty face, I knew he'd gladly kill us if he got his huge hands on us. He then frantically looked around for a weapon.

He glanced down at the deputy's gun belt but seemed to think better than to reach for his pistol. Instead, he hurried to the fireplace and grabbed the wrought iron poker from the stand.

"Without you three, there are no witnesses," he bellowed and lunged toward his wife. He was holding the poker above his head and clearly had murder on his mind.

Valerie screamed and used her arm to cover her face. Lance and I ran over, and both gave Morgan a violent shove from behind. He stumbled, then turned to face us, the poker again held over his head.

Fortunately, Deputy McGill wasn't completely out of commission. He grabbed Morgan's ankle and held on for all he was worth.

Angry that he couldn't bash in his wife's head, Morgan instead smashed the poker down on the deputy's side. We heard the meaty *thump* of the iron rod making solid contact.

Deputy McGill yelled in pain, and Morgan was able to yank his leg out of the lawman's grasp. He took a step toward Valerie when Lance and I again crashed into him from behind.

Morgan landed on the floor with an *"Ooof."* His head had made solid contact with the hardwood planks, and he was momentarily knocked senseless.

This was the opening Deputy McGill had been looking for. He crawled over to Morgan, and the two men began to wrestle.

The deputy had pulled out a collapsible baton and used it to smash Morgan's kneecap repeatedly. The big man responded by hitting the deputy hard in the face with his fist. Porter hurried over to help break up the fight, but by this point, it was clear that the two men wanted to beat each other into unconsciousness.

Within a few seconds, Porter, Morgan, and Deputy McGill were a tangle of cursing men and twisting limbs. Dalton was hovering close to the fight but had decided to stay out of it, at least for the moment.

"Let's get out of here!" Valerie shouted at Lance and me.

I wanted to leave but hesitated, knowing that if Morgan came out on top, he'd likely try to kill the lawman. Deputy McGill briefly looked up and saw the three of us standing near him.

"Go!" he shouted, then turned his attention to Morgan's

hand, which was groping around, blindly trying to grab the deputy's face.

The three of us took off. As I ran past the sideboard cabinet, I grabbed my purse and Lance's phone. I was surprised my pistol was back in my bag, but when I pulled it out, I could tell that the bullets had been removed.

Running onto the porch, we paused and looked around. Two pick-up trucks and two sedans were parked in the clearing in front of the house, but the deputy's SUV was nowhere to be seen.

The sky was still overcast, and the misty rain was falling harder. I gave Lance his phone and slipped the bag's strap over my shoulder.

"It's almost an hour's hike down to the cable car," Lance said, echoing my thoughts. "If Morgan escapes, he'll be able to get into one of these vehicles and run us down."

"Where do they keep the keys to these ranch trucks?" I asked Valerie.

"Um, the key rack is in the office," she said, sounding a little distant. "But that's next to the living room, and they'd see us for sure."

I then looked over to the hitching post and saw four brown horses tied to it. They each had a saddle and seemed ready to ride.

The horses were swishing their tails and munching on hay that had been placed in the troughs in front of them, seemingly ignoring the rain. I could only assume they belonged to ranch hands who'd needed to come to the house for something.

"Do you know how to get down to the construction cable car?" I asked Valerie.

"Well, sure," she said, a look of confusion on her face. "But that thing's a rusty death trap. Please don't tell me that's how you planned on crossing the river."

"If we take the horses, we could head directly down to the cable car," I said. "Even if someone did come after us in one of the trucks, they couldn't go cross-country like the horses can."

Valerie looked between me and her son as if we were both slightly insane. "The cable car isn't so bad," Lance said in a quieter voice. "Can you get us there?"

Lance's mom blew out a sigh of disapproval. Then, by mutual agreement, we hurried over to the hitching post.

Valerie chose the smallest of the four horses and untied it from the post. She stuck her foot in the stirrup and lightly hopped on.

Lance chose the largest and also managed to mount his steed. His climb into the saddle wasn't nearly as graceful as Valerie's, but he made it.

I hurried to the smaller of the two remaining horses but then had to remember which foot to put into the stirrup. I hadn't been on a horse since vacationing in Mexico in high school, but I hoped it would be like riding a bicycle.

Unfortunately, it wasn't.

It took a couple of tries, but I was able to swing my leg over and make it into the saddle. Valerie took off like a shot through the parking area, and Lance followed.

Valerie seemed to be at one with her mount, and they effortlessly flew down a path parallel to the main road. After about two hundred yards, she veered off and went down a wide, well-used dirt path that seemed to head in the right direction towards the cable car.

Lance was going significantly slower than his mother, but he eventually made it to the turnoff. A few seconds later, his horse was also running down the new path.

Chapter Twenty-Two

My horse followed behind the other two, and at first, everything went okay. But I soon realized that there was a big difference between the gentle tourist mounts I'd ridden on the beach in Rocky Point all those years ago and a horse belonging to a working cowboy.

I attempted to get him to slow down so I could better position myself in the wet saddle, but he ignored me. I then tried to steer my horse using the reins, but that only seemed to annoy him.

After going at a fast trot for about a hundred yards, the horse seemed to realize that I didn't know what I was doing. He then decided he'd simply do his own thing, and I could come along for the ride, assuming I could hold on.

He took off at top speed to catch up with the other two horses, who were now a good hundred yards further down the trail. Channeling my old high school self, I tried to remember how to use my legs to bounce up and down in rhythm with the horse.

Unfortunately, this only worked for a few seconds. I soon got out of tempo, and my butt violently started to slap against the hard leather saddle.

Ouch, ouch, ouch!

Using one hand to hold the reins and one hand on the horn, I used my legs to stand up in the stirrups. This stopped my ass from being beat to hell, but I was completely unstable as the horse bounced me around.

Crap. This isn't fun.

Hanging on for dear life, my horse gradually caught up with the other two. But rather than slowing when I reached my partners, Valerie only sped up.

"Do we really need to go this fast?" I yelled. I was on the verge of falling off and didn't know how much longer I could stay on my mount.

"Someone's started up a vehicle at Longview," Lance shouted back. "I doubt it's good news."

I turned my head in time to see one of the ranch pickup trucks speeding out of the gravel drive in front of the house. From the way the mud and rocks were flying, I didn't doubt that it was Morgan.

Even though we had a good half-mile head start, I knew Morgan could go much faster in the vehicle. Fortunately, the truck had to take the long, loopy road while the horses could go straight to the river.

"Does Morgan know about the cable car?" Lance loudly shouted to his mother.

"He used to jump off it as a kid," Valerie shouted back. "He'll know exactly where we're going."

We kept up the fast pace, and I somehow managed to keep myself in the saddle. I glanced back three or four times, and the pickup truck was still speeding down the road, but with the wide switchbacks across the mountain, it was only slowly catching up to us.

Four or five minutes later, we reached the trail down to the steel tower. At this point, the path became steeper and was covered in loose rocks and pieces of broken asphalt.

We got off our horses and began to run. The wet pieces of broken pavement were slippery, but we still sprinted down the trail at full speed. We were all pretty much soaked after riding through the rain, and I was so cold that I'd started to shiver.

We raced up the rusty steps and reached the platform when we saw Dalton come over the lip of the hill, running down the trail. He was waving a big revolver and yelling that he was going to mess us up.

Shit, he's got Deputy McGill's Peacemaker.

Surprisingly, from over the hill, the ranch truck revved its engine, and the noise quickly faded away.

So, who's driving the truck, and where are they going?

We jumped into the basket, and Lance started to frantically pull on the tow cable. With the expected screech, the car began to move.

Valerie ducked behind the basket's metal sides as I helped pull on the thin metal line. Dalton was running with surprising speed, and as he reached the steps at the base of the tower, he pulled the hammer back on the Colt and fired at Lance. The shot from the ancient revolver was incredibly loud, but fortunately, the bullet missed.

We'd just cleared the lip of the tower when Dalton ran up the stairs and leaped off the edge of the platform. He let out a loud *"Ooof!"* as he landed awkwardly on his side on the basket's metal floor but quickly scrambled to his feet.

I could tell that the hard landing had injured his left shoulder. He grimaced in pain as he held his arm tightly against his side.

"Stand still, you bastard nephew," he yelled at Lance as he raised the pistol and cocked it with his right hand.

Dalton was blinking rapidly and shaking his head to clear it as he attempted to aim the gun at Lance. He was about to fire off another round when I balled up my fist and hit him on the side of his head as hard as I could.

The pistol went off with the explosive sound of the .45 caliber bullet flying from the gun. Fortunately, the shot went wide, and Dalton was momentarily staggered.

Lance used the brief opportunity to lunge at him, knocking him backward. Dalton took a step back, then tripped and fell.

The older Mercer brother would have been okay, except he happened to hit the gap on the side of the basket. In our rush to escape, I hadn't refastened the safety chain. Dalton hit the opening and began to fall out of the cable car.

As he realized what was happening, the older Mercer brother tried to grab at the edge of the basket, but the sides were slick with rain, and his hand slipped. Screaming and flailing his arms, Dalton went down, landing on the rocks at the edge of Oak Creek, some thirty feet below.

Snap!

Lance and I winced as we heard the unmistakable sound of a bone breaking, followed by Dalton's scream of pain. With a sense of relief, I knew he wouldn't be coming after us anytime soon.

Dalton's fall caused the cable car to swing violently. Valerie was standing against the front of the basket, leaning back as far as she could to avoid the fighting.

She started to fall backward and grabbed for the railing. Unfortunately, like Dalton, her hand slipped on the wet edge. With a loud scream, she tumbled over the side of the basket.

We rushed to the front in time to see her land in the river with a loud splash, three or four feet from the shore. She hit the water badly on her head and neck. Despite me yelling her name, she didn't come up for air.

Lance didn't hesitate for a second. He leaped off the front of the basket and landed in the water ten feet from his mother. After several seconds, he swam over, pulled her head out of the river, and began to pull her to the far bank.

I used the tow cable to pull the basket across the river as fast as I could. Unfortunately, the wheels holding it on the cable hadn't gotten any better, making it hard to go more than a few feet with every pull of the tow line. Although with the main cable being wet, the screeching sound was a little bit softer than before.

I'd made it a little over halfway across when a shot rang out from the east riverbank. There was a loud *clang!* as a large caliber bullet ricocheted off the side of the steel basket.

What the hell?

Across the river, Dalton was sitting up and using the Peacemaker to take potshots at me. Even in the dim light of the overcast morning, I could see that his leg was bleeding badly and bent at an unnatural angle.

Shit!

Two more shots rang out, and there were loud *clangs* as the bullets bounced off the sides of the metal. Fortunately, Dalton had landed in an area strewn with large boulders. From where he was sitting, I didn't think he'd be able to see Lance or Valerie as they slowly crossed Oak Creek.

When the shooting had stopped for about a minute, I lifted my head over the side and looked to the far riverbank. From the way Dalton was panting, blinking his eyes, and grimacing, he seemed to be in a great deal of pain. I knew from experience that this would have the effect of making it impossible for him to aim accurately.

He must have seen my head poking over the basket

because his vision seemed to clear, and he fired off another shot, likely emptying the pistol. I ducked when I saw him raise the gun, and the shot only hit the side of the cable car.

After another thirty seconds, I popped my head up again. Dalton didn't seem to be doing very well. He was leaning badly, and as I watched, he slowly collapsed to his side.

I didn't think he was dead. It was more likely he'd simply passed out from the pain and perhaps loss of blood.

Lance had reached the bank on the far side of Oak Creek, maybe twenty yards downstream from the tower. He pulled his mother partway out of the water and laid her on the wet ground.

As I watched, he began to perform CPR on her. Her face was deathly pale, and I began to fear the worst.

With the additional strength caused by the adrenaline surge, I was able to pull myself the rest of the way across the river in two or three minutes.

I hopped out of the basket and ran down the three flights of stairs. In the back of my mind, I was surprised that they didn't collapse as I barreled down them.

Valerie was still lying on the muddy riverbank with her legs halfway submerged in Oak Creek. Her mouth was partially open in a frightening, dead sort of way, and her face had grown even more pale. Lance was hovering over her, giving her chest compressions, with a look of misery on his face.

Valerie's leg gave a sudden kick, and she gasped in a deep breath of air. This started a violent coughing fit but also had the positive effect of forcing out the water from her lungs.

We picked her up and helped her to her hands and knees to help cough out the rest of the water. After thirty or forty seconds, she began to breathe more easily, and color rapidly returned to her face.

"We've got to hurry," I said. "I heard the pickup truck speed away right before we saw Dalton. I think Morgan's going over the bridge. We need to get out of here before he can find us."

Holding Valerie between us, we hurried on the path back to my car. She was still lightly coughing and hadn't fully come to her senses but seemed to be out of any immediate danger.

We reached the clearing, and Lance helped his mother sit against a large tree while I hurried to get my car out from under the thick branches that were helping to hide it. I unlocked my doors and was about to climb in when I heard Morgan's deep and angry voice.

"Stop right there. None of you is going anywhere."

Morgan stumbled into the clearing. He was limping badly and had a twisted and furious look on his face.

I looked to see if he had a gun and was momentarily relieved that he didn't. Instead, he was holding something, and it took me a second to realize it was an old wooden baseball bat.

Shit. Not good.

"You thought you could escape me, huh?" Morgan growled, looking down at Valerie. "I knew exactly where you'd be, bitch. As soon as I saw where you were heading, I knew you'd cross the river using the old cable car. There's only one place to park around here. I knew all I had to do was wait, and you'd eventually show up."

"Morgan, you don't have to do any of this," Valerie pleaded. Her voice was weak, and her breath came out in shaky gasps. "I'll go back home with you. Just let these other two people go."

"It's way too late for that, don't you think?" Morgan

smirked as he began to limp towards her.

With each step, his face winced in pain. Apparently, Deputy McGill hitting him on the kneecap so many times had caused some serious damage.

The younger Mercer brother had the baseball bat in one hand and began to swing it back and forth lazily.

"Morgan, please, no," Valerie cried out.

"So, you think you could simply run away to Scottsdale? Huh?" Morgan growled, standing ten feet from his wife. "Well, I'm here to show you different. First, I'm going to mess up your pretty face to make sure you can't pick up any new boyfriends. Then, I'm going to hurt you bad for thinking you could blab to the police about what we did to your damn lover last year."

As Morgan was yelling at Valerie, Lance and I glanced around the clearing, hunting for weapons or a way for everyone to escape. I reached down and picked up a softball-sized rock. I wasn't sure what I would do with it, but I felt better having something in my hand.

After looking around and concluding that there was nothing else he could do, Lance ran at full speed towards his father. Morgan seemed to anticipate the charge. He stepped back, with a nasty grin on his face, and swung the baseball bat, hard.

Lance had his arms outstretched to grab onto Morgan, and the bat caught him solidly on his left side with a wet-sounding *thud!* All the air then flew out of Lance's lungs with a painful *"Ooof"*.

Lance was staggered by the blow, which only made Morgan smile and chuckle. "You like that, boy? Huh? Well, there's plenty more where that came from. Why don't you come over here and let your daddy take another swing at you."

Lance took a shaky step towards Morgan as if to continue the brawl. But he soon thought better of it and dropped to his knees, grimacing in pain.

Seeing that Lance had given up, Morgan scoffed loudly. "Yeah, that's what I thought," he mocked. "You have no fight in you, boy. You ain't my son."

Morgan slowly turned back to his wife, who was now maybe twenty feet away on the far side of the clearing. She was crying, coughing, and doing her best to crawl away to the river.

Morgan lifted the bat and rested it on his shoulder. "Dear," he shouted, now with a lunatic grin on his face. "I think it's time that you and I have a quickie divorce."

Valerie looked back at Morgan and raised her arm to protect herself. She shook her head back and forth and began to whimper in terror as her husband limped toward her.

Morgan only chuckled and began to whistle a familiar tune. It took me a second to recognize it was *Pop Goes the Weasel*.

Lance was trying to get up, but his eyes were glazed over in pain. I knew he'd be out of the fight for at least a minute or two.

Now that Morgan had his back to me and was focusing on his wife, I knew this would be my only chance to take him out. I held the rock high over my head and ran at the man.

Morgan must have heard me coming because he spun around to face me. His eyes had gone a little crazy, and there was spittle flying out of his mouth.

Seeing me running at him with a rock in my hand seemed to please him. He grinned and brought the bat around like a baseball player waiting for a pitch. He then stood his ground, ready to swing at me as soon as I got into range.

There was a sudden movement in the bushes, and a woman stepped into the clearing next to Morgan. She was tall and athletic, and her long, dark hair was pulled back in a ponytail.

She wore a tight, black leather outfit with a deeply plunging, scoop-neck bodice outlined in blood-red trim. I was a little shocked at the outfit since her boobs were all but falling out.

Morgan paused mid-swing as he turned to gawk at the beautiful woman. She looked back at him and lifted her hand to give him a playful finger wave.

"Hello, asshole," she said, giving him a wide smile.

I was still holding the rock above my head but had stopped running at the shock of seeing my friend.

"Gabriella," I called out. "What are you doing here?"

Morgan turned to glower at the new person standing in the clearing. His lips slowly curled up in a smirking, perhaps at the thought of fighting with a beautiful woman, but he also had a slight look of confusion on his face.

"Who the hell are you?" he bellowed while staring down at Gabriella's abundant cleavage. "Stay the hell out of my way before I smash in your pretty face. I warn you. I have no problems hurting a woman."

"I see you did not bring gun," Gabriella said in her odd Russian accent. Her face had a rosy, pink glow, and her breaths were coming in short pants of anticipation.

"That is good," she said. "Now I not have to shoot you. Shooting is too quick for me to properly enjoy."

Chapter Twenty-Three

Gabriella was carrying her black Ferrucci Spy Bag, which I knew held several pieces of combat gear, including an Uzi submachine gun, a Marine Corps fighting knife, and even a few hand grenades. Giving Morgan a wink, she let the bag slip off her shoulder and fall to the ground.

"You like to hurt women?" she asked as she raised her fists in the classic boxer's stance, inviting him to fight. "Thank you for warning. But I also have no problem hurting men. In fact, I like it. I like it a lot."

Morgan again lifted the bat and held it over his shoulder. He gripped it tightly, like a major leaguer waiting to hit the next pitch out of the park. As he advanced towards Gabriella, he grinned and began to chuckle.

"So, you think you want a piece of me? Well, come and get some. Go ahead, sugar tits, give it your best shot. I'm going to pop you right in that sweet little mouth of yours. Maybe I'll knock out a few of your teeth. What do you think? I love making the pretty girls cry."

Gabriella quickly moved up to Morgan in three fluid strides. He swung the bat with all the strength he could put into it, but she easily dodged the blow.

Gabriella's fists and feet then flew out in a blur of motion that was hard to keep track of. All I was able to catch was a spinning kick to the face, a hard knee to the crotch, and several solid punches to his face and throat.

After fifteen or twenty seconds of dishing out this brutal punishment, Gabriella stepped back. Her breath was coming out in short gasps, her face was flushed, and her mouth hung open in a look of erotic ecstasy. I then watched as a powerful shudder of pleasure swept through her body.

Wow, go figure. That happens every single time.

The bat fell out of Morgan's hands and landed in the mud. The big man then slowly fell backward and landed with a solid *thud* next to his bat. It was a little like watching a giant tree falling into the forest.

Blood had begun to stream from his face, and he slowly rolled to his side. He sucked in a wet breath, then began to moan loudly.

Gabriella walked to Morgan and bent over. "Are you good, bro?" she asked. "Did you have enough, or do you want to try and hurt me some more?"

"You dirty bitch," Morgan gasped out as he stared up at his assailant. "You better hope I never find you. I'm going to hunt you down, then I'm going to fuck you up. I'm going to take my sweet time and hurt you so bad…"

Ooof.

Even as Morgan was making threats, Gabriella used her combat boot to give him a vicious kick to the face. His head snapped back, and a fresh wail of misery bellowed out from his bloody mouth.

"That was for calling me sugar tits," she said as she closed her eyes, and another intense shudder of pleasure washed over her body.

Damn, that woman is so unusual.

In a way, watching Morgan roll in the mud and moan in pain was a little like watching a car crash. I didn't like what I was seeing, but I also couldn't look away.

Lance didn't have a problem looking at his father. Holding his arm against his ribs, he stumbled over to the prone body of his mother's long-time antagonist in several limping strides. He let out a yell of disgust and then began kicking Morgan in the side.

After the second or third kick, there were the distinctive *popping* sounds of ribs cracking and breaking. Morgan tried to roll over to block the kicks, but his body had stopped responding, even to this new level of pain.

Altogether, Lance gave Morgan four or five solid kicks before his emotions began to drain out of him. He then turned and stumbled back until he got to my car.

"Very nice," Gabriella said to Lance, clearly approving of the violence. "It is good to let it out, no?"

"I shouldn't have done that," he gasped in pain as he held his arm tightly to his side. "I think I made my injuries worse."

"Hopefully, Porter and the deputy are okay," I said.

"Let's call it in," Lance said, again wincing with pain. "Assuming he's able to respond, we'll have Deputy McGill come down to pick up this piece of trash. He'll also need to get Dalton. I doubt he was able to get very far away."

"No, I stay to watch other man who had gun," Gabriella confirmed. "He crawl down to river, but then he pass out. He not go anywhere now. You do good work on him."

I looked back at Morgan, who had tightly curled up in the fetal position. All the talk about how he was going to hurt Gabriella and Valerie had apparently faded from his mind.

Gabriella walked over to her bag and pulled out two pairs of police flex cuffs. She then efficiently slipped them over

Morgan's wrists and ankles.

"Stay, good boy," she said with a slight smile as she lightly patted his cheek.

Morgan's eyes watched as Gabriella talked with him, but he now was smart enough not to mouth off to her.

Lance stepped to the side and pulled out his phone. As he dialed 9-1-1, I walked over to Gabriella.

"Thanks for showing up. You really pulled our bacon out of the fire. But what are you doing here?

"Max say you were going into harm's way, and he ask if I help keep an eye on you."

"How did you know where we'd be?" I asked, but my thoughts trailed away when I looked at my Miata.

"Max activated the tracker in my car?" I wasn't sure if I was upset or grateful.

Gabriella only looked at me like I'd said something stupid. "I came here in case you need my help when you get back to your car. We found the towers with the cable over the river, and I set up there to see when you come back over."

"What about him?" I asked as I pointed to the moaning man in the mud.

"This man show up ten minutes ago," she said, looking at Morgan, who had started to calm down. His face was bright red, and he was still taking shallow breaths to help manage the pain but hadn't shouted any further insults.

"He tried to get into your car and was about to smash your window with his bat when he heard noise of gunshots and gondola going over river. He then set up ambush for you here. He did not notice I was always ten steps behind him."

"Thanks for doing that," I breathed out. "But if you were so close, why did you wait until he was about to cave in my chest with the bat before you stepped out?"

"I not want to spoil your fun. I thought you might want to enjoy taking him out on your own. It was only when I saw you attacking man armed with baseball bat, but you only have little rock, that I thought you need assistance."

"It looks like I owe you again. How long have you been out here?"

"We got here a little after midnight. Your car was still warm, so we knew you had parked recently."

"You were here all night?"

"It is no problem," she scoffed. "I have set up in much worse places. This is very nice compared to the winter mountains of Azerbaijan. It has been very quiet in Scottsdale since you were trapped under the building in the desert. Max ask permission from Johnny to borrow me for couple of days. He knew I would enjoy some light field work for nice change."

"Did you say 'we' got here last night?" I asked. "Did Max come too?"

"Max and Carson both come. They watch for you at bridge. We thought that would be where you would cross over river. Max had me watch old cable car only as backup. I didn't think you would try to cross river in something that look like that, but Max say that you might. They heard the shots and are on their way here."

Even as she said this, an engine roared, and a black SUV drove into the dirt clearing with Carson behind the wheel. Max hopped out, holding a semi-automatic pistol, and quickly assessed the situation.

He hadn't shaved, and his black cargo pants and T-shirt were badly wrinkled. It was the closest I'd ever seen my boyfriend to being messy in public. I have to say, he looked pretty good.

Carson got out and stood next to the vehicle, taking in the situation. The man was huge and didn't need to say anything to be intimidating.

"Are you okay?" Max asked, looking me over.

"I'm in one piece," I said. "Thanks for bringing Gabriella up here. She was a lifesaver."

Max nodded and turned to Gabriella. "Gabby, what about you?"

"I'm not injured," she said. "I had nice fight with scumbag lying in mud. He not put up much resistance, but it was still very enjoyable."

"I didn't think you could be up here?" I asked Max as I wrapped my arms around him, not surprised to feel the hardness of his bulletproof vest under his shirt. "Doesn't that sorta violate the criminal gang rules?"

"Well, it may slightly violate the spirit of the agreement," he chuckled. "But as long as we don't go onto the actual Mercer ranch, we'll be fine. Now that I know you're okay, I won't push it any further. Have you called law enforcement yet?"

"I just did," Lance said as he walked up to us. His eyes darted between Max and Carson, but he decided not to ask who they were. "They said they'd send a couple of ambulances and some deputies down from Cottonwood. That's the next town to the west from here, and apparently, there's a big hospital there. They should start showing up in about fifteen minutes."

"Alright," Max said as he hugged me again and gave me the sweetest kiss. His face was stubbly, and I wondered what it would feel like if he ever grew a beard.

"Since it looks like things are stable here, we need to disappear," he said. "It's best if our names don't appear in any of the official reports. Let me know if you have problems dealing with the local sheriff's office. Call me as soon as you get back to Scottsdale."

"I will," I said as I squeezed him again. "Thanks for keeping an eye on me."

"I don't mind watching your back, but you owe me," he laughed. "I'm going to want an entire weekend with you."

"As soon as we can arrange it," I said as I smiled back at him.

"Feel free to rough him up a little before police come," Gabriella said, pointing at Morgan. "He is bad man, and hurting him will make you feel better. I would say give him nice kick to face, but you not have on boots. Why do you not wear boots for hostage rescue?"

"I know," I said, feeling a little frustrated. "I've been regretting it all night. Next time, I'll wear my hiking boots."

I really hate that there'll probably be a next time.

While we were waiting for the sheriff to arrive, I explained to Lance that it would help me out if he didn't tell the police that a woman had appeared out of nowhere, taken out Morgan, and then disappeared.

I also asked him to forget about the two men who had come to the clearing after the fight and then vanished as well. Lance only considered it for a moment before agreeing.

I went to Valerie to see how she was doing. She had begun to stare blankly across the clearing, and her face had again grown pale.

Concerned that she could be going into shock, I had her sit in my Miata. I'd then taken an old *Power Puff Girls* blanket from my trunk and wrapped it around her.

I asked her if she was still good with going down to Scottsdale to speak with the detective. "It's okay. I'd still like to go through with it," she said. "Especially after we went through all of this."

Valerie's voice was still weak and shaky from the events of the morning, but I couldn't blame her. It had been an eventful day.

"It would be best if an attorney is present when the police question her," I told Lance when we were out of earshot from his mom. "Would you like Lenny to represent her in this?"

"That's a good idea," he said. "I doubt that the police will let me attend the interview, and I don't want her to go in there alone."

The first of the sheriff's patrol cruisers from Cottonwood pulled into our clearing about ten minutes after Max, Carson, and Gabriella had taken off. Two uniformed deputies piled out, looking for a fight, and were somewhat surprised at finding Morgan trussed up like a Thanksgiving turkey.

By this point, the younger Mercer brother had started to recover from the fight. He cursed loudly and made threats to the deputies as they searched him for weapons.

A few minutes later, two additional deputies and a sergeant arrived, closely followed by an ambulance. People piled out of their vehicles to assess the situation and check on the wounded.

A pair of EMTs checked Morgan's condition and quickly assessed his injuries before a deputy handcuffed him to a gurney. They then loaded him into the ambulance for the trip to the hospital.

While this was going on, I led the sergeant to where I'd last seen Dalton. When we found him, he'd crawled the remaining few feet to the river, but he'd passed out again, this time with his arm dangling in Oak Creek.

"Deputy McGill's Peacemaker is probably lying next to Dalton," I said. "I'm pretty sure it's out of bullets, but you should be aware it's there."

When the next ambulance arrived, the sergeant guided the EMTs back to the river to pick him up. I was somewhat startled when I heard the screech of the cable car as the men went over Oak Creek to bring him back. But considering the situation, it was probably the best way to transport an injured man on a stretcher back across the river.

After telling the EMTs what had happened to Valerie, they checked her vitals and looked her over. They thought she was in no immediate danger but suggested she should go in to be more fully checked out. Valerie insisted that she was fine but agreed to have one of the deputies drive her to the hospital.

Lance was also examined, and it appeared that he had three ribs that were cracked or possibly broken. With assistance from the EMTs, he was able to climb into the back of the same sheriff's SUV as his mother to be driven to the medical center in Cottonwood.

I spent the next hour in the clearing, showing various law enforcement members my ID and filling out report forms. The local detective soon arrived and was initially suspicious of my story.

This was mainly because it was obvious I was hedging on

a few key details, such as where the flex cuffs had come from. My made-up explanation that I always carry restraints in the trunk of my car didn't seem to impress the detective.

While in the middle of this uncomfortable questioning, Deputy McGill radioed in a report of the incident from Longview. Fortunately, it fully corroborated my account of the events. This went a long way toward keeping local law enforcement friendly and to the point.

I learned from the detective that Deputy McGill had been roughed up pretty badly but would likely be okay. Porter had also suffered some injuries, but no one knew how bad they were. Fortunately, an ambulance and the paramedics were en route to Longview to treat both men.

Deputy McGill had listed Morgan and Dalton Mercer as wanted murderers who escaped custody and were considered armed and dangerous. I was sure several other charges would be added as the process unfolded, including attempted murder, resisting arrest, and assault on a peace officer.

Chapter Twenty-Four

The detective released me an hour and a half later, after I'd promised to make myself available if needed. I then drove the twenty-five-minute route to the Verde Valley Medical Center in Cottonwood. I wanted to find out what had happened to Deputy McGill and Porter Mercer and make sure that Valerie and Lance were still doing well.

When I arrived, I wasn't all that surprised to see five sheriff's cruisers parked in front of the emergency room. I was glad to see they weren't taking any chances with the Mercer brothers.

I found my client coming out of the emergency department as I was going into the hospital. He walked stiffly but seemed to be otherwise okay.

"They took some scans of my mom, and she wasn't seriously injured from the fall," he said. "But they're going to watch her for a while. They said some problems can sneak up on you after a tumble and from passing out. They're currently treating her for having river water in her lungs and will move her up to a room when they're done."

"I'm glad it was nothing more severe," I said. "How are you doing?"

"Three cracked ribs, but none of them broke," he said. "They said that the current treatment is to do nothing, not even tape them up. They gave me a prescription for pain pills to help me breathe and told me to avoid stressing the area for the next six weeks."

We found Porter's room and were relieved to see that he was awake and alert. He had an IV in his arm and was hooked up to several monitors.

"Mr. Mercer?" I asked. "Is it okay if we come in?"

"You might as well," he grumbled when he saw us standing at the doorway. "I haven't been able to get a straight answer from anyone here about what's going on. Maybe you can clue me in on what's happened."

"We can try," I said. "How are you feeling?"

"I feel like I've been in a barroom fight," he said as he shook his head slowly. "But so far, they tell me I only have some cuts, bruises, and a mild concussion. They're going to monitor me for a while to make sure I didn't do any serious damage to myself."

"It was very brave of you to jump into the fight like you did," I said.

"That wasn't a big deal," Porter scoffed. "Morgan was acting like a jackass. What do you know about my boys? After Morgan knocked me out, he must have taken off Dalton's cuffs, and they ran off. The deputies I've talked to say they've both been admitted to the hospital here, but they won't tell me their conditions."

"Dalton is the worse off of the two," I said. "There was a fight on the old cable car over the river, and he fell out. He landed badly on the rocks on the riverbank and broke his leg in a compound fracture. I don't know about any other medical problems he has."

"Dalton was fighting with you when he fell out?" Porter asked, looking at Lance with an appraising eye. "What about

Morgan?"

"Morgan suffered more injuries," I said. "But I don't think any of them are life-threatening. He was in two fights today, starting with you and Deputy McGill in Longview and again in a parking lot down by the river. He was limping pretty badly after the tussle with Deputy McGill. The second fight added some additional wounds and injuries, but mostly cuts and bruises."

"Morgan was never the brightest boy," Porter grumbled. "But he always had the heart to go on. He wouldn't have given up as long as he could still raise his fists."

"That's true," Lance admitted. "Morgan didn't stop fighting until his body was too badly beaten to move."

"Very well, thank you for telling me what you know," Porter said, now looking at Lance. "I'm glad you're here. Our discussions last night and again this morning cleared up a few things but also brought up some additional problems."

"What kind of problems?" Lance asked a little hesitantly.

"I first want you to understand something very clearly," Porter said. "I dearly love Cici and Jeannie, and I want both of my granddaughters to be happy. Cici must never know who her true father was. I made sure not to tell Morgan or Dalton the truth about her this morning. If you really are my blood grandson, which I now see as likely, then I want Cici to believe you are her brother. And I mean her *full* brother. I don't want any foolishness my daughter-in-law did to ever put a cloud over that."

Lance nodded. "The things we've discovered this week have been a shock to me as well. I've learned that my biological father shot and killed the man whom I loved as a dad and who raised me as his own. I won't do anything to push that sort of guilt on Cici. I understand that the birth certificate lists Morgan as her father, and I won't do anything to lead her to believe otherwise."

Porter thought about it for several moments, all the while looking down at the gold watch on his wrist.

"It's going to be hard enough when Cici and Jeannie learn that their fathers were arrested for the murder of Bill Tillman. They're going to need love and support from as many family members as possible. Will you pledge to be there for my granddaughters and do whatever you can for them?"

"Being with my mother and sister is more than I could ever imagine," Lance said. "It doesn't make up for my dad being murdered, but I can't change what happened. Knowing the truth about my mom and dad helps put everything in a different perspective, and it's something I'll need to live with. I'll be there to help my sister and cousin in any way I can."

I excused myself from Porter and Lance, who were making small talk and trying to learn about each other. I needed to make a couple of calls to get the process going from my end.

Taking a deep breath, I pulled out my phone and called Jackson Reno. I felt some mixed emotions as I waited for him to pick up.

Reno had been my on-again, off-again boyfriend for the past couple of years. I hadn't stopped seeing him for good until right before I started dating Max.

Fortunately, when we broke up, he didn't seem to take it too badly. Since he worked as a senior detective for the Scottsdale Police Department, I still used him occasionally for information that would be otherwise hard to get.

"Hey," I said when he answered. "It's me. How have you

been?"

"Laura Black," he said with a sigh. "You seem to pop up at the most unusual times. Are you calling to ask me out again?"

"Um, nooo," I said. "Not today."

"Okay," he said with a slight chuckle. I got the sense that he was somewhat disappointed. "So, what can I do for you?"

"Do you happen to remember a home invasion that occurred last June on Orange Blossom Lane? One man was killed. His name was Bill Tillman."

"Oh, sure," Reno said. "The Tillman name stuck in my head. I don't think they ever closed that one. Do you have any information on it?"

"Yeah, the two men who did it are currently in sheriff's custody in Cottonwood. We also have a local deputy and a couple of witnesses who can describe the events surrounding the murder. Do you know who's working the case?"

"You always were efficient," he said with a snort of laughter. "I'll give you that. I heard they reassigned that one to Chugger two or three months ago when the case started to grow cold. Even if he's not still on it, he'll know who has it now."

"Thanks," I said. "It's good knowing I can still ask you about things like this. Um, how are you doing? Anything new happening with you?"

"Not really," he said. "I tried dating Cynthia Redburn again for a few months, if you remember her, but that eventually petered out."

Cynthia Redburn? The skanky blonde woman who liked to have her nasty toes sucked on? Eeewww.

"Besides, you know how my schedule is," Reno

continued. "It's almost as bad as yours. It makes dating someone with a normal job a challenge. What about you? Are you still closely associating with known criminals?"

"No, of course not," I lied shamelessly. "It's not my fault that my job sometimes has me mixing with some of the more colorful members of society."

"Alright," Reno chuckled. "I know Chugger will appreciate your help in closing his case. Even after a year, there's still pressure in the department to wrap that one up. Nobody likes the idea of a violent home-invasion gang roaming unchecked through the city."

"Alright, I'll give him a call. But, um, before I go, can I ask you a question?"

"Sure," he said with a chuckle. "I remember that tone. You always used it before you asked me about saving the world."

"Shut up," I said. "Listen. This has been bothering me for a long time. You arrest a lot of people, and that can cause them to leave their jobs and families, sometimes for years at a time. A lot of innocent spouses and children can get caught up in the process when a family member goes to prison. Do you ever feel that your job is causing more general harm than good?"

"Not really," he said after a pause. "I felt that way a few times when I was a rookie, but now I'm senior enough that they let me have some leeway on who I take in. If I don't think they're guilty, I don't arrest them. Why do you ask? Are you still trying to save the world?"

"No, maybe not the world. Not anymore. But I do want to feel that I'm doing more overall good than harm."

"That's a great goal. But Laura, I know you and how you operate. Everyone in the department texts me whenever they run across you, and they always tell me what you're doing. I think I've heard about every crazy caper you've been involved with since you blew up that truck in the desert near Casa Grande last year. Try not to overthink it. I believe you're doing alright for yourself."

Reno knows that I blew up that truck full of military supplies? What else does he know?

"Thanks," I said. "I appreciate that. Okay, well, I'll talk to you later. You take care of yourself."

"Thanks," he said, sounding somewhat thoughtful. "You take care of yourself, too. Feel free to call anytime something comes up. Or, I suppose, you don't even need a reason."

I disconnected, then took a deep breath to clear my head.

Why do I always feel a little sad when I talk to Reno?

I next called my old friend Chugger McIntyre. I'd grown up with Chugger, and we'd gone through elementary school together. After several years as a patrol officer, Chugger had recently become a detective.

"Well, Laura Black," Chugger laughed when he picked up. "It's been a while. What's going on with you? Are you calling in to report another dead body?"

"Not this time, but I have some information on an old case."

"Aw, that's too bad. You know, the office pool on you finding another dead body is still going strong. I think Arny was the one who won the last time you called one in. Although, you seem to be slowing down. It's been a few months since you've called anything in."

"Do you want the information? It's on the Bill Tillman home invasion murder from last summer."

"Oh, sure," Chugger said, his attitude quickly shifting to a detective's neutral. "What have you got for me?"

"The murderers are Dalton and Morgan Mercer. They live

at the Laughing Armadillo Ranch near the town of Sycamore Springs. The Sheriff's deputies are currently holding the brothers in Cottonwood. I also have a material witness, Valerie Mercer. She's Morgan's wife and knows all the details of the murder. She had a long history with Bill Tillman, and the brothers murdered him for revenge."

"Who else knows about it?"

"The local deputy, a man named Dan McGill, overheard the brothers' confession, and so did their father, Porter Mercer. You can talk with the deputy, but I'd be surprised if Porter would talk with you. Rumor is that his family used to be involved in some things that may not have been strictly legal."

"Oh, it's like that?" Chugger asked thoughtfully.

"I'm afraid so. You might want to keep that in the back of your mind as you investigate."

"Alright," he said. "You'd better get me Deputy McGill's number, and I'd like to get the wife's story in person. When can you bring her in? What about Monday, ten o'clock?"

"That should be good, but let me check," I said. "Lenny will be with her to make sure things don't get out of hand."

"Jeez," he laughed. "I thought you were helping me out. Lenny's the kind of lawyer who gives other attorneys a bad reputation."

"It'll be fine," I said with a laugh.

My last call was to Lenny. "Hey," I said when he answered. "I've finished the Lance Tillman assignment. We found his mother, and we also found the two men who murdered his dad. They're currently in jail in Cottonwood."

"Jeez, Laura," Lenny grumbled. "Finding his dad's killers was noble and all, but it was outside the scope of the investigation. Do you think our client will squabble when I bill him for your time on that?"

"He shouldn't," I said. "Lance's mom knows all the details of the killing, and we've got a tentative appointment at ten o'clock on Monday to talk with the detective on the case in Scottsdale. Lance has already asked that you represent his mother during questioning."

"Oh, really?" Lenny perked up. "That's a nice extension to the investigation. Depending on how things shake out, we should be able to soak up the rest of the retainer plus bill for another ten or fifteen grand. Good job."

I next went to find Deputy McGill. When I walked into his room, I was surprised to see Sally in a chair next to his bed, holding his hand. I was even more stunned that he seemed to be holding her hand back.

Sally had hung some crystals in the window, and they were shooting out bright rainbows throughout the room. The music of Peter, Paul, and Mary was softly playing through a phone with a purple case that sat on the counter.

I also caught a hint of patchouli oil. Since this was a hospital, I figured it was likely from Sally's perfume rather than from anyone burning incense.

"Hello, Sally," I said. "It's good to see you again. Deputy McGill, how are you feeling?"

"Miss Black, I'm glad to see you in one piece," he said. "From what I've been told, you and Mr. Tillman took on both Mercer brothers and came out on top. Truth be told, I heard you beat the hell out of both of them."

"We only did what we had to do," I said. "Dalton and Morgan both wanted to kill us so they could get away with the murder of Bill Tillman. When they came after us, it became a matter of self-defense more than anything else."

"From what I understand, Morgan and Dalton are in custody here in Cottonwood. Perhaps they're still somewhere in the hospital being treated. Did I hear correctly that Dalton broke his leg?"

"Um, yeah," I admitted. "That did happen. He and Lance were fighting on the old construction cable car, and Dalton fell out of the basket. He landed on the rocks on the east bank of Oak Creek, and his leg snapped."

Sally's eyes grew large as she listened to our conversation. "You crossed over the river on the old cable car?" she asked, her voice becoming emotional. "You're braver than I am. That thing's a rusty accident waiting to happen."

"I also heard that Valerie Mercer is going to interview with the homicide detective down in Scottsdale about the murder of Bill Tillman," the deputy said.

"That's the plan," I said. "I told you I work for a law firm. My boss will be representing Valerie until everything surrounding the murder is cleared up."

The lawman nodded his approval, but I could tell that he wasn't all that happy. "Is everything okay, Deputy McGill?"

"To tell you the truth, Miss Black, I'm a little pissed at myself. I had a suspect swing and connect with me while I was trying to arrest him. Now, I don't like to think of myself as a soft man, but Morgan knocked me senseless. He took my weapon, released his brother from the cuffs I'd put him in, and escaped with murder on his mind."

"I was there," I said. "From my standpoint, it looked like you did everything you could."

"Not hardly," he scoffed. "It was a foolish rookie mistake. I think I let my friendship with the Mercers cloud my judgment. I know it caused you and Mr. Tillman a lot of trouble to make up for my error in judgment. I hope you can forgive me for that."

"There's nothing to forgive," I said. "I appreciate that you took on Morgan and let us escape. Things could have really gone south otherwise. Oh, I let the detective on the scene know where your Peacemaker ended up. It may have a few new scratches, but hopefully, he'll get it back to you."

"He's already stopped by to let me know he had it," the deputy said. "I appreciate you doing that for me. That pistol has been in my family since 1876. I would have hated to see it disappear."

"It's no problem," I said, reflecting inwardly on how the gun had been used to shoot at us.

"I've been going over the facts of the case," he said. "Between what Valerie knows and what you and I heard this morning, I think the Maricopa County DA will be able to put together a pretty solid case against the Mercer brothers. I'm not sure if I'll be able to convince Porter to talk with the police, but stranger things have happened."

From the deputy's tone, I could tell there was something deeper going on other than guilt over messing up the arrest. "Are you sure you're okay?" I asked.

"Miss Black, I can't tell you how much this whole thing is tearing me up. I've known Morgan and Dalton since the day I started this job, twenty-two years ago. Jeannie was going into kindergarten back then, and Cici had just gotten out of diapers."

"I could see how that would make things difficult," I said.

"I feel especially bad for Porter. The boys may not be the most upstanding citizens of Sycamore Springs, but Porter certainly is. He's a big part of the glue that holds this community together. If we lose him, I could see the town starting to fade."

I could tell that our discussion was straining the deputy. He lay back on his pillows and winced in pain.

"Sally, it's only been three hours since all of this happened. How did you know the deputy was here?"

"It's a small town," she said as if that was the only explanation needed. Maybe it was.

Chapter Twenty-Five

I met up with Lance, and we went to Valerie's room. I was pleased to see that she was awake and alert. When she saw Lance, she broke into a wide grin, confirming for me that she was doing okay.

She verified that the doctors had all but cleared her and only wanted to keep her overnight for observation. I was again thankful that she hadn't been more seriously injured.

Lance and his mom made plans to return to Longview the next morning so she could pack enough clothes to stay at his place in Scottsdale for a few days. They also wanted to explain to Cici and Jeannie what had happened, the truth about Lance being part of the family, and why their fathers wouldn't be coming home anytime soon.

I was sort of glad I wouldn't be there for that. It would be a difficult conversation for everyone involved.

Since his mom needed to spend the night in the hospital, Lance decided to rent a car for the drive back to Scottsdale the next day. I offered to take him down to the rental office to pick it up, but he thought he could get someone else to drive him. He then texted Gwen to share the news with her.

Even after everything that had happened during our eventful day, Lance smiled sweetly as he read her reply.

I took that as a good sign.

By four in the afternoon, things had pretty much settled down at the hospital. They'd released Deputy McGill, but Porter and Valerie were still scheduled to spend the night. I hadn't asked anyone about Morgan and Dalton, but the number of sheriff's cruisers in front of the hospital had dropped to two, so I assumed that both brothers were in the local jail.

When I went up to say goodbye to Lance's mom, there was a deputy outside her room at the nurse's station. He said that the case had a high profile in the sheriff's office, and there would be someone on the floor until Valerie was discharged the next morning.

Gwen had come to the hospital to pick up Lance. She also stopped by both Porter's and Valerie's rooms to check on them. I was still a little surprised that everyone in Sycamore Springs seemed to know everyone else. But, as Sally had said, it was a small town.

After I'd said my goodbyes and worked out the details with Valerie and Lance for the meeting with Chugger on Monday, I climbed into my Miata and took off. As soon as I got to the interstate, I called Grandma Henderson.

"Hi, Grandma," I said when she answered. "How's Marlowe doing?"

"He's feeling much better. Doctor Dusty said it was only a minor upper respiratory tract infection. She gave him a shot, and he seems much better today."

"Oh, that's such good news. I've been stuck up here in Sycamore Springs, and I've been worried about him. How much do I owe you for the vet?"

"The entire visit was $75," she said. "The receptionist said she'd send you the bill."

"Perfect. Thanks for taking Marlowe in. Do you need a break from him yet? If not, I'll hopefully be with Max tonight and tomorrow."

"Oh, there's no need to hurry home," Grandma said. "Marlowe's feeling like his old self again, and other than having to clean some boogers off my couch, my outfits, and his chair, he hasn't been any problem at all."

"Thanks, Grandma," I said. "I'll be back to my place in a day or two."

My next call was to Max. "Hey," I said when he picked up. "Thanks for coming up last night to watch over me. I didn't think that I'd need any help with this one, but I guess I did."

"It's no problem," he said, and I could picture him smiling. "Gabriella was in a great mood the entire drive back to Scottsdale. It's rare for her to talk non-stop like she did. She must have really beaten the crap out of that man I saw lying on the ground."

"Hard enough for her to have two intense orgasms," I said with a chuckle. "It's so, um, odd. I never know what to think when she does that."

"I try not to think too much about it," Max laughed. "Gabriella's a unique woman, and I'm only glad she's on our side."

"We didn't get much of a chance to talk this morning, but are you free tonight?" I asked. "The assignment is pretty much over, and I'd love to spend some time with you."

"I'm free all weekend and was hoping you'd be available," he said. "Swing by the house around cocktail time. Beatrice has been shopping, and I know she's looking forward to cooking you something special."

I drove straight to Max's house and parked in the circular drive. It was only after I'd rang the doorbell that I looked down at myself.

I was still wearing the outfit from the previous night, and I looked terrible. My arms were full of scratches and bruises. Mud caked my shoes and pant legs, and I had various dirt, mud, and rust smudges across my top.

I'd been so distracted on the drive back to Scottsdale that I hadn't put any makeup on, and I could only imagine what my hair looked like. As I thought about it, I hoped I didn't smell too bad.

Jeez, this isn't the way to greet my boyfriend.

I was about to go back to the car to quickly brush out my hair and dab on some makeup when the door opened. Max looked me up and down, then began to laugh.

"You don't need to knock," he said as he continued to chuckle. "I knew you were coming and unlocked the door. You can come right in next time."

"I know," I said. "You've told me that before, but I feel sorta creepy doing that."

Max continued to chortle as he stepped aside to let me in.

"Hey," I said, feeling a little annoyed. "I know I look and probably smell like crap, but it's not very nice to laugh at your girlfriend."

"You're right, and I'm sorry. But it looks like you've been out in the field for a week."

"I've had a hard twenty-four hours," I said. "But now, you're going to need to spend the rest of the weekend making it up for laughing at me."

Max held his arms out, and I snuggled against him. I was about to kiss him when I had another thought. "Um, I also haven't brushed my teeth today."

"I'll risk it," he said as he bent down for a kiss.

Max made me a scotch, and we drank it while standing on his deck overlooking Paradise Valley. It felt great being with my boyfriend and not having to dodge the bad guys.

"I'm going to take a shower and get myself presentable," I said after the drink. "I know I have plenty of clothes over here."

I stepped into Max's shower and turned the water to hot. I stood there and let myself relax while the water cascaded all over my body.

I'd finished with my hair and was thinking about getting out when I heard the bathroom door open and then softly close.

I'd wondered what had been taking him so long.

Thirty seconds later, Max joined me in the shower. "I hope you don't mind some company," he said. "But you said I needed to make it up for laughing at you. Maybe I can help by scrubbing your back?"

"Nope," I teased. "I've already done that part. You'll need to come up with another way of pleasing me."

"Oh, really?" he asked. "Well, what about this?"

Oh my god!

"Yup," I moaned out. "That will definitely do it. Um, how long do we have until Beatrice's dinner is done?"

"I'd say we have at least an hour."

"Okay, that's long enough for a really good start," I moaned out as I reached up and kissed him. "Then we can continue after dinner."

"You're reading my mind," he said as he bent down to kiss me back.

Yes!

I knocked on the door to Grandma Henderson's apartment a little after nine on Monday morning. When she opened the door, she was in her purple jogging suit, holding a bottle of Diet Pepsi.

"Good morning, dear," Grandma said brightly as she motioned me in. "I bet you're here to see Marlowe."

"Hi, Grandma," I said. "You're right. I've been worried about him."

"Well, like I told you, he's fine. With the medication Doctor Dusty gave him, it only took him a day to get better."

"Thank you for doing that. It was frustrating being stuck in the mountains and not being able to take care of him."

As we were talking, Marlowe sauntered out of the kitchen. He looked up at me and gave me one of his squeaky meows. He then walked up and rubbed against my leg, all the while purring loudly.

I'm so glad he's better.

I walked into my apartment holding my purring cat and was thrilled to be back home.

I made it into the office a little after eleven. Gina was working at her desk, and Sophie was flipping through her tablet. Both of my best friends looked up as I entered.

"Hey, Laura," Gina said. "We heard about your adventure up in Sycamore Springs this weekend. It sounds like you not only found the client's mother, but you also found the men who'd murdered his father."

"The news story only hit the internet this morning," Sophie said. "But from what we read in the Cottonwood paper, both of the Mercer brothers were severely injured as they resisted arrest. The story also said that two civilians helped to capture them. Somehow, knowing you, I don't think that tells the full story."

"Yeah, well," I said. "You know how it goes. The papers sometimes exaggerate things."

"The news said that Dalton suffered a compound leg fracture and that Morgan had a cracked kneecap," Gina said, a slight grin on her face. "Are you saying that you had nothing to do with that?"

"Nope," I said, shaking my head. "I'm totally innocent for both of those."

"Yeah, right," Sophie snorted and rolled her eyes.

As we were chatting, Debbie walked into the back offices. "Hey, Laura, I'm glad you're here. Lenny's been in a great mood all morning. You must've done good work up there. He was so distracted about going down to the precinct offices with Valerie Mercer that he forgot to give you any new assignments. If I were you, I'd head home before he comes back and remembers."

"I'm only here for lunch," I said, holding my hands up. "After that, I'm heading home for a nap."

"Well, Lenny likely won't be back until after two," Debbie

said. "Count me in for lunch."

After forwarding the phone, flipping the sign from *Open* to *Be Back at 1:00,* and locking up the office, the four of us headed down the street toward Dos Gringos. As we walked by the Desert Vistas art gallery, it looked like it was about ready for the grand opening.

Olivia saw us walking by and motioned for us to come in. Susan was also there and hurried over to unlock the door.

"I'm glad you came by," Olivia said. "Evelyn Tasker from The Art Loft in Sycamore Springs called to chat this morning. I think she said that you'd been up there to see her and that your client might start dating her daughter. Did I get that right?"

"Yeah," I said. "It seems like it might work out that way."

"Evelyn talked about Cici, and it turns out that we were right. She's a new artist at the gallery. Evelyn sent me some images of her work, and she's quite good, especially considering her age. I let her know I still had space for a half dozen pieces, and she's arranging it with the artist."

"That's great," I said. "I got a chance to meet Cici while I was up in Sycamore Springs. She's nice, and I'm glad she'll be able to show her paintings in Scottsdale."

As we were chatting, a small sedan with heavily tinted windows drove by and tossed something out the window. There was a loud crash, and the front window of the gallery shattered.

Susan shrieked, and Olivia ducked behind her desk as an old quart milk bottle bounced across the floor and landed against the far wall. It was filled with an amber liquid and had a rag jammed into the top. It didn't break, but the liquid began to seep out slowly.

Crap.

I caught the smell of gasoline and hurried over to pick it up before more could spill on the floor. Gina saw that I was dealing with the fire bomb and ran out the front door to try to get the license plate.

She came back a moment later, shaking her head. A note in bold black lettering was taped to the side of the bottle. Being careful not to handle the Molotov cocktail any more than I'd already done, I placed it on Olivia's desk as we gathered around to read it.

Bitch, I'm back. Be afraid. Next time, I'll light the wick.

"Who would do something like this?" Olivia asked, anger and worry in her voice.

"Shit," I blurted out.

"What?" everyone asked in unison.

"That," I said, pointing to a colorful doodle on the corner of the note. It was a crude drawing of a red rose with a green stem.

"What about it," Sophie asked.

"Oh, shit," Susan said. "That's his tattoo."

"Whose tattoo?" Olivia, Gina, Sophie, and Debbie all asked at once.

"Jonathan LaRose," I said. "The former head of security at the Black Castle Casino."

"You mean that creep who tried to kidnap Susan and was going to leave me to die of dehydration?" Olivia asked, a look of surprise and fear on her face.

"But you told us that he was dead," Susan said. Her face had gone pale, and she started to shake.

"I thought he was," I said. "But it seems like he's back."

Susan and Olivia looked at each other and then at me.

"What are we going to do?" Susan asked.

Later in the day, I met with Johnny Scarpazzi and Gabriella and shared what had occurred at the Desert Vistas art gallery. I then reviewed the details of my earlier interaction with the former head of security at the Black Castle Casino.

Gabriella had already briefed her boss beforehand, but based on his questions, I was able to provide some of the missing information. This included Jonathan's sadistic side as I described the pleasure he derived from watching Susan and me suffer at his hand.

The guy was serious scum, and I'd thought he was already dead. It was hard to express my disappointment that he wasn't.

Two weeks later, things seemed to have settled down. I'd gotten a new assignment from Lenny, but we hadn't heard anything more from Jonathan LaRose or anyone else from Las Vegas. According to Max, it was likely only the calm before the storm, and everyone on Johnny's side of the business was on alert.

I was working in the back offices with Gina and Sophie when Debbie got on the intercom to let us know that a box had been delivered and that it was addressed to me. We all went to the front, where a wooden crate about three feet high by four feet wide was leaning against a wall.

When we opened it, it was Cici's painting of Bell Rock, the same one we'd watched her sign on our first day at The Art Loft. Along with the painting, Cici had enclosed a note:

Dear Laura, I've been gathering bits and pieces about what's been going on in Longview for the past year. Jeannie and I have always suspected there'd been some sort of trouble, but according to Grandpa, my dad and my uncle murdered Bill Tillman, who turned out to be Lance's stepdad. He also said that Lance is actually my brother. I don't really understand everything that went on, but I know that you were the one who set things on the right track. I saw in your eyes how much you liked this painting, and I want you to have it. I know you'll appreciate it more than a random collector would. Think about me whenever you look at it. Cici.

"Wow, that's a beautiful painting," Gina said. "You're right about Cici. She's really good."

"*Awww,*" Sophie said. "I remember that place. It's where we looked for the vortex and found our rock."

"Where are you going to put it?" Debbie asked.

"Too bad there isn't any room in the back offices to hang something that big," Sophie said, sounding a little disappointed."

"I think I'll take it home and hang it over my couch," I said. "My apartment could use some classing up. Besides, it will be great to have something on my wall to remind me of our trip to Sedona last year."

Epilogue

The trial of Morgan and Dalton Mercer for the murder of Bill Tillman was held at the Maricopa Superior Courthouse in Mesa. Between the physical evidence and the testimony of Valerie, Lance, Deputy McGill, and Val's old diary, the outcomes were never in doubt.

Porter Mercer didn't testify, but he sat in the front row of the courtroom every day of the trial. The news reported that he was emotionless during the proceedings, but after getting to know him, I could only imagine the turmoil that must have been going on in his heart.

What made it worse for the Mercer brothers was that they turned on each other during the trial, each saying the other was the mastermind of the murder. They each claimed that they only went to Scottsdale to make sure things didn't get out of hand with the other brother.

Destroying their testimony was the coroner's report that Bill Tillman had been shot with bullets from two different guns and that either wound would have been fatal on its own. Surprisingly, the person giving the testimony was Doctor Wilson, the county medical examiner I'd gotten to know a few months before.

It only took the jury three hours to return their verdicts. Both brothers were found guilty of murder in the first degree.

Before sentencing, the brothers begged the court for mercy, but with their prior criminal records and the heinous nature of the crime, the judge threw the book at them. When the sentences were handed down, each brother faced life in prison without the possibility of parole.

My schedule had been open enough to let me attend a couple of days of the trial. I couldn't help but notice that Porter Mercer had seemed to bond with his newly found grandson.

I was glad since Lance was still hurting from the loss of his father, and Porter was in the process of losing his two sons. I knew that both Lance and Porter could have somewhat of a new beginning.

It's crazy how these things sometimes work out.

About a month after the trial of the Mercer brothers, Lance and Gwen invited me to dinner. By now, she was back to teaching in Tempe and said they had some news.

Gwen mentioned that she hoped I could bring my boyfriend, and Max was good-natured about it when I asked him to join us. When Lance saw who I was with, his eyebrows rose in surprise, but he didn't seem to want to ask any questions about the fight by the river. That was fine by me.

The first bit of news was the sparkly engagement ring on Gwen's finger.

"Congratulations," I said when I saw the ring. "That's fantastic news."

"That's not all," Lance said. "Over the past few months, I've been getting to know Porter. He told me that he'd always been disappointed that neither of his sons or granddaughters had ever shown a knack for business. He was concerned for the future of the ranch after he wasn't able to run it anymore. He'd even contemplated having to sell it when he retired."

"Okay," I said. "Was that your news?"

"No," Lance laughed. "A few weeks ago, Porter told me that if I'd consider moving up to the Laughing Armadillo, he'd have me take over the day-to-day operation of the ranch."

"That's a great offer," I said. "Are you going to do it?"

"I am," he said with a nod. "I'm still in the process of learning about my mom's side of the family, and this will definitely help with that. My grandmother also thinks it will be good for me to connect with more of the family."

"With you living in Tempe and Lance living full-time in Sycamore Springs, what will you do?" I asked Gwen.

"I guess that's the last part of our news," she said. "Ever since my dad died, I know my mom's been a little lonely. I'd love to be with her all year round, but I've built a good life in Tempe and always hesitated to go through with it."

"What about now?" I asked.

"I know the elementary school in Sycamore Springs is always looking for teachers, and I gave them a call. There're a couple of positions opening up, and I'm heading up next week for an interview."

"That's fantastic," I said. "I'm sure you'll get a great job."

Max lifted his glass. "To new friends Lance and Gwen. Congratulations on the new beginnings."

The last I heard, Lance had moved into Longview to be with his grandfather, mother, sister, cousin, and new fiancée. I even heard that his grandmother was considering moving up as well. He then sold his home in Scottsdale as well as his business.

Gwen got a job teaching second grade at Sycamore Springs Elementary School and was scheduled to start at the beginning of the spring semester.

She even promised to invite me to the wedding.

I can't wait!

On the following pages, please enjoy a special preview of:

Hula Homicide:

A Kristy Piper Aloha Lagoon Mystery

by B A Trimmer.

Hula Homicide:

A Kristy Piper Aloha Lagoon Mystery

by B A Trimmer

After divorcing her cheating husband, Scottsdale wedding planner Kristy Darby, now Kristy Piper, had finally achieved her lifelong dream of moving to paradise when she took a job in Hawaii as the Aloha Lagoon resort wedding planner on the gorgeous island of Kauai. Sun, surf, sandy beaches, and glowing brides... what could possibly go wrong?

Turns out, everything...

GEMMA HALLIDAY PUBLISHING

HULA HOMICIDE

NOT CROSS

CRIME SCENE DO NOT C

Aloha

Lagoon

B.a. Trimmer

Hula Homicide

A Kristy Piper
Aloha Lagoon Mystery

B A Trimmer

Chapter One

"Kristy, my necklace is missing," Aunt Audrey moaned as she dropped into one of the chairs at our table. "I'm sure it's been stolen."

"Stolen?" I asked, my voice rising. "Are you talking about that gorgeous diamond and ruby necklace you wore last night?"

As the wedding planner for the Aloha Lagoon Resort, I was responsible for the wedding party's happiness and ensuring everything went smoothly. Hearing that somebody stole a necklace that must have been worth two hundred thousand dollars was a lousy way to start the week.

"I'm afraid so," Aunt Audrey said, anger and disappointment etched on her face.

Audrey Wentworth was a spry-looking seventy-five-year-old with a kind disposition and dark hair pulled back in a neat bun. She was the aunt of the bride, Carly Clarkson, who would marry Justin Cooper on Saturday, four days from now.

Due to Aunt Audrey's generosity, the ten members of the wedding party were spending the week at the resort. From what I'd been able to gather, she was a wealthy, childless widow who'd always had a soft spot for Carly, her only niece.

"Well, you definitely had it last night at the reception," I said. "When did you discover it was missing?"

Even though the Aloha reception was for Carly and Justin, the star of the show was Aunt Audrey. Hanging around her neck was a stunning diamond and ruby festoon necklace on a shiny gold chain. The pear-shaped center diamond must have been four or five carats, and the dozen side diamonds and rubies appeared to be over two carats each.

I'd been immediately impressed and completely jealous. Several resort guests in the reception lounge had commented on how beautiful it was.

"I think it was taken while we were at breakfast today," Aunt Audrey said, her voice tinged with disgust. "When I was dressing to go down to the beach, I thought I would check on my necklace, but it wasn't in the jewelry case that I always keep in my suitcase."

"Didn't you have it in the room safe?" I asked, slightly confused. "I'm pretty sure all the Huts have them."

"It's obvious now that I should have. But I've always heard those room safes are easy to break into and are the first place a thief would look."

"Have you alerted the resort?" I asked, although I knew there was usually not much they could do about a theft.

"I just spent an hour with Jimmy Toki, the head of resort security," Aunt Audrey said, looking depressed. "I showed him my room and the luggage where I kept the necklace. My next stop is the local police station to file a report."

"Would you like some company while you do that?" I asked. Taking an Uber to the police station didn't sound like much fun.

Aunt Audrey's eyes softened with gratitude as she looked at me. "No, I'll be fine. Jimmy's arranged everything. It's just that the piece has a lot of sentimental value for both Carly and me. I'd planned on giving it to her as a wedding present."

After again assuring me that she didn't need me to accompany her, Aunt Audrey left the table.

I looked over at my assistant, Leilani Alana. She'd silently followed the entire exchange.

"Wow," Leilani said. "That really sucks."

Leilani was not only my assistant at work but also my best friend. I met her the day after I arrived in Kauai almost six months ago, and we've been inseparable ever since.

Although people had told us we were nearly identical in personality and attitude, Leilani and I looked nothing alike. I was twenty-nine and tall, with long, mostly natural blonde hair. My eyes were green with flecks of gold and blue that seemed to change colors depending on the day and my mood.

Leilani was twenty-seven and wasn't quite as tall as me. She was graced with the long, luxuriant, dark hair of a native Hawaiian. She had huge brown eyes, a broad smile, and a gorgeous, expressive face. She was as close as I'd ever come to having a little sister.

Our table was one of many scattered around the outside patio of The Lava Pot, the resort's beachside tiki bar. As required by management, we both wore khaki shorts and our official Aloha Lagoon blue polo shirts.

This was our favorite spot to hang out whenever we scheduled a beach day. The location allowed us to keep an eye on the wedding party, and the big table umbrella gave us plenty of shade.

As always, it was a beautiful day in paradise. The temperature was perfect, delightfully warm, with a gentle touch of humidity.

A light breeze ruffled the fronds of the coconut palms along the beach. Fluffy white clouds dotted the sky over the emerald blue of the ocean, signaling fantastic weather for the foreseeable future.

Per the bride's request, the first full day of the week was

spent on the beach. Leilani and I watched as the members of the wedding party played a friendly game of three-on-three beach volleyball in one of the sandpits next to the tiki bar.

Typical for the middle of the afternoon, The Lava Pot was doing a brisk business. People were wandering up in a steady stream from the beach to order a beer, a Shark Bite, a Mai Tai, or the house's signature cocktail, the Lava Flow. People on the deck were bobbing their heads to the upbeat classic rock pumping out from inside the bar.

We'd barely begun discussing the disappearance of the necklace when we heard a high-pitched scream from a woman on the beach.

"Jeez," Leilani moaned. "What now?"

As we looked toward the noise, we saw one of the bridesmaids, Roxanne Grant, kicking and screaming as she was hauled down the beach over the shoulder of Alex Adair. It appeared that the good-looking groomsman was intent upon tossing her into the Pacific.

Somehow, I wasn't surprised. I'd already pegged Roxanne as the troublemaker of the group. Since arriving the previous afternoon, she'd openly flirted with every guy she'd come across, whether they were married or not. It had been only a matter of time before something happened with Roxanne as the center of attention.

Since I meet so many people at these weddings and names are always hard for me to remember, especially during the first few days, I typically give everyone a private nickname. For these two, it had been easy; he was Movie Star Alex, and she was Flirty Roxanne.

Judging by their body language, Roxanne had apparently said something snarky to Alex as they'd stood together on the beach, watching the group volleyball game. In retaliation, he'd snatched her up and was carrying her down the sand to the surf, her long red hair swishing against the back of Alex's legs.

The way she was twisting and struggling had me worried. Her neon-strawberry bikini top was already a size too small, barely covering her oversized, perfectly tanned boobs. It appeared we were about to have a severe wardrobe malfunction.

Some of the other guys in the wedding party, and a few tourists walking along the boardwalk, must have been thinking along the same lines. Many of them were watching the scene with blatant interest.

"Kristy?" Leilani asked nervously as her eyes followed the spectacle on the beach. "He's not really going to toss her in. Is he?"

By now, the rest of the wedding party had paused their volleyball game to watch the scene unfolding on the beach. There was some laughing and a few good-natured shouts of "Do it!"

One of the groomsmen lifted his beer and called out, "Roxanne, you're going to sleep with the fishes." Even a couple of the bridesmaids were smiling at the exhibition, no doubt thinking it was karma for the shameless way she'd been teasing the men.

"Damn," I groaned. "I think he might actually throw her in."

Instead of smiling and laughing as I would have expected if it had been part of a joke, Alex's jaw was clenched, and he looked like he was fuming. What had Flirty Roxanne said to him? Had she insulted his mother? His manhood?

The bridesmaid twisted and struggled to free herself. Unfortunately, Roxanne's arms were pinned to her sides, and she couldn't do more than kick her legs and shout what I had to assume were vile insults.

As Alex marched with his helpless captive down to the waterline, several sunbathing tourists swiveled their heads to see what the commotion was about.

Although I was appalled by his actions, I had to acknowledge that Alex was classically handsome with his boyish face and medium-length blond hair, as well as a decent body. He'd even arrived in Hawaii with a golden tan.

Once Alex was up to his ankles in the water, he paused. Roxanne stopped struggling, likely thinking he'd changed his mind. But it was clear that Alex was only waiting for the next wave to roll up to the beach.

When it did, he easily tossed the bridesmaid a good six feet out into the ocean. With arms waving and another frantic scream, Roxanne landed with a splash we heard all the way up at The Lava Pot.

Although most of the wedding party clapped and thought it was hilarious, the bride and a couple of the other bridesmaids looked at each other, shock and worry on their faces, before rushing down to the surf as a group to help a soggy Roxanne out of the water.

"Should you go down and referee?" Leilani asked, her head tilted and her eyebrows raised.

"Hmm, not yet. Her hair didn't get too wet, and she's got plenty of people there to help her out. When's our new photographer supposed to arrive? A photo of Roxanne screaming as she flew through the air would've made some fun wedding memories."

I was finding it hard to sympathize with Roxanne's plight. It wasn't something I was proud of, but women like that rubbed me the wrong way.

"Jake should've been here already," Leilani said with a deep sigh. "I told him the wedding party would have their first group get-together at noon, here at The Lava Pot."

I gave her a look to show what I thought of the friend of her brother we'd hired to shoot photos of the wedding. I tried to make the look somewhere between irritated and thoroughly annoyed.

"I don't know why he's late," Leilani said as she raised her palms and shrugged her shoulders. "Don't give me that look. I'll give him a call."

She pulled out her phone and scrolled through her contacts. "Maybe he's just on island time?"

I shook my head. When you're a wedding planner and have events timed to the minute, *island time* isn't a term you ever want to hear, especially in connection with someone you'd just hired.

Finding a wedding photographer had turned out to be a lot harder than I'd expected. The good ones tended to be artistic souls who'd go wherever the spirit took them. Hawaii has too many beautiful locations to keep any of them tied down in one spot for more than a month or two.

Leilani's older brother, Kai, had recommended his friend, Jake Hunter, insisting he was an incredible artist who had his own photography business. Of course, I'd met Kai several months ago. My impression had been that the only things he seemed to be interested in were girls and surfing. I wasn't sure if his judgment of what made a good wedding photographer would be all that reliable.

I sighed. Truthfully, I was beginning to get desperate. If this new guy didn't work out, I'd have to pull out the ancient digital SLR camera we kept in the office for emergencies and start taking the pictures myself.

* * *

Twenty minutes after the incident on the beach, the ten

people who made up the Clarkson-Cooper wedding party seemed to be in a festive mood again, and the celebration itinerary was back on track. The volleyball game had settled into a steady rhythm with plenty of good-natured laughing and gentle teasing.

Members of the group who weren't actively playing were clustered around the sandpits, chatting and sipping colorful drinks. Almost everyone was smiling, laughing, and seeming to be enjoying themselves. For a wedding planner, that was the best possible outcome.

Clearly, Roxanne had recovered from being tossed into the ocean as she was back to chatting with the groomsmen. Her target was now Angry Eddy Martin.

I'd only briefly met Eddy the night before, and I didn't know a lot about him. I found him to be more rugged than handsome, with a square face, short dark hair, and a thick mustache. He was a barrel-chested man with hairy arms that were covered with tattoos. He was a little shorter than the other men in the group, but he appeared to be powerfully built.

From what I could tell, he wasn't a man who liked to smile a lot. In fact, every time I'd seen him, he'd struck me as being aggravated and spoiling for a fight.

Carly Clarkson, the bride, had mentioned that Eddy worked in trucking and warehousing. However, she hadn't known exactly how he was involved in either.

Like the rest of the wedding party, Eddy had been friends with the bride and groom since college. From what I could tell, everyone in the group still lived scattered throughout the San Francisco Bay Area.

Flirty Roxanne held a Mai Tai in one hand while her other hand rested on Eddy's shoulder. As she talked, she leaned in and rubbed up against him. I watched her "accidentally" press herself against him three or four more times before he narrowed his eyes, cocked his head to the side, and gave her a questioning look.

She flashed a shy little half-smile and shrugged her shoulders to acknowledge he'd caught her. The muscles in his jaw tensed as his gaze quickly flicked over to Alex and the best man, Wealthy Derek Williams. They were both talking near the patio of The Lava Pot, slightly apart from the rest of the group.

Eddy turned his attention back to Roxanne, and they spoke to each other quietly for a moment. Eddy then relaxed, now looking much less irritated, and nodded his head.

Her mission accomplished, Flirty Roxanne sauntered off to talk to other people in the group with a smug smile on her face. Meanwhile, Eddy took a long, thoughtful sip of his drink as he watched her backside sway seductively as she walked away.

I glanced down at my watch, then raised an eyebrow at Leilani. "Well?" I asked. "Where's our photographer?"

"He just sent me a text," she said, breathing a sigh of relief. "He's on his way." Her look implied that none of what happened was her fault.

"Well, he's almost missed group beach day," I said with a disappointed shake of my head. "Not having beach pictures on top of a missing necklace isn't how I wanted today to go."

* * *

Once the volleyball game finished, everybody took a break to head back into The Lava Pot for drink refills. The best man, Wealthy Derek Williams, detoured by where Leilani and I were sitting.

I'd met Derek the night before at the Aloha reception. He was about the same age as the rest of the group. After college, he'd started a network technology company in Silicon Valley that had made him rich.

With a slightly soft body and short dark hair sticking out at all angles, I got the impression that Derek wasn't the type to take care of himself. Most of the time, there was a hint of a smile on his face, as if the idea of hanging out with his old college friends was mildly amusing.

The Dolce & Gabbana camouflage cargo shorts and Valentino print shirt he wore matched well with his diamond-studded Rolex watch but were a bit over-the-top. After so many years of drooling over luxury fashion on the internet, it was always entertaining to see someone wearing it.

"Hi, Derek," I said. "How's everything going?"

"Kristy," he said in the clipped tones of an employer addressing a subordinate. "I want to talk with you about my bungalow. According to what I was told, I'd have an ocean view."

Everyone in the group was staying in one of several high-end guest villas scattered between the main building and the beach. The resort had labeled these as *The Huts*, but the name really didn't do justice to the beautiful two-story private cottages.

"Oh no," I said. "Did you not get one?"

"Well, technically. If I stand on the corner of the second-story balcony, I can see the ocean. But it's hardly what I'd call a great ocean view. I'd like to have it changed to something more reasonable."

These types of problems and requests frequently came up throughout a typical wedding week. As a result, I always encourage the guests to use me as their personal concierge, travel agent, party host, and all-around problem solver. If I could tell jokes or juggle flaming bowling pins, I'd probably be asked to do that as well.

"No worries," I said. "Check back in a few minutes. We'll make sure to get it changed around."

It was clear Derek had been building up for an argument and seemed to deflate slightly when he realized there wouldn't be one. "Oh," he said. "Very well. Thanks for getting that done."

When Derek took off to rejoin the game, Leilani called Summer at the front desk to make the updated arrangements. I then noted the room change on my tablet.

"There he is," Leilani said with relief as she looked toward the entrance to the bar. She stood up and waved to get his attention.

I turned to get a look at my new photographer, prepared to give him a proper chewing out for being so late.

Oh my.

The person standing at the entrance of The Lava Pot turned out to be not what I had been expecting. For one thing, he was incredibly handsome in that tall, broad-shouldered kind of way, and for another, he was somewhere in his early to mid-thirties. I don't know why, but I'd been expecting someone a lot younger.

A tight black and green University of Hawaii Rainbow Warriors T-shirt showcased the muscles of his chest and arms, while a pair of casual khaki cargo shorts showed off his well-defined legs. Even the man's feet were attractive in his leather sandals, and I usually am not the kind of person to check out a guy's feet.

He had the kind of deep tan that a Mainlander gained by living on the island full-time. But what really struck me were his curly dark hair and piercing blue eyes. The man was serious eye-candy.

"Sorry I'm late," he said, flashing me a brilliant smile as

he walked up and extended his hand. "I'm Jake Hunter."

"Look, Jake," I started after we shook, prepared to lay into him. "If you're going to do this, I can't have you stroll in late to…"

"How much longer will everyone be out here?" he interrupted, pulling a high-end Nikon camera out of his bag and removing the lens cap. From the gold band next to the focus ring, I could see the lens was a professional model.

"About forty-five minutes," I said as I glanced down at my watch. "Maybe a little less. But listen, I can't have you…"

"Plenty of time," he interrupted *again*, even as he smiled at me with a lopsided grin. "By now, they've all had a drink or two, and no one will be shy about getting their picture taken."

Turning, he hopped onto the sand and made his way to the volleyball pits. Frustrated that I didn't get a chance to vent, I mentally crossed my fingers and hoped he at least knew what he was doing. A lousy photographer could leave a bride in tears and cause lasting problems for the wedding planner.

For the next twenty minutes, I watched as Jake wove in and out of the group, easily inserting himself into the moment. Judging by his cocky attitude, I figured he'd be completely lame when it came to taking photos. Honestly, I'd dreaded the worst, like a puppy who's adorable but still destroys your house.

Instead, I was pleasantly surprised by how effortless he made it seem. His photography style appeared to be a combination of casually chatting with people and taking pictures.

Jake quickly worked his way through the entire group, making sure to get shots of everyone. Unlike some photographers I'd worked with who were intrusive, everyone seemed to be relaxed with Jake.

When he got to Flirty Roxanne, I couldn't help but notice she spent several moments positioning herself in some rather suggestive poses. Although she'd obviously tried to entice him, he'd waited until she relaxed into something more presentable before taking the photos.

Jake then gathered everyone together for a group picture as the players switched sides. It didn't take him more than a minute or so to correctly stage everyone, complete with a breathtaking backdrop of palm trees and the beach.

I heard the rapid *ping-ping-ping* as he took a burst of eight or ten shots. He glanced at the back of his camera, then looked up with a dazzling smile. "Perfect. Thanks, everybody."

The group quickly scattered, everyone going back to the game. I was utterly amazed. Jake had done in two minutes what I'd seen other photographers struggle with for ten minutes or more.

As I watched Jake work, I noticed the way the light breeze coming off the ocean ruffled his hair. It looked so soft that I started to wonder what it would feel like to run my fingers through it.

Clearly, my lack of male companionship over the last six months had affected how I looked at men. I was starting to get hungry. I hated to admit that I hadn't been on more than two dates in a row with anyone since I'd arrived at Aloha Lagoon.

Chapter Two

Carly-the-bride wandered over to join Leilani and me at our table. In her early thirties, she was a pleasant-looking, somewhat curvy woman who seemed to be one of those people totally happy in her own skin.

Her smile was sweet, her brown eyes crinkling at the corners. I loved how the shag cut with curtain bangs and subtle highlights flattered her.

I'd met her in person the day before when she'd flown in with Justin Cooper, her husband-to-be. Fortunately, she'd been my favorite kind of bride to work with, realistic and organized.

Carly was decked out in full bride-to-be gear. She sported a white one-piece swimsuit that flattered her curves. Gold cursive lettering proclaiming *The Bride* was splashed across her chest. And a sparkly silver tiara graced the top of her head.

From her happy laughter, it was apparent she hadn't yet heard about the missing necklace. I briefly considered telling her, but the news would ruin her afternoon, and I didn't want to be the one to do that. I was confident her aunt would tell her soon enough.

"Kristy"—she beamed at me—"you were right about everything. The beach is fantastic. How are we doing on time? I have the schedule on my phone, but I left it in the bungalow."

So much for being organized.

I pulled my tablet from my bag and flipped it open. "We'll

wrap up here in about fifteen minutes," I said. "That'll give everyone plenty of time to clean up, get dressed, and make it to the Ramada Pier for the luau by six-thirty. They'll serve dinner and start the show at seven. Tomorrow morning is sightseeing. We'll meet at the entrance to the lobby and leave at nine."

Suddenly, we heard a frantic scream. We looked up to see that Movie Star Alex had grabbed another bridesmaid. His latest victim was the maid of honor, Lauren Maxwell.

"Jeez," Leilani grumbled. "What's up with that guy?"

"Kristy?" Carly moaned, looking at me like his actions were something I had control over.

Again, Alex had his victim slung over his shoulder and was effortlessly holding her with one arm, her slim frame making his job easier. His other hand held the remains of a Lava Flow.

He took a few steps towards the surf but then turned to smile back at the group. They all shouted out, "Boo!" and "You suck!"

Somewhere along the way, Lauren had lost her oversized black plastic-framed glasses. She pounded on his back and kicked her legs in front of his face.

When I'd met Lauren the day before, she'd struck me as painfully shy. Now, she was loudly shouting a string of profanities at Alex, something that surprised me.

The night before, I'd been amused to see her dressed in an aloha shirt decorated with colorful Pokémon characters. Today, her pink one-piece swimsuit sported a picture of the anime cartoon character Sailor Moon. I was starting to think of her as Anime Lauren. The cobalt-blue tips and highlights in her shoulder-length brunette hair coordinated well with her suit.

Unlike earlier, when Alex had snatched up Roxanne, it seemed like he'd grabbed Lauren simply for the fun of it. There was a wide, goofy smile on his face before he laughed and tossed back the rest of his drink, flinging the plastic cup on the beach. He then turned and started walking towards the surf.

"Loser!" one of the bridesmaids yelled out to Alex.

I sighed and stood up, knowing that as the wedding planner, I needed to go out and have a heart-to-heart with Alex. I'd have to remind him he was here because of Carly and Justin, the happy couple, and he shouldn't do anything to spoil the occasion.

I'd just stepped onto the sand, and Alex hadn't made it more than five or six steps toward the ocean when Jake stepped in front of him. Alex tried to go around, but Jake again blocked his path.

Alex absentmindedly let go of Lauren, and she landed on the beach with a thud. He casually stepped over her to get in my photographer's face. I was still too far away to hear what the men were saying, but after several moments, Alex got an icy look on his face and gave Jake a hard shove.

Surprisingly, Jake didn't budge. Instead, he returned the shove, and Alex was knocked back several steps before toppling to the sand.

No, Jake, you can't do that to a guest.

Alex quickly jumped up, rage on his face. His fists were tightly clenched as he readied himself for a fight.

The groomsman stared at Jake for a moment, breathing hard, before seeming to think better of it. He then turned to go back up the beach and almost ran into Lauren, who had climbed to her feet.

She stood, hands-on-hips, directly in front of Alex. She

was also breathing hard, her face red from anger and embarrassment.

Without warning, she swung her arm and, with a resounding *crack*, connected with a solid slap to his face. It appeared he hadn't been expecting it and didn't have time to avoid it.

"Ka-Pow!" somebody shouted from the volleyball pit. Most of the men and a few of the women started to clap—some were also laughing.

The blow was loud enough to be heard over the pounding of the waves, like a branch that had broken off the side of a tree. It staggered Alex, and he fell back onto the sand again.

"Slimebag!" Lauren shouted at Alex before turning and stomping up the beach in the direction of the bar.

Alex climbed unsteadily to his feet, angry and apparently looking to continue the confrontation with Lauren. Jake again stepped in front of him and shook his head.

By now, the encounter had lost its entertainment value, as Alex wisely chose to slink back to the volleyball game. I noticed everyone in the group avoided making eye contact with him.

"I'm starting to regret inviting Alex," Carly said with a deep sigh and a shake of her head when I returned to the table. "Lauren's right. He's acting like a jerk. I suppose he hasn't changed a lot since college."

"If you knew he was a bully, why'd you invite him?" I asked.

"Oh, he was Justin's roommate all through school. I couldn't invite everyone else and not ask him. I'm glad your photographer was there to stop him. He seems like a handy guy to have around."

I was starting to think I agreed with her.

Carly got up to retrieve Lauren's glasses, which had fallen on the beach. Then she followed the maid of honor, who'd stomped into the bar, obviously upset and wanting another drink.

I let everyone know they had time to relax and get ready for the luau. Several people seemed relieved as they packed up and headed back to their rooms. After what had just happened, many appeared to welcome the chance for a change of scenery.

* * *

The Ohana Luau was always one of the highlights of any wedding week. Ohana means family and people of all ages would attend the event. It was held at the Ramada Pier, an area of the resort on the beach set aside for larger events.

As I arrived, traditional Hawaiian music was being played on the main stage by a three-piece group featuring a steel guitar. The music was upbeat and foretold of a fun evening ahead.

Guests dressed in colorful aloha shirts and muumuus filtered onto the pier from the central part of the resort. They gathered around the bar and gradually filled the tables.

Several guests, most holding a complimentary beer or rum punch, had collected around the *imu,* the in-ground barbeque pit where a whole pig had been slowly roasting all day. With a great deal of ceremony, two shirtless Native Hawaiian men in colorful skirts removed the pig from the pit. They then carried it to an open-air kitchen along the side of the venue, where men in white coats and chef's hats prepared the pork in a style known as *pua'a kālua.*

I walked into the seating area and saw one of the groomsmen, Orson Cross, standing at the bar with two rum punch cocktails in front of him.

Orson was tall and thin, almost to the point of being

skinny. As with most of the wedding party, he was in his early thirties. His skin was pasty white, and his long brown hair was pulled back into a ponytail, emphasizing his skeleton-thin face and oversized nose.

Orson's eyes were riveted on a video game he was playing on a handheld gaming console.

"Hi, Orson," I said as I walked up to him. "Can I take your drinks to the table?"

He briefly looked up and smiled. "Hi, Kristy," he said. "Hold on. I'm almost done with the level."

With a final flourish, his fingers danced over the buttons. The video game played a happy fanfare, and Orson relaxed.

"We issued an update to this game today," he said as he shoved the device into his pocket. "I was making sure it was uploading correctly."

"Carly said you design computer games. Was that one of yours?"

He blushed pink and looked down at his feet. "Yeah, um, I'm the lead developer at the company. We're about to launch volume seven in the *Orc's Apprentice* series. The last release won Fantasy Game of the Year, so we're hoping for some decent sales."

"Wow," I said, thoroughly impressed. "I had no idea."

"Are you a gamer?" he asked.

"Um, no. I haven't played video games since I was a kid."

"You should try it," he said with a knowing grin. "The graphics and gameplay have come a long way since the old Nintendo Game Cubes and PlayStations."

I walked with Orson over to our table. Alex was off to the side, talking with Wealthy Derek. I noticed Orson went out of his way to avoid them.

Alex didn't look so much like a movie star anymore. The side of his face was red, and there was the start of a nasty bruise under his left eye.

When we reached our table, Orson delivered one of the rum punches to Anime Lauren, who also seemed to be actively avoiding Alex.

She'd changed into a short yellow dress with the Pokémon character Pikachu across her chest. I was glad to see she wasn't showing any ill effects from the earlier encounter on the beach.

"I'm here, on time," a voice behind me said. I turned to see Jake standing three feet away. He had a grin on his face as if he'd pulled something over on me.

That man has the most dangerous smile.

He'd changed into a tight black T-shirt and was wearing some kind of sensual cologne. I caught traces of wood, musk, and leather. I could picture Jake as a cowboy, sitting in front of an open fire with a soft drift of smoke.

There were parts of me that were slowly starting to wake up, parts that hadn't been awake in a long time, maybe not since my divorce, now almost seven months ago.

"I'm glad you made it," I said, doing my best to keep my voice even. "We have maybe thirty minutes until the buffet opens and the show starts."

"No worries," he said with his lopsided grin. "Let me know if there are any specific shots you want."

"Tonight should be simple. Take some general memory photos of the luau and the show. I'll also need candid photos of everyone and some small group shots. We have permission to use the luau stage for a group shot if you can get everyone up there, but don't force it."

"Okay, I'll see if they're in the mood for it."

"During dinner, they do the quieter part of the show," I said. "Nani Johnson does her ukulele numbers, and she sometimes has a singer with her."

"That should be easy. What else?"

"After that, the Aloha Lagoon Hula Wahines do some dance numbers with the guests. They already know about our wedding party. They'll pull Justin, our groom, up to hula in front of everyone, so make sure to get that."

"I'll shoot that in video," Jake said slowly as though he was mentally planning the shot. "If I stand behind the stage, I can rack focus to get some reaction pictures of Carly as he dances."

"Great idea. I can already imagine how well that'll work out."

"How late should I stay tonight?"

"Well, after the Hula Wahines, the Ahi Fire Knife Dancers come on stage. The house lights are then basically off for the rest of the show. You might as well take off after they start up."

"Perfect," he said as he nodded and gave me a wink. "I should have all the time I need."

Oh my god. He winked at me. I liked it, but who does that anymore?

"Don't forget," I reminded him. "We're meeting in the lobby tomorrow morning at nine o'clock for a group visit to the Fern Grotto. Make sure to get there a little early. The grotto's a beautiful place. It'll be a great setting to get candids and small groups."

"I'll be there," he said. "I looked at the raw images from this afternoon. Some of them are pretty good. I'll clean them up, and we can review them tomorrow whenever you have some time."

His cologne was starting to trigger thoughts that were definitely inappropriate for the workplace. I wondered if I could find out what it was so I could sprinkle a little on my pillow.

Jake started to circulate through the crowd. He worked the wedding party, chatting with people and shooting pictures. His muscles flexed and bunched as he turned the camera to capture different angles.

Jeez, I really need to find a boyfriend.

While I was mesmerized by Jake's physique, Aunt Audrey walked up to the table. Rather than one of the complimentary drinks, she held a glass of the resort's high-end reserve pinot grigio.

Reluctantly pulling my attention away from the view, I asked, "How'd it go with the police? Is there anything they can do about your necklace?"

"It doesn't appear so," she said, clearly disappointed. "I'd place more faith in Jimmy Toki. He seems a little more on the ball. The detective I talked to, Ray something, says there isn't a lot he can do."

"I'll work with Jimmy to see if he's learned anything yet."

"Thank you, dear. That necklace has always been Carly's favorite piece of jewelry. As a child, I'd let her wear it, and she'd pretend she was a princess."

On the stage, a shirtless native Hawaiian man wearing a colorful lavalava skirt blew a loud musical note on a conch shell, signaling the start of the feast.

* * *

In the relative calm between dinner and the main part of the show, I spent a few minutes chatting with bridesmaids Madeline and Victoria Trapp, a pair of identical twins. They were both tall and athletic, with similar hourglass figures.

Physically, the only thing that set them apart was their hair. Although both women had the same honey-blonde color, Victoria had long flowing tresses, while Madeline's locks were cut shoulder length.

"Hello, ladies," I said as I took an empty seat next to them. "You were both fantastic in the volleyball pit today."

"Thanks," Victoria said with a shrug. It was hard not to think of her as the sister with the long hair. "I thought we were terrible. We haven't played together since college. We were pretty good back then."

"Well, we *were*," Madeline said absentmindedly as she looked out at the rest of the wedding party. "But that was a long time ago. My serve is terrible, and I can barely set the ball anymore."

I caught a distracted tone from both women. I wanted to help if I could. "Is everything okay?" I asked. "Is there anything I can do for you while you're staying at the resort?"

"If you could turn back time about ten years, that would solve a lot of problems," Short-haired Madeline said in a wistful tone. There was a somewhat distant look in her eyes as her gaze lingered on Movie Star Alex and Wealthy Derek, who were now chatting with Carly and Justin, the bride and groom.

She turned and saw my puzzled look. She then gave a small laugh and shook her head. "It's okay," she said. "We're good."

"It's sweet of you to keep asking," Long-haired Victoria said as she flashed me a beautiful smile. "But we're fine."

"Okay," I said, a little discouraged. "Let Leilani or me know if anything comes up. We'll take care of it."

I didn't want to be overly pushy, so I let it go. As long as nothing spilled over to the rest of the wedding party, I'd gladly let them keep their secrets and work out their problems on their own.

By now, nearly everyone in the group was smiling and laughing. The lone exception was Angry Eddy Martin. He stood near the bar, looking out at the ocean, so I went over to talk with him.

He didn't look as grumpy and intimidating as he had earlier in the day, but he still didn't look all that friendly. He now seemed annoyed and frustrated, as if something was gnawing at him.

"Hi, Eddy," I said. "How's everything going?"

"It's alright," he said in a quiet, steady voice. "The resort is gorgeous. Carly and Justin chose a great place to get married."

"Have you known them both a long time?" I asked.

"We all started as freshmen together in the same dorm. Justin started dating Carly our sophomore year."

"That's a long time to know a group of people."

"Yeah," he said as he glanced over at Flirty Roxanne. "It's interesting seeing everybody again. I'd lost track of most of these people over the years."

"Do you know why Carly only invited people from college to be in the wedding party? I'm sure our bride and groom have family and friends they could have asked."

Eddy snorted out a laugh and nodded his head. "I hear it happened because Carly and Derek, the billionaire, have apparently stayed pen-pals all these years. The rumor is that Derek said he'd come to the wedding and even be the best man, but only if Victoria and Madeline Trapp were bridesmaids."

"Why those two?" I asked.

"He used to date Victoria. I think he even dated Madeline

for a while before that. So, since the first three people in the wedding party were part of the old circle from college, it snowballed from there. Carley has several sisters, and she used Derek as the excuse why they all couldn't be in the wedding party. I suppose it saved her from hurting anyone's feelings. As I understand it, the rest of the friends and family will show up later in the week."

"Deciding who to exclude from the wedding party is never easy," I agreed. "What did you think about how it happened?"

"Hey, we get to come out to paradise a week early, courtesy of Carly's aunt. I was all for it." He grunted and held up his beer. "One last time to get the old gang together."

* * *

Like the rest of the audience, I was entranced when the Ahi Fire Knife Dancers took the stage. This unique event combined athletic skill, unflinching bravery, and ever-present danger.

Jake spent a few minutes shooting the fire dancers, then returned to the table. Since he was done taking pictures for the night, I expected him to take off. Instead, he pulled out an empty chair and sat next to me.

A whiff of his cologne drifted past, and his presence pressed in on me. As the fire dancers transitioned from one scene to the next, Jake leaned in closer, his mouth brushing my ear, sending tingles along every nerve ending.

"Those guys are pretty good. Do they ever miss as they're tossing around those flaming knives?"

I turned so I could talk to him without having to raise my voice, which brought our faces to within a few inches of each other. As soon as I realized what had happened, my heart sped up a notch.

"In the six months I've been here, they've only missed a

couple of times," I said. "Haven't you ever seen the show before?"

"I haven't been to a luau in years. But we were always going to them when I was a kid. Whenever family would come over from the mainland, my parents would take us to one of the luaus. I've always loved them."

"Same for me," I sighed. "The first time I went to one was on my honeymoon, seven years ago. The marriage didn't work out so well, but I'll never forget the fun I had at the luau."

"How long ago was the divorce?" he asked. His deep blue eyes met mine, and I could sense he was genuinely interested in my answer.

"It was final about six months ago," I said with a shrug. "There weren't any kids, and he wanted to move on with his life, so it was a simple process."

He looked at me for a moment, then nodded. He reached out and lightly rested his fingertips on my arm. His touch felt both exciting and comforting.

"I understand what you must have gone through," he said quietly, a somewhat distant look in his eyes. "It's not easy when someone you care about no longer wants you."

He seemed to realize he'd brought down the mood, and he pulled his fingers away. I was a little sorry to feel them go.

He again gave me that lopsided smile and spread out his arms. "But it's hard to be sad when you live in paradise, huh?"

"It certainly helps," I said with a laugh. "Not living in the same city as before helps as well. Too many things there reminded me of my ex-husband."

"How did you end up at Aloha Lagoon?"

"I was lucky. I found out about the job through an ad the resort put in a wedding planner's magazine. The interview process was quick, and I've been working here ever since."

He looked like he was gearing up to say something else when he seemed to change his mind. "Okay," he said. "I'd better take off and start to clean up the pictures from tonight. I'll meet you down in the lobby a few minutes before nine tomorrow morning."

He got up, and my eyes followed him as he left the Ramada Pier. I knew I'd be thinking about him tonight.

Chapter Three

I made it to the Aloha Lagoon Wedding Center a little before eight the following day. The office was just off the cavernous main lobby, past the concierge desk, between the gift shop and Gabby's Island Adventures.

As I walked in, the bell above the door jingled. It was a pleasant and happy sound that always made brides smile.

Dorothy Campbell sat at her white desk concentrating on a document while Leilani stood next to the coffee pot, pouring herself a cup of Dorothy's custom-roasted Kona blend.

Dorothy had been the office manager at the Wedding Center for the last thirty-five years. Her parents had come to Kauai from Jamaica when she was a small girl. She pretty much considered herself a Hawaiian native, even though she'd managed to retain a slight Jamaican accent.

As always, Dorothy's clothes were neat as a pin, and her curly black and gray hair hung down to her shoulders. Her signature double-strand Mikimoto pearl necklace was draped around her neck, making the regulation resort polo look somewhat fashionable.

Dorothy's eyes were bright, her mind was sharp, and not a lot got past her scrutiny. She was one of the most organized people I'd ever known, and I was grateful to have her. She effortlessly took care of the hundreds of details that went into planning a destination event and could mentally keep track of twenty weddings at once.

I grabbed a mug of coffee and plopped down on the chair behind my desk. Unlike Dorothy's spotlessly clean workspace, mine always seemed to have several stacks of catalogs, magazines, and notebooks on it.

"How did it go yesterday?" Dorothy asked, her eyes shifting to Leilani. "How'd Jake do? I was a little surprised when you said he was a photographer. I didn't think he had any interests outside of computers and surfing."

"He seemed to do alright," Leilani said, maybe a bit annoyed that Dorothy would question her friend's abilities.

Dorothy didn't have a mean bone in her body. But since Leilani had recommended Jake, Dorothy would be pinning his results on her.

"Jake did fine," I echoed. "But yesterday was a mixed bag. There was a little friction on the beach in the afternoon. And I suppose you heard about Aunt Audrey's necklace possibly being stolen?"

"Leilani was telling me about it," Dorothy said. "It seems to be quite valuable."

"The center diamond alone must have been four or five carats," I said, a touch of envy in my voice. "There were another dozen diamonds and rubies besides that."

"Oh, really?" Dorothy asked. Her eyes sparkled at the thought.

"It totally bites that some jackwagon stole it," Leilani said.

"Why didn't she have it in the room safe?" Dorothy asked.

"When I asked her about it, she said she didn't think the room safes were all that secure," I replied. "She also mentioned that she'd planned on giving it to Carly to wear at the ceremony with her gown."

"Jeez, that would've made a nice present," Leilani moaned

enviously. "I should've been born to a wealthy family." She then shrugged it off. "What's the schedule for today?"

"The group had breakfast on their own," I said as I pulled out my tablet. "I imagine most of them went to the Rainbow Buffet or the Loco Moco. We have about half an hour before we need to go to the lobby and gather everyone up for Gabby's shuttle to the boat for the Fern Grotto."

"I always like it there," Leilani said as she nodded her head. "Standing on the grotto overlook is an excellent place for selfies."

"After that is a group lunch back here on the Ono Terrace at noon," I said as I flipped through the schedule. "They have the afternoon off, and I imagine most of them will head back to the beach. Tonight will be dinner and karaoke at the Loco Moco, starting at six."

With a thrill of anticipation, I knew I'd be working with Jake again. Hopefully, he'd be on time today. I didn't want to give Dorothy any reasons to be disappointed with him.

As I thought about my photographer and how good he'd smelled the night before, I realized I was beginning to develop a bit of a crush on the man.

"Maybe it's time to start dating again," I mumbled to myself.

"What?" Leilani asked, surprise in her eyes. "I thought you said you were through with men. I remember about a month ago, you said they were all scum and the world would be better off without them."

"Well…" I admitted, "Maybe I did. But I'm starting to rethink that position."

"Really?" she asked, confused. "With who? Are you talking about Alex Adair? He doesn't seem like your type."

"No," I confessed with a guilty grimace. "Jake Hunter."

Leilani laughed and wrinkled her nose. "Really?"

"Why would you say that? He likes girls, doesn't he?"

"Oh sure, he dated a woman named Michelle for about three years. I figured they'd get married, but four or five months ago, she dumped him for a condominium developer from Oahu. I guess she had some daddy issues. The guy was close to fifty years old."

"So, what's wrong with Jake?" I pressed.

"Nothing's wrong with him. But I've known him since I could walk. It's hard for me to think of him as dating material."

"It won't creep you out if I talk about it, will it?"

"Go ahead," she laughed. "Knock yourself out. Jake's always been nice to me, and he seems like a decent guy. So, go for it. Drag him behind a coconut palm if you want to."

Dorothy shook her head and gave us an eye roll. Fortunately, she had a pretty high tolerance for the things Leilani and I discussed.

We started going over the week's events when something caught Leilani's eye, and she stared into the lobby. "Uh-oh," she groaned. "Management doesn't look so happy today."

I sighed, knowing what was coming after the problems we'd had the day before. Actually, I'd sort of been expecting it.

The door to the Wedding Center opened with a friendly jingle, and David Mahelona walked in.

David headed the resort's human resources department. He was a large man with an islander heritage. Even after working at the resort for six months, I hadn't learned anything about him other than he was in a continuously lousy mood.

As he walked into the room, I could feel him occupying much of the office space. His shoulders were broad, his long dark hair was pulled back, and his expression was downright intimidating.

"Hello, David," Dorothy said, using her most soothing *dealing-with-a-client* voice. "What can we do for you today?"

"Good morning, ladies," he said to Dorothy and Leilani. He then turned to look at me. His smile was stiff and didn't make it up to his emotionless eyes.

"Kristy, we received a complaint yesterday afternoon from someone in your wedding party, a Mr. Alex Adair. He said he was on the beach when he was attacked by your photographer, Jake Hunter."

Leilani rolled her eyes and barked out a quick laugh. She quickly quieted when David glared at her. I sighed and shook my head.

"That's not what happened," I said. I knew I sounded annoyed, but I couldn't help it. David just rubbed me the wrong way.

"Alex had grabbed one of the bridesmaids and had thrown her over his shoulder. She wasn't happy about it and was screaming to be let down. Alex was walking down the beach, seemingly intent on tossing her into the ocean, when Jake stepped in front of him. Alex got annoyed and gave Jake a shove. Jake pushed him back. That was it. Jake actually resolved what could have turned into an ugly situation."

David stood impassively, but it was apparent he wasn't going to listen to anything I had to say.

"I do understand how guests can be, especially when there's alcohol involved," he said, trying to sound reasonable but completely failing. "Still, we can't have anyone associated with the resort involved with assaulting a guest. Next time something like that happens, he's out. If you're not able to control your employees better, you'll find yourself out as well."

David turned and left the office. The bell over the door jingled as he went.

"Well, he was more cheerful than usual," Leilani said.

"I don't know," Dorothy said, sounding worried. "He seemed pretty serious this time. You better keep Jake on a tight leash. I don't want to see anyone getting into trouble over something like that."

"Come on," I said to Leilani as I looked down at my watch. "Let's go find our group and our naughty photographer."

* * *

Leilani and I arrived at the front of the massive lobby, where we started to gather the wedding party. I imagine preschool teachers go through much the same process before beginning class.

The space was a hive of activity, as it always is in the morning. Bellhops were pushing carts full of luggage while people stood in line waiting to check out.

Flirty Roxanne and Gamer Orson had already arrived and were chatting near the lobby entrance. Leilani and I walked over to greet them as Orson noisily sipped on the remains of a Bloody Mary. Roxanne's long red hair looked especially fluffy today.

A few minutes later, we were joined by Victoria and Madeline, the blonde twins, as they entered the lobby from the direction of the conference center. They both wore matching outfits that showed off their long legs.

After saying hello to everyone, I stuck my head out to check the parking lot. I confirmed that Koma had the van from Gabby's Island Adventures waiting to take everyone down to the Wailua River to start the morning's excursion.

I've always liked Koma. At twenty-three, he and his twin sister Lana were full-blooded Hawaiians who worked for Gabby. He was handsome, muscular, and good-natured. All the ladies loved him.

I looked around, but Jake hadn't arrived yet. I hoped he wouldn't be late again. No matter how great he looked or smelled, I couldn't work with someone who didn't show up on time.

Aunt Audrey strolled into the lobby wearing white plastic sunglasses and an oversized sun hat. Walking behind her were the bride and groom, Carly and Justin.

Carly was wearing a sundress that flattered her curves, the sparkly silver tiara, and *The Bride* white sash. With his medium-length brown hair, medium height, round face, and slightly soft body, I was once again struck by how completely average Justin looked.

Angry Eddy came in and stood with the others. Looking at his solid build and the many tattoos covering his arms, he seemed somewhat intimidating. I noticed he surreptitiously eyed everyone and glanced around the lobby before joining the group.

At nine o'clock, Wealthy Derek and Anime Lauren wandered into the lobby. Derek's hair again looked like he'd towel-dried it and then forgot to comb it. Lauren had a nice outfit that showcased her fantastic figure and blue-tipped hair, but she also wore a headband with pink cat ears. It looked like she'd even used makeup to place a large black dot on the end of her nose and had drawn cat whiskers on her cheeks.

I conducted a final headcount and noticed that we were one person short. "Does anyone know if Alex is coming today?" I asked.

Victoria Trapp, the sister with the long hair, gave a little snort to show she didn't care if Alex came or not. Some additional snickers and murmurs of agreement joined her. *Loser* and *jackhole* were the two terms I heard most clearly.

"If we're voting, I'd say leave him here," Lauren said with a wicked grin.

"Or, why don't we take him but then not bring him back?" Roxanne suggested.

"I saw him earlier when I went to the gift shop," Derek volunteered. "But that was probably a half-hour or forty-five minutes ago. I think he was walking toward the meeting rooms," he said as he pointed down the hallway that led to the conference center.

"Alright," I said. "I'll give him another few minutes, then track him down. Has anyone seen Jake Hunter, our photographer?"

There were some blank looks, along with a few mutters and shaking of heads. Roxanne's eyes sparkled, and she bit her lower lip, apparently in appreciation of Jake.

I looked over at Leilani. She gave me two palms up and a slight shoulder shrug.

I felt a surge of irritation. Although Jake was utterly adorable, he was starting to become more trouble than he was worth.

Jeez, it's always one more thing.

We waited another five minutes while the wedding party milled about the lobby entrance. I walked over to Leilani. She had a slightly guilty expression.

"Um, I'm sorry," she said as she scrunched up her face. "I don't know where Jake is. I tried calling, but he didn't answer. Maybe he wasn't such a good choice for a photographer after all."

I sighed and shook my head. "Let's not worry about him

now. Run back to the office and grab the old camera. I'll get everyone on the shuttle. Go out with the group and take as many pictures as you can. I'll find Alex and drive him to the boat, assuming he still wants to go."

"Okay," she said as she beamed at me with her bright smile, eager to make up for Jake's tardiness. "I can do that."

As she turned to scamper back to the office, I led the group out to the van. I heard Carly telling Justin that the trip would probably be a lot quieter without Alex there to cause trouble.

Once everyone was settled, Leilani ran out of the lobby, holding the office camera bag. She climbed into the van, and I wished her luck with the excursion. As I headed back to the resort to start my search for Alex, I briefly paused to watch Koma maneuver the big vehicle out of the parking lot.

I sighed and shook my head. The wedding week had started out on a sour note. I only hoped it got better from here.

As I headed down the hallway that wound toward the conference and events center, I knew I only had about ten minutes to find my lost guest. If I couldn't track him down by then, the excursion boat to the Fern Grotto would leave with the wedding party, and Alex would miss the outing.

I passed the Kealia and the Alaka'i conference rooms within the conference center, and both appeared to be locked. I knew a door at the end of the hallway, next to the bathrooms, led out to the main pool, so I headed that way.

Traditional instrumental music played softly through overhead speakers as I quickly walked to the end of the hallway. I'd almost made it to the exit when I passed the Halelea conference room. Its door was slightly ajar, and the lights were on.

With a bad feeling, I stepped in and quickly glanced around, hoping to find a meeting in progress. Instead, I saw something on the floor and froze.

Jake lay crumpled against the back wall. He held his hand to the side of his head, and his leg was kicking out weakly. As I approached, I could hear him moaning almost inaudibly.

Oh my God.

A colorful tiki statue lay on the floor near him. It appeared to be one of the cheap versions you can pick up in any souvenir shop on the island. It was about two feet tall and looked to be made of wood or maybe hard plastic.

I hurried over to him and bent down. My mind was racing, and my questions tumbled out all at once. "Jake, what happened? Are you alright? Who did this to you?"

Jake kept blinking, as though his eyes weren't focusing very well. He didn't seem to recognize me. I knew he was injured, possibly severely.

Jake pointed across the room before his arm dropped back to the floor with a thud.

I glanced in the direction Jake had indicated. There was a table with a white cloth sitting in the center of the room. Sticking out from behind it, I could see a pair of men's legs, ending at a pair of brown leather sandals on the feet.

Oh no.

About the Author

Halfway through a successful career in technical writing, marketing, and sales, along with having four beautiful children, author B.A. Trimmer veered into fiction. Combining a love of the desert derived from many years of living in Arizona with an appreciation of the modern romantic detective story, the Laura Black Scottsdale Series was born.

Comments and questions are always welcome.

Email the author at LauraBlackScottsdale@gmail.com

Follow at www.facebook.com/ScottsdaleSeries

www.ingramcontent.com/pod-product-compliance
Lightning Source LLC
Chambersburg PA
CBHW071101250626
47159CB00002B/545